THE DARK ISLES

SIMON WHITFIELD

The Dark Isles by Simon Whitfield

First published in Great Britain in 2024 as eBook and paperback

Copyright © Simon Whitfield 2023

The moral right of Simon Whitfield to be identified as the author of this work has been asserted in accordance with the Copyright, Designs and Patents Act, 1988.

All rights reserved. No part of this publication may be reproduced or transmitted in any form or by any means, electronic, mechanical, photocopying, recording or otherwise, without the prior permission of both the copyright owner and the above publisher

Paperback ISBN 979-8-8634-1650-2

This book is a work of fiction. Names, characters, businesses, organisations, places and events are either the product of the author's imagination or are used fictitiously. Any resemblance to actual persons, living or dead, events or locales is entirely coincidental.

The author notes that the system of government used on the Orkney Islands does not include a mayor. In fact, they operate a significantly more sensible method of governing. The mayor has been wholly invented for the purpose of telling this story.

ACKNOWLEDGEMENTS

Firstly, I'd like to thank a couple of dead people. Raymond Chandler and Raoul Whitfield influenced the style for this novel, and I thoroughly enjoyed reading their books over the past few months.

I'm grateful to my family, my wife especially, for their support and encouragement.

There are others I could name, who read and provided amazing feedback to help me shape this story. You know who you are.

It would be remiss of me not to thank Flint. Yes, he's a character, but he sprung to life in my head one day and dictated the first chapter to me whilst I was driving through Suffolk. I had to pull over and start a voice recording so I didn't lose him!

Finally, thank you readers. I'm hopeful that you'll find something you enjoyed. Working full-time and writing is a tough combination, and it's rewarding to have anyone who isn't a friend and relative reach out and tell me that they enjoyed my story.

I hope you enjoy reading this as much as I enjoyed writing it.

Simon Whitfield

1. NO REST FOR THE WOUNDED

A knock at the new door. Grabs my attention more than the constant hammering of the October rain on the roof. Like an RSVP from winter. On my way. Don't mind me running a little late.

A dark figure stands out there in the night, blurred by the frosted glass. A silhouette. Looming like a bad noir movie poster.

Sleep and I are like squabbling siblings anyway. It's been months since we've seen eye to eye. These days, we go together like Mashed potato and custard.

We were coming together around a table for peace talks when someone's done enough to jolt me awake on the sofa.

I unpeel myself from the new light grey leather sofa. It nudges the wall. Fresh plaster. New, pale green paint. This ain't the refurbished part of the house. This is new. Painted a subtle colour. Easy on the eyes.

I splash some water on my face on a nearby glass. But damn it, it ain't water. The stuff stings my eyes. Blinking ain't doing a damn thing.

I shrug. Too late to fix it now without being rude.

Been wearing the suit all Monday. Got a week or so of thick stubble. Now wearing the smell of the booze like it's cologne. Whoever's on the other side of that door should prepare to run away. Head somewhere, anywhere. Could throw a stone out there and hit a more respectable detective.

Can't ignore the guy at the door any longer. Even if he's tapping at the thing like he's knocking out dents.

I get on my unsteady feet. Turn on the green glass lamp on my desk. On its lowest of three settings. It's still trying to burn out my retinas.

I might as well be crawling to the door. I fling it open and turn and stumble into my high-backed chair.

A short woman's standing at the threshold. A face I might've seen before. Maybe at school a couple of decades ago. On a toothpaste advert. It'll come to me.

She looked more menacing through the glass in the shadows. She's got a greying blonde bob and thick-rimmed glasses. A cute face that's all screwed up in anger. Dark grey eyes as alluring as manhole covers. She's so thin she might have last eaten when I last did some meaningful exercise. Might be attractive to someone who's turned on by long-handled garden utensils.

She's got a small tote bag on one shoulder. Looks like a suitcase on her tiny frame.

I wave at the chair the opposite side of the desk. She shakes her head. She ain't in a mood to take a load off.

She holds the bag with one hand and reaches in with the other.

The look on her face gives nothing away. She's the kinda gal that's built for one of those bluffing TV game shows. The kind where you keep spinning yarn about a word or a person you've never heard of with a level voice. Like you're reading out an Act of Parliament. See how much wool you can pull over people's eyes. If she wants to earn an extra few grand, she's gotta look into it.

The hand in the bag comes out with a gun in it. One of those tiny things they probably market for women in the USA. They get a discount on them when they get a new purse. Silver barrel. Pearl grip handle. Got all the punch of an electric toothbrush. But it can still kill a man when it's close enough. When it's aimed right. And when the safety isn't on.

A little more like the menacing mirage through the opaque glass a moment ago. Not a whole lot more than that. She's turning into quite the trick-or-treater, but she's about a week early.

I'm blinking the sleep outta my eyes. Some things are good at waking you up. An imminent threat of death would do that for most. Adrenaline kicks in when you go from one sleep to the verge of a bigger one.

I'm looking down the barrel of a piece she might not even know how to load. For now, I've gotta assume she knows all there is to know about it. That she spends her spare time on a firing range. That this little thing is all she needs to get the job done.

The fog in my head clears for a moment. I can see straight through to a recent memory.

I sit back in my chair like I'm watching the morning news. "Got something to say, Mrs Debenham?"

She shuffles closer. The little strides of someone with jelly legs. Her right elbow's pressed against her side. Some vain attempt to stop her hand from shaking. "You think you know me?" There are tremors in her voice.

I shake my head. "I think I know some of the stuff you've been up to. That doesn't amount to much."

"You think you've got me sussed? You think I killed her?" Her voice is getting shriller with every word. Louder too. "You don't know anything!"

"I know things," I say. My voice is lower. Steady. Reassuring.

If I matched hers, that gun would go off in seconds. I move my hands to the back of my head like I'm sunbathing. "I know, for example, you might be a tad more convincing without the iron."

She shakes her head. "It gets people seeing things the way I want them seen."

I nod a little, head cocked to the side. "I get that. I'm in the business of the truth. Not interested in conjecture. What only one side considers truth is of no use to me."

I know a little more than I let on. I usually do. Gotta benefit on occasion from having a face like mine.

I know she knows how to use that gun.

She's used it before.

Walking in, pointing that thing at me's like a confession. Same calibre. They'd find the same striations on the bullet that kills me if she goes through with this.

Her face explodes in tears. "I didn't kill her."

I sit forward. "Stop pointing the gat at me then. Might go some way to convincing me."

She takes the last couple of strides to the polished oak desk with its leather top. She's got a purpose. Like she's returning the weapon for her money back. She ain't happy with it. I'm not too pleased with it either.

She puts the thing down in something close to a slam on the corner of the desk. The barrel's facing neither of us. I wanna say the furniture's new. Expensive. Be careful. Don't want a gun-shaped dent in the stuff in my office for at least a few more weeks. Someone told me good furniture doesn't get damaged. It gets character. Still don't have a clue what they meant.

I pull a tissue from the box. I reach over and pick the thing up. Stick it in the top drawer to my right. Cold. At least she hasn't pulled the trigger again on her way over here.

The stern face melts into a mess of self-pity. She lets out a howl.

That kind of wailing sob should come with a warning first. Scared me as much as the weapon. Maybe more.

I still ain't got a clue what to do with a crying stranger. All I ever manage is to look at my shoes. Hope the waterworks call it a day and we can start throwing words at each other again.

While she's emptying her tear ducts, I'm thinking about the new desk. With the fancy electronics built right in. The two buttons on my side. One starts and stops the hidden recording machine. The other, which I also pushed when I sat down, sets off the silent alarm to your choice of number. I was never gonna have a private security team. The police might not be at my beck and call twenty-four hours a day, but they're a damn site cheaper.

Looked at the contraption a while back. I'd said something about being able to look after myself. Gonna look pretty stupid when Flick's back. When she stands there, on the money again. Still, could've looked worse. Could've had a hole in my head.

"What about I hire you," she says through the sobs and the hands covering her face. "You find something to make the police think it wasn't me. Make all this go away."

I shake my head. "Was already hired by your late wife. Bit of a conflict, don't you think?"

I got the local fuzz well-trained by now. They know the drill. Show up with a whisper and a sneak. Only charge in when they hear or see something that ain't right.

"Why don't you just come clean?" I say. "Get off the lam. Tell the law it was an accident. You could claim self-defence. You could say whatever you like. But your hand was on the shooter when it went off."

She looks down. She nods and keeps right on sobbing.

"The fact that the other Mrs Debenham already hired me ain't gonna make your ride all sunshine and daisies. But it's time to face the facts. Jealousy got the better of you. Could happen to anyone."

The tears stop. She lifts her head and looks at me. Her dull grey-blue eyes are clearer somehow. They look all innocent. Like she's the kind that puts spiders out the window instead of squashing them with her slipper. No one told her she's killing them all the same, whatever she's doing.

She looks over at the door she left open. Probably remembering what it's like to be born in a barn. No real harm done. The rain's more polite than my guest and it's getting no farther than the mat.

A man and a woman get to the doorway. He's a little over five-ten, she's a tad under it. Both have dark hair, serious faces. Both dressed head-to-toe in black. They step across the damp threshold. Thick vests that ain't the kind you wear for a dinner party. Bright yellow tasers pointing at my guest. They both look as old as the door they just walked through. Like a sudden gust of wind might slam it and set off their twitchy trigger fingers.

"It's okay, officers," I say. "I've got the piece now. About all she can do is whack me with the desk lamp."

They keep pointing the tasers like she's thinking about it.

The Mrs Debenham with the still-beating heart drops her shoulders. Looks like she just lost a cup final. Like her whole world's fallen apart. It has, and she put the first few holes in it.

***

It ain't long until they've got the bracelets on her. They're leading her to the cop can like she's a recovered dog on its way to the pound.

The cops might prefer she's strapped to a gurney. Mask. Unable to do so much as scratch her own nose. A little like Hannibal Lecter. But the cuffs are gonna have to do.

The female officer walks back to the door I'm now standing beside. I'm letting the cold rain clear my head for a beat. She's a little taller than her partner makes her look. Not a bad looker too, when you can see past the uniform.

"You're gonna have to start charging us pretty soon," she says. "You keep reeling them in, we'll snag them in the net."

I shrug. "Not like I plan it. This one was gunning for me. Literally."

"What's it, two from your place this month?"

I shake my head. "Only been doing business two weeks."

She sneers at me. "How long you expect to be running this racket at this rate?"

I give her a polite smile and a nod. "It's only a side gig until I'm done with my sabbatical."

She looks at me like I'm talking about some fancy new wine. Or some new invention that's gonna change the world. If not, some crazy new pills from the doctor I've gotta take twice a day. Either way, it's over her head like a bad throw in a game of catch in the park.

"Unpaid leave." Gotta talk at her level.

She's gotta be grateful of the looks. She's already leaned on them too heavily. Left herself with a head full of air.

"Was talked down off a ledge by a couple of senior officers that care about me. Gotta get my head straight before I show up and pick up a pay cheque again."

She raises her eyebrows, turns and walks back to the car. "Gotta keep that head long enough to get it straightened out."

"That's the plan."

I give Mrs Debenham a wave as they start to drive away. She's not gonna wave back.

I get back in where it's dry and warm. I close the door and turn the key. Turn off the lights.

I hit the sofa again.

Life's supposed to be easier away from the fuzz. It ain't turning out to be the case.

A few more weeks of being self-employed like this, and no one's gonna have to worry about when I'm coming back.

I need better clients. I need to start charging more while they're still breathing.

I need to shut my eyes for a while. Pretend there's not a line of people out there somewhere, all wanting to put holes in me.

2. A RISKY BUSINESS?

It's all there in the minutes he's typing up.

They've all got their doubts about getting into bed with such a loose cannon. Who wouldn't?

Okay, it came close to working last time.

The plan might've worked too. If it wasn't for that overweight, balding, spiteful mongrel of a person.

But it's all early stages.

That's the point of these early projects.

Test the waters. See what works.

People are expendable. They can sit in a prison cell. They can lay in the ground. Makes little difference to the end game.

Noted. Everyone on the encrypted video call agrees.

They've got their man. Yes, he's mad, but to do that sort of thing, you've got to be mad.

Has to be someone who's gonna cause problems. Gonna build up layers of complexity, like the world's least appetising trifle.

See how much it takes to completely upend the apple cart. Forget upsetting it.

One community. One subset of people.

A sample. A cross-section, if you will.

If it works there on the scale they're thinking, the same plan, with a few tweaks could succeed elsewhere. Scale it up a little. There's no telling how far it could go.

Okay, experiment one ended in failure. No other way of putting it. The goods on the truck never made it. Too many greedy people along the way. Too many noble people stick their oar in. Too many spanners in the works. There were too many moving pieces to begin with.

Someone points out they went too big. That was the problem. Too ambitious.

This time, start out simple. A more or less controlled environment.

That's the way to work it.

Observe the island community. Read their news. See their reactions on social media. Watch them like rats in a lab.

People say crime doesn't pay.

What do they know?

Yeah, if you're robbing houses and getting caught, it's far from lucrative.

If you make tanks and you can get some people riled up, start a war? Well, then you've gotta say it's pretty damn profitable.

What if you can find the perfect recipe for making a whole society do exactly what you're expecting them to do? Find a way to tear it apart and put it together. Custom-made society, exactly how you want it.

That's gotta be worth something.

You take a person, anyone, on their own. You're looking at someone complex. An enigma. Make them one of a crowd and reassess. Mobs are so predictable it's pathetic. Got to be a way to harness that. Monetise it.

It's all got a few of them wondering.

Is this the right guy to hang so much on?

Is this even the right place to start?

Some have voiced their concerns. It's all written down. All laid out on the figurative, digital table. A few discussed and resolved. Some stick in his head like a bad earworm. He notes the remaining, unresolved objections too.

They're all done with the talking. Time to see where everyone stands.

Only one way to find out.

He keeps a tally for the official minutes. One vote in favour. Another. A third. On and on they go.

Turns out, it's a unanimous vote in the affirmative.

Looks like they're giving it a go.

It's a risk worth taking.

This file will be encrypted. Saved. Sent on to those in attendance using secure channels.

This time, it's a solid plan. The rewards will speak for themselves.

3. LOOK INTO MY ISLES

I gotta start asking more questions when I pick up the phone.

Someone says I've got to meet them on Tuesday morning. Some nearby café. I need more than that. What kinda hairstyle are they wearing? They got a red carnation? They gonna utter some cryptic phrase so I know it's them?

> The sparrow flies south for the winter.

> Yes, but the berries he searches for remain at home.

Except we're not spies. And this ain't the Cold War.

Still, a hair colour, a coat, something. Anything would've been useful.

Details matter for clandestine meet-ups. Especially when the guy picked the largest, busiest coffee shop I've ever seen.

Someone told the folks who build these places that they all gotta look like a sawmill to be inviting these days. Even glancing around's enough to make me think I've got a splinter somewhere.

I catch a glimpse of my reflection through a window on the way in. Same dark suit. No tie. Same thick stubble. Hair (what little remains) is as tame as a rabid Shih Tzu on heat. Looks a little like a straw hat I can't take off. The stuff's splaying out everywhere like the limbs of a spider plant.

If I go sit outside, people are gonna chuck coins at me. Offering to buy me coffee. Help me get back on my feet. Get my life sorted out.

First, I look for a guy on his own.

Not gonna narrow it down much these days. We ain't a

nation of social coffee drinkers anymore. Not sure we ever were.

Even the ones who don't get a paper cup to go, sit there like they're drinking at some boring desk. Some dark office. Hoping the caffeine fix is enough to get us to the next moment when normal life intervenes.

I walk by folks taking pictures of nothing more than a cup. Posting them online. I wanna ask them why, but I'll get that look they give me. Like I'm the strange one.

The air smells like someone roasted every coffee bean in the country in some back room and set up a fan to waft it around. If the air in here gets any thicker with that aroma, moving between the tables is gonna feel like dancing in syrup.

I come close to losing a shoe on a sticky patch. What's' with the polished concrete floor? When did actual flooring become unfashionable?

I scowl like my angry eyes are gonna melt through the residue.

The java joint is getting more appealing by the second. Someone could bump into me. Call me grandpa. Make my nightmare complete.

But after gawking at a few cup-obsessed weirdos, Pretty sure I've found the guy.

He's wearing a light pink shirt and a red jacket. The kind of red that looked darker on the computer or phone screen, so he ordered it online. But it showed up and it's a little bright. Not what he thought. But he paid good money for it, so he's damn-well gonna get value out of it. The trousers are a kind of dark purple.

A little face paint and the guy's ready for the nearest exhibition of oddities. Shame no one told him they all closed down years ago because even strange people have human rights.

The truth is, everyone's got a little weird in them. For some folks, it's a little closer to the surface.

Me? I keep my weird on the inside. At least I think I do. I don't even let it out at New Year. Stays shut away at Halloween too.

The man with no sense of matching colours sits there. His effeminate features eyeing me. A wide nose. High cheekbones. Girlish mouth. Eyes the colour of a wet brown paper bag. Not-quite blond hair pulled back from his face. It's held there with some styling gloop of some description.

With the right make up and outfit, he could disappear in a crowd. This crowd, anyway. He could use gents or ladies lavatories without a second glance or a complaint from anyone.

But I'm not here to talk fashion. Not gonna offer the guy a job in some clandestine organisation. I'm not even gonna talk about the coffee.

"Mr Wallace?" I ask.

He looks up and smiles. A single nod.

He ain't getting up to shake my hand. No one does that anymore. You go around shaking hands and people stare at you. Like how come you're hell-bent on starting the next pandemic?

I sit and shuffle along the bench the other side of a booth. It's rough wood. No one's tried to get it smooth. No one's even thought a cushion was a good idea. Might as well be sitting on a crate in an alleyway.

"What was it you couldn't talk about on the phone?" I ask.

He looks at me with those dull eyes. A cheerful-sounding Scottish accent I can't place garnishes his words. It's a little more sing-song than I'm used to from north of the border. Not a million miles from Welsh. A careful listen tells anyone it's Scottish. Not the kind of Scottish a lot of the English would recognise.

"I didn't say I couldn't talk over the phone," he says. "Some things are better done in person, aren't they?"

I nod and pick up the menu.

It ain't even a menu. Some square box filled with random black and white patches. Gotta scan it with my phone to place an order. Not my cup of tea.

I didn't want a drink anyway.

"It's my sister," he says. "She's gone. Disappeared."

I put the menu-thing back down like I don't hate it. "You got police looking for her?"

He smiles with the right side of his mouth. The left side's not interested in joining the party. "They've had a couple of days. They've not got a clue."

I shrug. "What do you think I can do that they can't?"

He pushes his drink away from him. Maybe the drinks, like the rough pieces of furniture, are lacking something. "You come highly recommended. You're good at finding people."

I frown a little. "I've been working for myself for less than a month. I hadn't expected word-of-mouth to travel so fast."

He smirks. "I'm betting not as far, either. My neck of the woods isn't exactly local."

I let out a laboured breath. "What can you tell me to help me find her? What's left that the police don't know?"

He leans in closer. Like the people at nearby tables give a

damn. "She quit her job a couple weeks ago. She must have got herself another source of income, if you know what I mean."

"Drugs?" I say in my normal voice.

He shuts me down with wide, angry eyes. He looks at the table and shakes his head. "I don't think so. Not big business up in Orkney. Not yet, anyway."

"You've made up your mind about your sister, Mr Wallace. Tell me what it is you've decided."

He looks like he's one clue from completing a crossword puzzle, but he's been that way for a week. "Name's Moira. Moira Wallace. Twenty two. We've not got parents anymore. Not since a few years back, but we've got their debt, sure enough."

I pull out a small notepad from my inside jacket pocket and I take down a few details.

I ain't one of those fancy mega-memory detectives. I've gotta write stuff down as I go. Too many hits to the head if you ask me. You could tell me you've already asked me. All you'd get is a shrug and a smile. I ain't that bad yet. Still remember my name and where I live.

He coughs a little. "Before we go any further..." As he talks, he slides an envelope that's just appeared along the table towards me. "You guys still call it a retainer?"

This guy's sense of subtlety ran off somewhere with his dress sense. No signs either would ever be coming back.

I shrug. "When I'm in a fifties movie. But I can go with it. Why's my silence worth buying?"

He drops the smile. "I'm a serious man, Mr Flint. I don't take chances with anything."

"It's just Flint. Drop the mister. Forget the Enoch. No one uses that either." I look around the room at nothing, and then back at him. "Serious. Yet you've hopped on a plane from the other side of the UK. You're hiring someone who's been working as a gumshoe for less time than it takes to grow cress."

He slaps more paper down on the table. "I'll pay two hundred a day, plus expenses. Your flight tickets to Kirkwall Airport. Change at Aberdeen. Leaves tomorrow. Got you a hire car and a nice deal on a suite overlooking the harbour. All the details are there."

I reach for the tickets. "What makes you think I can drop everything and fly up there?"

He smiles at me. "I've already spoken to your employer, and to your lovely partner. I told you, I don't leave anything to chance."

He shuffles to the edge of the bench. He gets up. Not even a glance back at the forlorn cup.

"You got anything more for me?" I ask.

He reaches into his inside pocket. Pulls out a folded A4 envelope like it's a magic trick. "Photo. Details about her. Everything else you should need to know."

I look at the envelope like I've got x-ray vision.

"One more thing, Mr Flint." It bugs me that he's not listening to me. He takes a couple of steps. "Wrap up warm. You'll want a hat, not an umbrella. It's a tad windier on the isles."

He leaves me to it.

Whatever *it* is.

Got nothing to do but cast curious looks about the joint.

Gotta do the British thing and let the guy leave before I get up.

No idea why.

I'm less than informed about the direction my life's heading too.

You take on one job for a friend. You stumble onto the right answer.

You end up with another job you didn't ask for and someone ends up dead and you help someone else end up in prison.

Throw in the news reports about my Heathrow heroics. Seems to be enough for a promising career as a gumshoe.

But I didn't ask for this. I don't even want it.

I want to lie on that new couch.

I want to drink gin.

I want to watch TV and see something go wrong for someone else for a change.

I open the envelope.

Three grand. A hell of a retainer.

I guess I'm gonna go home and pack.

4. TROUBLE VISION

The trouble with moving in with a new dame is the clothes.

You had them for years. Worn them for all manner of situations without complaint. They used to be fine, but they ain't good enough anymore.

These days, everyone wants to point out that man, woman, either or both, or even none of the above, are all the same. That ain't the planet I've been living on. Maybe it should be, but some people are wired differently.

A man sees a woman for who she is. Sure, he knows she's spent at least twenty minutes choosing the outfit. Maybe the same again on the makeup. True enough, she's hiding her imperfections. She presents a version of herself that's too perfect. He knows there are imperfections. If he's a good one, he's willing to love the woman for what he sees, and whatever's hidden away.

I swear the women I've known haven't seen an attractive man. At least a man who ain't hideous. Who, on the hush-hush, spends almost as long getting ready. They see a project. A broken down house. Repairs needed. Let's see what value we can add with some new fixtures and a fresh coat of paint.

A man in a relationship must wear something befitting of his new status. None of those rude, funny t-shirts. Gone are the comfortable clothes no one ever saw anyway. You're allowed to keep one outfit for painting or gardening. Not gonna get away with wearing it where folks are gonna see it.

I could've argued the case for every one of my threads. In truth, they weren't worth a few crossed words. They'd had their time. I was right to show them all the inside of a waste bin.

Why not donate them? she'd asked.

So, what, they're not good enough for me, but they are for someone else? That seems a little inconsistent.

I'd had the time to get myself a new wardrobe, but none of the enthusiasm.

A few grand burning a hole in my pocket fixes something like that.

That, and the need to dress up warm. Get stuff that's gonna withstand the weather. A wind that tries to cut you in half. Horizontal rain that tries to freeze you in place until the wind's done its job.

I must've spent nearly an hour in the closest menswear store. Looks the type for fancy getups. Not a Saville Row establishment. I ain't that flush with cash. Truth be told, it's at most one step up from a Primark.

Nothing to show for my time here but gritted teeth.

How do people shop for fun? They wander around malls with armfuls of bags. Smiles on their faces. It's all foreign to me.

Can't stand it when it's essential. Staring at racks and racks of shirts, suits, coats. They all bleed together. A swirling black fog of wasted time and effort.

Every coat I liked was too small.

Every hat that looked good was too big.

Suits are either slim fit, regular, tall, generous fit. Don't think any of that describes me.

I'm gripping the collar of a coat like I'm squeezing the last drops of juice from an orange half. Some guy behind the counter sees me. He's tall, thin enough that he can't buy a suit off the rack. Got a narrow face that's miserable whenever he's not stuck on the Cheshire-cat smile. His nose points off to the side a little and his eyes are looking everywhere but at me. "We got some bigger coats in the back. I'll see what I can find."

I work my way through a table covered in hats while he's away.

I'm putting on a trilby. A pork pie. Even a damn top hat. The mirror tells me the same thing about each of them. Might as well be a monkey in a fez. Flat caps too seem to be a no-go.

My persistence pays off when I find the only hat that fits on my head. A slight snug fit. The wind ain't gonna rip it off me and chuck it in the sea. A dark grey, whale-tooth check fedora with a charcoal band.

The mirror's showing me a less-than-pleased expression on my part-white, part-Hispanic face. I knew about that already. The mirror also says that the hat's not perfect, but it's the best thing I'm gonna find in here. At least it covers the thinning, greying hair. Could even say it takes years off me, if you wanted to hand me a false compliment.

The assistant's found me a double-breasted beast of a trench coat. A kind of dark, speckled grey. New wool. Fancy lining.

I put the thing on. Sleeves are a sensible length. Fastened up, there's the right amount of space to move around a little. Length means the collar could fold up and cover my neck, and it almost falls as far as my knees. The lapels are so wide they nearly touch my shoulders. Thought that was a seventies thing. Seems to be a now-thing too.

My watch tells me I gotta get on with packing. The day's disappearing.

I pay the awkward clerk with the social problem. It's more than I think's fair for the hat and the coat.

I can cobble outfits together from the rest of my tired

wardrobe. I'd still look better than my new employer. Even if I look like a washed-out Dick Tracy.

***

"This the new look?" Flick asks as I close the door. She's running a hand through her shoulder-length chestnut hair. "Where'd you go shopping, New York in the thirties?"

I shrug. "Gotta stay warm where I'm going."

Her shoulders drop. "Flint, you're recovering, aren't you? Where are you off to now?"

I give her the lowdown of the guy in the colourfast threads. Show her the envelope stuffed with cash.

"So your compassionate leave is about to lapse, you're not ready to take up the day job again, but you're taking *this* on?"

Her girl-next-door cuteness is looking a little strained when she's close to going ape at me. She's still a little too cute to pull of a mean look all the way, like a puppy trying to act upset. Grief that would be forgotten as soon as the next treat's in view.

I take off the hat and set it on the little table by the door. The kind that used to hold a telephone. Now it sits there, holding the thin layer of dust you get when you're getting the place done up. Looks like someone forgot to throw it out when times changed.

The walls are a patchwork of browns and greys. The wallpaper's gone. That's a good thing. That stuff was an eyesore. Even before the cracks and the holes got filled in, it looked better. What carpet remains ain't worthy of the name. Yet that table's come with us from her old digs. It's defied every change. Weathered every storm. Still, it's sitting there.

"You think heading out there's gonna fix whatever's not

happening right here?"

I shake my head. "I don't think it's gonna fix anything. Someone needs me. That's all."

She turns and heads for the half-built kitchen. She walks past some long, thin pieces of something or other, still wrapped in plastic. Needed for whatever the builder's doing next. "Plenty of other people they can call on, Flint. Doesn't have to be you."

"It's a little dough when I'm still on unpaid leave. Helps grease the wheels." I give the place the up-and-down from where I'm standing. "Could pay to fix up a few more things round here."

She looks at me like I called Toby ugly. "We've got enough to fix up the house, thank you. Maybe not enough for that *and* your drinking money."

I shrug off the coat with the comment. I put it on an old hook on the wall. It's threatening to come out with the weight of the thing. "I'm gonna head up there. Try to find a girl. Head home again. A few days."

She shakes her head and looks to the wall covered in tester pot patches instead of at me. "Is it ever that simple with you?"

"It's gotta be about time that it was."

She's looking back at me again. "It's about time you admitted something to yourself. You can try to leave the job alone, but it's gonna come looking for you. Might as well pick up a salary and a police pension doing it."

She storms to the base of the stairs. "You know where the suitcase is. Pack it yourself. You get back within a week, I'll eat that new hat of yours."

I wanna ask what's gotten into her. Why she made me kit

out an office with stuff I ain't gonna use. Why she got me to buy the one with the fancy panic alarm. That's not stuff you throw good lettuce at for a hobby.

She wants me to take the job seriously. Be professional. Be the best problem-solving sleuth I can be. This is it. This has gotta be the start of what success looks like.

Me? I can look like I live under a bridge. I can turn my back on the boys in blue. I can call anyone who walks through my door whatever I like. Hell, I can get most of them in cuffs. People still crawl out from anywhere. They want my help.

Someone from the other side of the UK found me this time. Not someone else. From a lotta folks in the classifieds, the wanted ads, on every Internet search. He couldn't have found me any of those ways, but he found me anyway. That's gotta mean something.

How am I supposed to turn down someone like that?

I'll be on that plane in the morning.

Get there. Find the girl. Fast.

Call it a day and head home.

Pick out a bottle of sauce. Maybe some haggis from the duty free at the airport. Something for Flick to enjoy with the hat.

5. A MAN WITH ONLY HIS PRINCIPLES IS A POOR MAN INDEED

Encrypted messages. Unknown people.

How'd they even get his number?

Not that it matters.

The stuff of dreams. Someone say they'll pay you for doing the exact thing you've always dreamed of doing.

The plans needed a little tweaking, but less than he might've expected.

The big question was how these mysterious people knew what was going on in his head.

He'd never told a soul.

Had he?

Had he let slip some idealised plan to someone in college a few years ago?

Had he joked with someone about the desires he had?

Sure, like all nutcases, he'd found an outlet online, but that was anonymous. Plus, there were thousands of them. How'd you distinguish one nut ball from another in the nuttiest places on the planet?

No one knew where his dark stories had come from.

No one knew the authors of the plans of how to teach society a lesson.

They were user accounts that went back to burner email addresses.

They were only ever accessed using a secure web browser. The kind that bounces your location and identity all over the world.

He was careful. He made sure he followed all the guides on staying anonymous online.

Some people made a mistake. They signed up to some VPN and signed into their personal email on the same connection. Or they bought something on the dark web. Did the untraceable crypto payment, but had it delivered to their home address. That was how they got you. Some personal link in amongst the anonymous stuff.

But he hadn't done that. Had he?

Had he always been sure that he'd stopped the cloud storage syncing? Had he definitely stopped his email app from refreshing? It all counts. Can all get you unstuck on one of these allegedly untraceable connections.

Maybe he had let something slip. There could surely be no other way.

But at least this wasn't the police. Wasn't the NCA or even the FBI seeking extradition.

Couldn't be.

They have some dodgy ways of working in these organisations. No way they'd cross the lines he's already crossed. Not for anything.

Still, what's the point in second-guessing it all now?

Some people liked his ideas.

They loved that they could lead to big things. That was the whole point.

They would cover his expenses. They would put some extra in too. Some nice laundered cash. All chucked in an account of his choosing. As it turns out, quite a lot of cash.

He didn't think he was the kind of person that could be bought off.

Not for sale. Not somebody's lapdog.

Turns out, he was wrong.

Someone writes a big enough cheque, maybe everyone's the same.

Principles are great, but they don't pay the bills.

They don't pay for the glamorous overseas properties he's now looking at online.

But these guys will.

The beauty is that he's already pretty much a third of the way there.

He attaches the photos as evidence.

Yeah, the police don't know what they're dealing with yet, but they will.

Some bright spark will spot the clues. He left enough of them.

He gets a thumbs up emoji.

That's it?

Not a group of many spun-out words, are they?

The emoji disappears.

Just says one thing.

    [deleted]

Another message arrives.

    Photos have been copied. Please remove them.

He obliges.

Needs to keep these people onside.

Needs to follow every rule.

Stick to the plan. No matter what.

He's already got the next one lined up.

He's been watching her for some time.

Gonna have some fun here.

No way the police are gonna write this one off.

By the time number four happens, it'll be pandemonium in the police.

He can sit back, watch the chaos. Claim his expenses. Get things ready for that life in the sun.

Crime certainly does pay.

It's gonna keep on paying.

No one in this community has a clue what's gonna happen. They're not clever enough to stop him.

That's why they hired him.

That's why he's gonna succeed.

6. FLYING OR FLEEING?

"Scared of flying?" asks the guy next to me.

He has to shout for me to hear him over the sound of the engines.

Thick glasses cover bushy, blond eyebrows. Got a fair-haired comb-over so obvious it's not fooling anyone. A chubby, round face that's often mistaken for a jolly countenance. He's wearing the garish suit of an insurance salesman.

I turn away from the little window, and my view of the endless blue you only get when you're above the clouds. My right hand had started trying to crush the armrest all on its own. I manage to prise my fingers off.

How do I answer that question? I little bit of a yes, but a whole lot of a definite no.

I hate the beige-interiored, tubular coffins with wings. A hundred dials are telling the pilot about problems. Problems that can become catastrophes. Makes you wonder if this is a sensible mode of travel.

It might be quicker than a train, but it's noisy as hell. Hot too. Those little air vents are kicking out a weak stream of barely cold air. As useful as the guy who stands nearby and says, 'let it all out' when you're tossing your cookies.

But the small plane's stayed up so far. Flight's only about half an hour. What's that, an episode of The Simpsons? Seems longer. Hasn't got the same capacity for a good laugh, though. Not even an average one.

Fifty people or so are trying to pretend that they're not as terrified as me. Two seats on the right of the tiny aisle, single seats to the left. Don't know why so many people are heading north at a cold, miserable time of year. They must have their reasons.

Some bird, thin, blonde, tanned, the Instagram-type, in a red tartan dress is pushing a trolley. It rattles along a miserable dark blue strip of carpet. Got a drink of water and some shortbread. Handed over with something close to a smile. It's what you get for free. Want anything harder to make the flight a little easier? It's gonna cost.

I'm on the clock. Best stick to the water.

The frequent flyer to my left chirps up again. Mouth full of biscuit crumbs.

If he tells me to take off my socks and shoes and make fists with my toes, I ain't getting off. I'll stay on this plane when it gets to Aberdeen until it heads back to London. But I guess Kirkwall's way off Nakatomi Plaza.

"You're not much of a talker, are you?" He asks.

The seats are too close together. He's getting a little personal in his questioning.

Why couldn't I sit the other side of the aisle in a single seat?

I shrug. "I mostly get paid to listen. Figure things out."

He looks confused. Looks like the kinda guy that's used to wearing that expression.

He gives me a polite nod and goes back to looking at the woman working her way further forward with the trolley. Maybe he's eyeing up the gal. Could be he's gonna chance asking for another piece of shortbread when she heads back the other way. Hard to tell.

We've lost a little altitude. Dropping beneath the clouds.

We're already making our descent. Everyone else has to feel it too. Like the air around you's not your friend anymore. It's gonna get in your ears and try to crush you as much as it can.

Fields, sea, bunches of trees are down there. A long way from us. Better stay that way for a few more minutes.

The small lurches downward don't seem to bother the tarted-up, tartan woman. She's used to the landings in these compact contraptions. That feeling in the pit of your stomach. Like a rough fairground ride. Like someone hitting a humpback bridge too fast while someone punches you, takes the wind out of you.

That sinking feeling's been with me since we were gaining altitude. Could be the destination. Wondering if a change of scenery's gonna change anything at all.

Flick's words rattle around my head with every sudden movement. That gal's got a knack for saying what I don't wanna hear. They'll shake loose at some point during the trip. No doubt when I need them most, or least.

But am I running away? Isn't this doing a job, nothing more? Is the need to investigate, to problem solve, somehow part of my DNA?

Is there anywhere I could hide where trouble ain't gonna come and drag me out by my heels and give me a good kicking?

Buildings are more than specs on the landscape now. Cars too.

If I'm such a trouble magnet, a plane's a bad idea. I'm the type to bring the thing down. Hell, I've already been the cause of at least one plane going to ground early.

A drop, deeper and longer than all the ones before. Enough to make me think I'm every inch the problem everyone thinks I am.

I swear a couple of passengers look at me like I'm the bad luck charm. Like the rough landing's my fault.

Landmarks that looked like decorations on a model train set grow larger by the second. It ain't long before we're the same size as everything on the ground again.

Wheels thud into the runway. I let go of a breath I've been holding. No idea I was doing it. Breathing in feels too good, so I must've held it longer than was a good idea.

The guy next to me's wearing a goofy, I-knew-it-was-okay-really smile. Makes me wanna force feed him shortbread until it comes out of his nose.

A couple of hours to wait for the next flight.

Plenty of time to regret some of my life choices all over again.

7. LIKE BANGING MY HEAD AGAINST A KIRKWALL

You know that moment you book yourself a trip based on someone else's snaps of the place?

You see the best of what they saw.

You see the hills that could inspire a thousand Scottish poems. You don't see the patch of wet mud they had to stand in to get that picture just right.

Beaches stretch farther than the viewfinder of a camera. Endless. White sand. Unspoilt. Empty. They don't tell you why they're empty. Like standing inside the world's largest, sandiest refrigerator.

You stand there long enough, the cold wind's gonna pelt you with every single grain of sand. Someone lost the feeling in their fingers taking that photo. Had their face exfoliated by force, too.

I came too late in the year, I'm told. The day light's already starting to fade at two in the afternoon. You get near-endless sunlight in the summer. The weather's better. Not as good as it is when you head south, but better.

The rain's gotta be a little warmer. It's mixed in with a little more sunlight. Same strong wind though. All year.

Never seen so much blue sky overhead while it's raining. You could look up and not even know where it's coming from. Might not be raining at all. Could be some local behind a hedge pointing a hose up in the air and laughing at me.

Cold winds and cold rain fit Orcadian life like traffic noise suits Londoners. With any luck, I'll be back in a place not much like either before Thursday.

I'm the first through the door of Moira's place. Davie

follows. He puts away his spare key. Pushes the door closed until the lock clicks. Gotta fight feeling trapped in here with a near-stranger. If he wanted to hurt me, surely he wouldn't have flown me up here.

He's still wearing that red jacket, but the rest of his outfit is a little more sensible. Dark blue jeans. White shirt with an open collar. V-neck jumper. It all makes the jacket stand out. Look even worse than it did in that café. Still the female facial features though. Doesn't matter how he dresses.

Mail's piled up. Cards about missed meter readings.

The one-bedroom apartment, or a flat to most in the UK. Behind and above a newsagents on the high street. The place is far from immaculate. If Moira had a system of organisation, she had lost it in there somewhere. Could take her months to find anything.

Maybe she ain't even missing at all. She could've tripped on her way in the door one day. Disappeared under layer upon layer of trash and unwashed clothes and old magazines.

But I look a little closer. This is the untidiness of someone who's coming home in a couple of hours. Maybe finally getting round to the tidying up they've been putting off for weeks. Or months. Couldn't have been years, but I ain't ruling it out.

Nothing useful, though. Unless it's hiding.

A few photos in little frames dotted around on tables, bedside cabinets. Some on the walls. The gal's alone in every single one.

Same chestnut brown hair down to her shoulders, like it's never grown and never needed cutting. Eyes pretty much the same shade. Same cute, roundish face. Cheekbones with definition some girls get from expensive surgeons. A button nose that she could've picked from a catalogue to match its surroundings. A fan of a kind of blue-green and khaki thing, given she's wearing the same type of threads in every photo.

Cheeky, ear-to-ear smile, but not a soul near her. Not in any of them. Not even a single snap with her brother.

Their relationship's not as close as he's got me thinking it is. Can't be. Chances are, he's not even related. He's playing some other angle.

He's closer to me right now than he's ever been to her.

He's by my side every step on that debris-covered cheap laminate wood floor. Wherever I look, he's gotta look too. Like he needs me to do it first, so he's got permission to snoop the way he wants. I peer into a drawer of her flat-pack pine-effect furniture. No way he's not gonna look too.

Her clothes are still there. Food still in the fridge. Most still in date. Dark emerald sheets straightened out on the double bed after a night's sleep. A couple of bowls still waiting by the sink for washing up. There's a shopping list written on a pink sticky note. The top of a stack of them near the front door.

She's anything but neat. Her handwriting is the opposite. You wouldn't know the same hands that penned those words had created this mess. Her lettering's a little girlish. The over-the-top curvy style. Circles instead of dots above anything with an I or a J.

From what I can see, she wasn't expecting to be gone long.

"Looked exactly like this four days ago when I was last here," he says. Still hanging around like he's paying for the privilege of being my personal shadow.

I head out the door. He looks around one more time and then follows.

He's gotta leave me alone at some point. Got a business to run, so he tells me.

Seems like he's happy to leave that to someone else. He's too curious. Too interested. Like he can't stand me knowing something he doesn't know.

But this ain't normal for a PI like me. No one pays two hundred a day for a dog and barks themselves.

We clear the small driveway. Get back to the narrow, cobbled stone high street.

He follows me up and down. Every style and shape of building from about the fifteen hundreds onwards is on show around here. Someone once upon a time had a bag of assorted houses. Someone picked them out blind and stuck them all next to each other.

Bridge Street down one end. It turns a corner and changes its name to Albert Street. A little way down is an old cathedral and a couple more name changes. It's like someone found more pieces of high street from somewhere. They tried gluing them together. They thought they looked okay, so they left them there.

I work my way to a place keen to point out it serves Orkney's best kebabs. An estate agent. A couple of travel shops.

I get the same kinda response from everyone behind every counter.

They look at me. A stranger who looks pretty weird. Must've got the wrong type of hat and coat for fitting in. They shake their heads when I show them a picture. Look all innocent or clueless when I say the gal's name.

They cast an eye behind me at the brother. Still hanging round like I promised to repay a debt when I pass the next cash machine.

Davie's got some way of affecting the people I wanna talk to. The ones who start to open their mouths cast one look behind me and forget whatever it was they were gonna say.

I'm getting nowhere with him. Ditching him round here ain't an option. It's not some sprawling metropolis where you can make yourself scarce.

We're back out on the street. I turn around. "Heading back to the hotel," I say. "Gonna make a couple of notes. Puzzle over this for a while."

He looks at me like I forgot something. "That it? You take a look around her place, ask a couple of people if they've seen her? What am I getting for my money?"

"You can have some privacy, if you want it," I say with my back to him.

He takes his voice up a few decibels. "Excuse me for my interest. For my concern over my sister."

I wanna tell him he's being ridiculous. That I ain't surprised his only relative has vanished. If he micro-manages everything in his life like he is here, no one's gonna put up with that for too long.

"How about we make a deal?" I say. I turn back to face him. "You don't need to pay from the moment I walk in that hotel door until the time I come back out."

He frowns. Stares at me. Nods. "I suppose I can work with that."

I start to turn around again. "Good. It's been a very long Wednesday, made up of short flights and some dull waits. Gotta recharge and hit things again in the morning."

He gives a stern, resolute nod. The last thing I see before I'm looking the other way. "When can I meet you tomorrow?"

"I'll call you," I say. I'm walking along the cobbled street. Both weighed down and carefree.

I walk in the door of the hotel. I ain't calling it a day yet. I'll leave it a few minutes. Ask a couple of people around here.

But I'm done asking questions about Moira, right now. People go missing all the time. They turn up, one way or another, or they don't. No amount of investigating finds someone who's determined to stay hidden.

I got a feeling that Davie's the guy I should be asking about. The guy's hiding something. Could be a whole warehouse full of somethings.

I get the feeling people around here don't like the kid. They think he's done something. He had to put on a show, hire some guy to show the folks of the city that he ain't the piece of work they think he is. *Look, I can't be at fault. Otherwise, why would I hire someone to find her?*

Yeah right. Something stinks about all this, and it ain't the stale smell of fish from the harbour.

***

The folks behind the desk of the hotel are either clueless or spineless.

The junior staff are the former. They've been there a few months at most. Probably got the only job going in this town at the time. Saving up some cash before they head somewhere with a younger average age.

The senior staff look like they're being honest like I look like Scrooge McDuck. All I gotta do is say the name and they're looking anywhere but at me. A clear of the throat. A swift shake of the head. They're asking me about my stay. Have I got enough towels in the room? How's the temperature? Anything other than the stuff I wanna know.

It's been half an hour, a little more, since I ditched my shady shadow. A quick trip to my room, splash some water on my face, pretend I've slept more than a couple of hours in the past forty. It ain't much longer before I'm out pounding the pavement.

I turn right and I'm at the edge of Bridge Street again. Gonna work my way down the stores on the right. Show the gal's picture. See who knows her. See who's got that glint of recognition in their eyes but their mouth's not playing ball.

First joint I get to's a fish and chip establishment. Big solid wooden doors look like something you'd find on a bank. They're closed tight. I stick my face against the window. Might be the kind of place that only opens at meal times. From the outside, I've got one of two ideas. Either the proprietor's one hell of a neat freak, or it's been a while since they swung open those doors. Fired up the deep friers.

Next along, an Indian restaurant, walls painted bright pink. I get nothing but darkness and emptiness from the front door, but there's an arch leading to an alley on the right. There's a guy down there who looks about right for working in a spot like this. Looks more authentic-Indian than the food is gonna be. Jet black hair, thick eyebrows doing their best to hug each other. Leathery skin. A moustache thick enough that it would make a decent broom if he shaved it off and stuck it on the end of a pole. A frown etched deep into his features, even when he sees me and puts on his customer-facing grin.

I show him the picture. "Seen this bird?"

He gets almost close enough to smell the gal's perfume. A shake of the head.

I watch him. Seems genuine.

"She used to work somewhere round here," I say. "In a café, I think."

He looks again, frowns, and there's a slight nod. His eyes brighten. "Yes, I've seen her. Not recently. You might try round the corner. Second place on the right."

I thank him and I turn around, catching a noseful of spices from a vent on the wall. Makes me feel a little hungry for the first time today.

I head into the travel agent next door. A Gal in her thirties is trying too hard to look twenty. The blonde hair is as fake as her smile. She's got a nose like a Norwegian carport. She looks down that considerable sniffer at the photo. A genuine blank look.

Next place along is a little different. A man with white hair. Skin's nearly the same shade. This guy's so pale he could be beach buddies with Dracula. His tall, thin and genial face greets me. Before he says a word, I know he ain't from around here. Funny how a few minutes into my stay, I can spot the English.

I show him the picture. He nods, but it ain't a happy nod. Like he's agreed to take the trash out that's been piling up, and it's not gonna go well. He gives me the same yarn about working for the café around the corner.

I ask about the brother. He gives me the headmaster look. It's like I'm eight again. Takes me a second to regroup. Remember I'm a grown-ass adult, and this guy's got no reason to make me feel so feeble.

"I hear things about him," he says. "Don't know how much

is true."

I lean on the counter. "Care to unburden yourself of some of those things?"

He looks down with sombre features. Shakes his head. "Best not give rumours credence."

I pull out my wallet. "I live for the rumours. I ain't gonna splash it across the front page of the Orcadian. Just gonna hold it in my head. Could be useful in finding the girl."

He looks at the wallet and then he looks away. "I'll tell you if it helps, but you didn't hear it from me."

I nod and let him win the battle with his own conscience.

"Rumour has it, he's got some shady business dealings going on. Trying to make something of himself around here. He lends money. Don't know where he gets it. If you don't pay up, something bad happens."

"What kind of something?" I ask.

"Little things at first. Maybe you find you've got a flat tyre next time you go out. Could be a window gets smashed. Or you come home to find your beloved pet's disappeared. Get the idea?"

I nod.

"Police never get far with these little things, even if they're reported. Never happens where there's cameras. If it does, they weren't working at the time."

I ask, "What happens next, if they still don't pay?"

He shakes his head. "Don't know anyone who needed a second warning before they got their cash together."

I look at him. He looks a couple of years older than when I

walked in the joint. "Why'd you say you don't know where he gets it?"

"Everyone knows about the debt their parents saddled them with. If he's got money, wouldn't he'd have paid it off?"

I nod, giving the guy permission to keep on spilling, but he dries up like an old sponge. Nothing left to squeeze outta him.

I thank him by way of a good old English banknote. He looks like he ain't seen one of those for a while. It's as likely to end up in a frame as in his pocket.

I head on down to the next place.

A sports store. The kind they set up, trying to cater for every sport and every athlete. They end up being a glorified seller of sports kits for the local school.

At least it ain't got the usual smell of sweat, new rubber and unemployment. That's reserved for similar establishments in bigger towns.

Someone's hanging up a shirt. Greasy curtains of brown hair hide some of the look he gives me. Not all of it. A frown like I'm hell-bent on setting off the fire alarm.

The older guy behind the counter's got a buzz cut and an attempted goatee. At his age, it ain't growing in any better, no matter how long he leaves it. Might get a little greyer. He's chewing something with that well-exercised jaw. He looks at me like I've come to try on every outfit, refuse to buy anything more than a ping-pong ball, waste their time.

The narrow look tells me I should turn around. Try the next place. He's got a face that was once chubby. Now it looks like it's imperfect. Made from wax. Since it got finished, someone left it a little too close to a fire for a minute or two.

Nothing but a no and a shake of the head. Whatever he knows, he's keeping it where it was. No foreign nobody's gonna drag anything outta him.

I don't even bother with the younger guy on the way out. He still gives me a look like he's Rangers and I'm Celtic.

I'm done wasting my time and that pretender's cash. Gotta head to the heart of this.

I round the corner. First place on the right started out as a convenience store. Not so convenient, now that it's come out the other side of a hipster brainstorming session. Still, people gotta know where to go to waste their scratch. Expensive-as-gold coffee, high-class fudge and artisan cheeses need a place to get sold.

Second place is a hunched up little building. Small windows either side of a low door. Gotta duck, force my head down into my neck, to cross the threshold.

Six tables are split down the middle by a straight path to a service desk and a tiny kitchen at the back. The table coverings are bright wipe-clean plastic in either red or blue. The red padded benches either side are cheap. Fitted by someone with a good shoehorn. If someone sits behind you and leans back, they've got a decent angle for sipping some of your drink.

A place that prides itself on its food as opposed to its décor.

There ain't many eateries open around here during the day, so they've only got one table free. I try to slide in the side opposite the window. Despite the vinyl covering, I've gotta put my legs to work. Plant them, stand up a little, shuffle and repeat.

I've soon got my back against the end wall, sitting on the diagonal. I can crane my neck around and see almost the whole place.

I double-take at the gal who stands at the end of my table. Her accent is as thick as a Glasgow ship-builder's, but it's at odds with her Asian features.

She's got huge, almond-shaped brown, black eyes, the kind of full lips that are never not pouting. Bright hair the shade of polished, new copper.

She's wearing a black t-shirt. All the staff are wearing them. She's combined it with a pair of washed blue denim jeans. They're so tight that they could snap like a balloon. Fly off. Land in someone's drink. All with a sound like someone blowing raspberries.

I order a large lemonade and she gives me a little longer to consult the menu. It's a bound collection of plastic covered pages. I'm starting to wonder if they clean this place by hosing it down.

The thing's thicker than a Jehovah's Witness tract. Options range from simple sandwiches to roast dinners. It's got chapters, each one starting a new page. Few menus can beat that.

I flick through until I find a light bite that looks good. One of the final few pages. Starting to think that I should finish flicking, scour the desserts, and then I'll be ready to leave a book review on Amazon.

Jenny returns with my drink, and with a less-than-sincere smile.

"You able to spare a minute?" I ask.

She sticks on a puzzled look, making those red lips stick out a little more. If she extends them any further, they'll put a plastic table next to her and call her the overflow.

"Can I ask a couple of questions?" I'm pointing at the menu.

She leans over a little. Beneath the grease-cooked smell there's some fancy jasmine perfume.

"Does Davie Wallace own this place?"

She gets up a little and glances to the back. In a flash, she's composed again and looking at the menu.

She points at another part of the page. "Yes, he does. So you're not asking about the food?"

I shake my head. "I'll get to that."

"His sister, Moira worked here?"

She nods and says, "yes, until a couple of weeks ago."

"You a friend of hers?"

She shrugs, standing up again. "As much as any of us were. None of us have heard from her since she left, so you be the judge."

"Thanks. Time to order, I guess."

She nods. Pad and pen at the ready.

"I'll have the details of the car she was driving, and a steak salad baguette please. Plus anything extra you can tell me on the side."

She nods and retreats to the kitchen

I take a moment to admire the random collection of Orkney photos on the walls. The place doesn't look like it's changed much in something like a hundred years. Same deal as the rest of the high street.

I hear rain hitting the window. I look up to see the little spots on the glass as confirmation.

Someone's stood by my side clearing their throat.

Davie Wallace. Looking less than pleased.

"I'm afraid we're not able to provide you with a couple of things you ordered," he says. "But I'll make sure your steak sandwich is with you shortly. On the house, of course, otherwise it's only coming back as expenses anyway."

I see Jenny mouthing the word, "Sorry" from the back.

I've pissed off the client, but at least I'm getting a free meal out of it.

Gotta look at the positives every once in a while.

With any luck, the rain will have stopped by the time I'm done.

Could keep ordering food until it does.

But then again, if folks around here are right, you don't wanna get on this guy's bad side.

The wrong kind of employer.

It's what I get for jumping into a situation like this without pause for thought. You end up opening all kindsa doors that should've stayed locked.

I've got a feeling there's a surprise or two behind doors number two and three.

8. FINDING MOIRA

I ain't the type to carry a lock-pick kit in my back pocket. Wouldn't have the first clue what to do with it if I did.

But I didn't start out as some meandering, skulking detective. Most of my training as a police officer stuck. Would be easier to break a bad habit than go against it.

I know you're thinking the boys in blue ain't got the cleanest of hands. What buttons do once they're trained is down to them. That training's better than the people it produces. Must be above the law to catch those filling their pockets on the far underside of the thin blue line.

I scout Moira's apartment from the street. No nosey brother this time. He stays in that café down the street. Pretends he earns his money on the up-and-up.

Back at Moira's place. Tucked away between the two old stone buildings. There's a patch of cracking concrete. Darker at the edges, but mostly a lighter shade, the rough shape of a rectangle. The steps up to Moira's door are a couple of feet away. This is her driveway. No car. One's been here. Parked here most nights until not so long ago.

Maybe she sold it. Parted ways to fund whatever new life she was looking for. Got out of here. Far away from whatever her brother had in-store.

Not that I got enough from the brother to be helpful. You'd think Davie would wanna give me the details of anything and everything he knows. Just so I stand a fighting chance of finding the dame. Instead, he's closed up tight. Might have better luck opening a stubborn pickle jar that's been set in concrete.

If I'm gonna find the girl, it's gonna be in spite of the

brother, not because of him.

First step, check her home again. A more thorough check. The kind that's not in keeping with someone watching. I ain't the mischievous kid, retrieving a wayward ball from an old lady's garden. I don't appreciate having beady eyes on me when I work.

I try the door. The wooden thing rattles in its frame. Some give there, but not enough. No clue how it helps me. I could mess around jamming credit cards places or twisting stuff in the lock, but I don't fancy my chances.

The door's at least sheltered from any onlookers, thanks to a protruding wall each side of the steps.

I got a bad idea, but nothing's challenging it for best-in-show.

The door's half solid wood and half thin glass. Nine small panes in a grid. A Yale lock that's twisted open from the inside.

There's one of those home improvement stores around the corner. They sell everything from ant powder to window latches. I stroll in, pick up a few items. A claw hammer. Glue. Small strip of wooden beading. Missing one thing.

I wander around, and bingo. Small single-paned rectangles of glass. The kind used to repair thousands of doors like Moira's. Looks to be a similar size, so I take a chance.

It ain't long before I'm breaking glass as a car drives past. I'm in.

I clean up the mess and set about replacing the broken section.

I'm no handyman, but this ain't exactly DIY SOS.

Glass fixed in place, I stand back and admire the result.

Admire's the wrong word. Look at it from a few steps back, at least.

The new piece is a different shade. I move around. Check from different angles. Barely different. Someone's only gonna spot it in just the right light when they're looking for it. No one's gonna notice otherwise.

I get a good look round, but when there's nothing to find, it doesn't matter how hard you try.

There's a light blue car in some of her photos. Gotta be hers because she ain't with anyone. Can't see enough to make out what it is.

I start hunting through sideboard drawers. I find a set of keys. Front door key, car key. A big chunky thing with Ford on the side. A small metal plate has a number stamped on it. It's a second key. I got her spare set. I'm looking for a Ford. Okay, that narrows it down to maybe one in six on the road. Gotta keep searching for something more useful.

Bedside units hold everything you'd expect to find except a diary. There's a pen, but nothing to write on. Maybe she writes reminders on her hand and hates putting down memories. Or a schedule. Looking around, she's not the kind to conform to a calendar.

The more drawers I hunt through, the more I build up a picture. I'm thinking this doll left because the task of tidying up was getting too much. I wouldn't blame her.

At the back of a kitchen drawer I find bank statements. Nothing out of the ordinary. No deposits to some rainy day account. No strange money coming in. Underneath it all, a car registration certificate. I've got the registration of her little blue Ford Fiesta. I write the details in my pocket notebook.

Light's starting to fade. I've gotta get outta here before I need to turn a light on and give myself away.

I take the keys and get out the door. It clicks shut behind me.

I get to the base of the steps when I hear a voice. Davie. Coming this way.

I crouch behind the wall, out of his way. Not quite out of sight. I hope he's too busy to notice me. Sure enough, he walks up the steps, head down the entire time. He's chatting away on the phone. Something about a game tonight.

I back away. I watch him from the edge of the driveway. He gets to the front door. Tries the handle. Gives a satisfied nod. Peers in through the glass for good measure and sees nothing. That's all the guy wanted. Make sure that pesky PI hasn't been back here. Making sure he can keep me on a tight leash.

I take a few steps back and stand round the corner.

He looks up when he gets back to the high street. Heads back the way he's come. He must've seen me. If he has, there's no sign on the guy's face.

He hangs up the call. Walks back towards his café, whistling like a man without a care in the world.

There's a whole heap of not-right about this kid. I ain't even scratched the surface. I trust him like I trust my stomach after a strong curry.

I haven't had any contact with the local law yet.

Might be time to get on the blower. See what they know.

I look up the number. The station's only about a minute's walk away.

Sure enough, it's seconds before I'm climbing the sandstone steps. This place has been the home of the police here for about a century, by the looks of it.

Solid sandstone construction, except for the fifties or sixties extension out the back. Huge windows. Imposing style. Other than some new Police Scotland signs, it looks like it's not changed much since it opened.

There's a woman behind some glass screen at the reception desk. She's got some getup on that looks a bit like a uniform but not quite. She's got a round face, a tiny nose and a mouth that could be big enough to hold the teeth of five pensioners. Dark hair somewhere between brown and black ends at her jawline.

"Help ya?" She asks.

No idea what's happened to the rest of that question these days.

I lay out my ID. Tell her who I am, why I'm here. Ask about the person assigned to Moira Wallace.

Her smile vanishes like I insulted the Scottish. "I'll be back in a mo."

She comes back with a man. He's got the stride of a long-in-the-tooth DC. His brown hair needs cutting, and intense brown eyes seem to bore their way through the glass towards me. His snub nose is twitching. So is his wide, stubble-covered jaw. A grey suit that needs dry cleaning. A shirt off-white but I'm not sure in which direction. No tie.

"You here looking for Moira Wallace?" He asks. His voice is as stern as his stare.

I nod.

"No one's told you yet? Who hired you anyway?"

I shrug. "I ain't been told a hell of a lot since I got here. Her brother hired me."

The piercing stare leaves. It's replaced by a confused is-someone-having-me-on kinda look. "Not more than an hour ago, I got off the phone to him. We found the girl's body in a farm outbuilding a few miles past Finstown."

9. IDLE TONGUES MAKE FOR BUSY PRIVATE EYES

It's well past closing time. There's a blackness to the wet air outside. Some tries to infiltrate through microscopic gaps in the ancient wooden sash windows. Some makes it, squealing as it goes.

It's a darkness that wants to creep everywhere, extinguish any light it finds. None of your soft, southern nights here.

The plastic tables and chairs are as clean as they ever get. The fryer is almost cold. The cash register's got nothing left inside it except maybe a couple of spiders. The sign on the door, bold white writing on a tartan background says, 'Sorry, we're closed.'

But the gang's all there, as agreed. As expected. Night after night, the same drill.

Young Bella could pass for any age from twelve to twenty. She's got the palest of blue eyes, a button nose and a mouth fixed in that sullen, teenager sulk. She's wearing a short purple party dress. It ain't the best colour for her dirty blonde hair, but somehow she makes it work.

Naomi's carrying a couple more years and a little more weight around her features. She's got a straight nose, dark green eyes and a cheeky smirk brought out by pink-red lipstick. Deep red ballgown. A split up one side to her thigh. The kind of outfit a bond girl might wear when she pulls a gun from nowhere in a shootout. A small black woollen cardigan makes her look more sensible. Her light brown hair would cover the shoulder straps of the dress if they weren't covered.

Fiona's black hair and plain face kinda make her the forgettable gal of the group. She's got an olive complexion, dark eyes, a Roman nose and a crooked smile. She's let her hair grow all the way down her back. She's gotta work harder for clients to remember her. Maybe the hair's what does it.

Jenny's still got the bright hair that reaches partway down her neck. A fan of bright in-your-face colours. She's in a tight-fitting yellow sweater and a shock pink pleated PVC skirt. She's got a pair of white knee socks covering most of her thin legs.

Shona's trying to be the footballer's wife-type. Gaunt face. Dark sunglasses, long slim-fit overcoat. No one's gonna find out what's underneath unless she says so. Black, wet-look shoulder-length hair. The bird could say more with a shrug than most folks can fit in an essay.

They gather and await the daily update on their friend and former colleague, Moira.

Into this room, from the door at the back, breezes Davie Wallace. He's looking like a man with recently repressed road rage.

"I've had the police on the phone," he says.

He looks at the floor and hunches a little. Could be putting this on for effect. There's a chance he's genuinely upset.

No one says anything for about a minute.

One by one, the girls start fidgeting. They tap their feet. They look at each other. They're getting looks back as confused as the looks they're giving off. It's like one of those tense, drawn-out pauses for effect on reality TV. Milk it before they announce the next person going home. Except this is more serious.

"They've found Moira's body. On the mainland. Near Stenness."

There are gasps. Hands over mouths. Tears falling from

pretty eyes and rolling down cute faces.

"I've got a couple of things to say," he continues, swallowing a lump in his throat. "First, you all know she was a kind woman who didn't deserve to have her life cut short. She strayed from here, and from the safety we could all provide. No one's gonna feel the sorrow of this more than me."

The girls nod. Each stands apart from all others, dabbing the corners of eyes with tissues.

"Second," he continues, "You might know I hired a private detective to find Moira. I'm now, of course, gonna send him home. That might take a day or two to arrange. Got to let him down gently. Persuade him to leave the rest to the police."

He looks up and looks each girl in the eyes in turn, from his left to his right. "You might also know that he's been poking his nose in about me. The way I run my business. My reputation. I want to make one thing perfectly clear."

He has their undivided attention now.

"No one is to speak to Enoch Flint about anything. Nothing at all. If he asks the time, even, you don't answer."

He starts taking small yet authoritative steps, pacing up and down the centre aisle.

"If I find out that Mr Flint has found out anything at all about me, I'll assume it came from one of you. If not from you, from one of our loose-lipped clients, who you should be keeping under control."

He's nearly reached the door. He turns around and strolls back the other way, like it's a summer's walk through a park.

"Private detectives and the police can't leave each other alone. It's just how it is. I happen to know he's already been in the station today."

He is walking past the end table when he lashes out and smashes a clenched fist down into it. The sound echoes around the room. The girls jump and a couple of them let out a whimper.

He spins on his heels and glares at them. "I cannot have the police getting wind of anything. Do you hear me?"

Three of the girls do a meek nod.

In a louder voice, he asks again, "Am I understood?"

They all nod like they want their heads to fall off and say, "Yes" in unison.

He walks back to the door at the rear of the room.

"I'll of course let you know where and when the funeral's gonna take place. I'll get a book of condolence if you or anyone else wants to write anything."

The girls are back to their meek nods.

"My wee sister's gone, and she's not coming back. I'm sad about that. I really am. But I've got to make sure, right now, that I... that *we* don't lose everything else."

He pulls a phone from his pocket. "Now, let's run over the schedule for tonight. Everyone knows what they're doing, where they're going. Pay attention, because I'm giving each of you a specific time to make your safety calls."

The girls nod and retrieve their own phones, ready to set reminders.

They earn pennies during their café shifts.

It's during these dark nights when they leave this place. Earn some real money.

10. A DAY THAT STARTS WITH A BODY AIN'T A GOOD DAY

I didn't need the directions. I could see the white forensic tent from the road.

I could've seen it from space.

Not today, though.

Not with that cold, merciless thick blanket of cloud sitting there, smirking at me. It's got all the power to pour down more misery on this scene any time it wants. There ain't a thing we can do about it. We sit around down here with our thicker atmosphere and wait.

The drive here would've been scenic, beautiful if I could've seen beyond the side of the road. But things cleared up a little a couple of miles ago. Distant hills poked through the haze like lurking giants in some fantasy movie.

Just past Stenness, DC Stephen Sutherland said. Past the standing stones, away to the right (if you can see them). It's on the right. Opposite a ruined barn.

The huge loch in the background. Looks like it's split in two by a kind of land bridge, but they're two different lakes. Enough landmarks around here to help find the place. Could even manage it without the white circus tent.

I get a quarter mile away before some PC waves me to the side of the road. He's got his tall helmet on with the big Police Scotland shield on the front.

Everyone's got the right gear on. The bigwigs are gonna show up and act like they know what's going on. Gotta look smart. Look attentive. The cops who do everything right, wear the right stuff, act the way you'd expect, go unnoticed. But you can be damn sure they'll spot the ones who've fallen a little short.

The guy by the side of the road's got a nose that got bent out of shape a few years ago. Looks like it healed badly. He looks east and that thing's pointing south east. Dark blue eyes are staring right at me, though.

Not sure if he's holding his slightly chubby jaw to one side for effect. Could be something was responsible for the wonk there too. Maybe the same beating. Or an entirely different one. Maybe he came off a bike and hit a tree hard.

I look around. Not a tree in sight. In fact, I'm not even sure I've seen one outside of Kirkwall. Plenty of dry stone walls. Could do the same kinda damage.

"You Flint?" he asks. How'd he know? Do I stand out that much? Might as well have a cow bell round my neck.

"You're here for the missing girl?" he says.

I nod with my head cocked to the right a little. "Yeah, but she ain't exactly missing anymore."

He purses his lips together and gives a grim nod. He shakes it out of his head and then points to my left. "Gotta park in the field opposite if that's alright with you."

I nod again. "Even if it wasn't, I'd do it anyway. Besides, this isn't even my car."

He gives me a polite smile and a nod.

I head on through a farm gate. I park a couple of feet from one of those unmarked-yet-entirely-obvious police cars. The type they've got everywhere. It's silver. Washed by someone who couldn't see or didn't care. It's got a couple of small dents no police mechanic is gonna sink time into sorting out.

I head across the road. Not as busy as a main route through a community should be, but that's fine by me.

There's a lane with chest-high hedges lining both sides.

The building ahead on the left is the house. It's got a fresher application of stucco than the rest of the structures. Net curtains behind small windows.

It's a small, hunkered-down sorta house on one storey. Thick walls holding up a slate roof. Would have to be solid to stay standing through bleak winters in a place this desolate.

Ahead, past the house, the property ends at the shore of the Loch. Could be an amazing view on a nice day. I don't suppose I'm gonna see one up here, though.

A couple of barely-standing concrete farm structures sit to the right of the lane. If they can store anything and keep it safe from the elements, then I'm best friends with Bob Hope.

The first unusual thing I spot is a bathtub. An old, free-standing one. Seems they dumped it outside as a large planter when indoor plumbing reached the island. Now, it sits in front of a disused coal shed, full soil and of dying flowers. Might make quite the feature in the summer months. Still looks strange outside of a garden centre.

Another officer's standing nearby. A short man with glasses and a smile that doesn't sit well on an otherwise stern face. "I'll warn you," he says, "it's not pretty in there." He points a thumb at the building behind him.

I give him a thanks and a nod.

As I walk past, he says, "we're not sure yet, but she might've been here a couple of days. The entrance is the far side."

I walk down the farm lane, barn (and bathtub) to the left.

It's bigger than it looked from the road. Could become a decent conversion. Four good-size holiday lets could be made out of it. Not so sure people would buy into it now, though, given what's turned up inside.

The walls are looking worse the farther along I get. The wall covering's cracking and coming away. Then there are chunks missing, revealing concrete blocks beneath. Then the blocks are broken. Then they're missing. Then the roof starts to disappear.

Its in bad shape. Worse than it first looked. It ain't ever getting converted into anything but rubble and a brownfield site.

The walk to the other end is a fast-forward through time and decay. Gotta check my watch at the other end to make sure I've not gone through some sort of time warp.

I reach the end of what may have once been a solid wall. There is no far wall. No door. A gaping hole at the end greets me. Like some farmer came outside one day and finds someone's had a go at stealing a whole thing.

No part of this structure shelters the inside from the worst of the weather. The white forensic tent helps, but that can't work miracles.

The body's laying there, halfway down the barn, right in the centre. Not a lot I can say about it from this distance.

They're not letting me get too close. Can't risk contamination. Got me wondering why I was even brought out here.

"We've not got dedicated CSI," DC Sutherland says, coming out of nowhere. "We've gotta make do with a couple of DCs who've been on a couple of courses. Someone's heading over from the mainland. They'll be here later today."

I nod. "A PC out there said she might've been here a couple of days?"

He nods. "Well, more than one, by the looks of things. Beyond that, we're not sure yet. Need the pathologist to say for sure."

He moves to get a little closer and gestures for me to come along. They're a friendly bunch, these Orkney officers. Show up on a Wednesday, introduce yourself, get invited to a crime scene on a Thursday morning.

We walk a little closer.

"Any idea what happened yet?" I ask.

A shake of the head. "Not really. Likely killed somewhere else, and the body dumped here. There's no blood pooling nearby. No spots on the way in, even."

He points at the ground. "We've covered all this area already, so we're safe to walk along here. Not so much as a footprint."

It can't have been possible for anyone to get in and out of this damp, dirt floor and to leave no trace.

I'm looking around at the walls. I wanna spot that magic clue. The one everyone missed that turns out to be crucial. Problem is, I'm no Sherlock. I ain't even his landlady.

"This is about as close as I dare get."

I look where he's looking.

About fifteen feet away, a girl is lying on her back. Arms and legs outstretched. She's wearing a pale pink blouse, torn open. No loose buttons. Black lace bra beneath. A dark grey pencil skirt. No socks or shoes. Something's sitting on her stomach.

The shoes are set off to the side. Neat. Like she slipped them off before having a lie down.

I point at them. "You found the shoes like that?"

He nods.

Then the smell hits me.

The nausea.

Memories of people recently deceased, and all because of me.

Jasper's dead.

Miami's gone.

Evie was close to joining them in the great blackness of wherever.

The ground underneath me has gone soft. It's gonna swallow me.

Everything's galloping around me.

What if Flick's next? Or Toby?

Breathing out was a mistake because I can't breathe in again.

My heart's jackhammering. My vision's blurring.

I start to keel over but DC Sutherland grabs me. Rushes me back outside the white tent.

I find a spot out back where I can lose my breakfast. It was much more enjoyable going in, not so long ago.

At least I can breathe again. And those thoughts of doom have gone back through whatever door they jumped out from.

It's a minute or more before I'm ready to stand up.

I head back inside and he's there, smiling. "No one warned you against eating, I see."

I shake my head. "Not that it's any use to me now."

He gives me a quizzical look. "You've seen stuff like this before though. You're not used to this sort of thing being a Detective from a big town?"

It ain't a big town unless you're from here.

I nod. "I've mostly seen the freshly dead kind. And no matter how many of them I see, it's not a sight I can get used to."

He pats me on the stomach and starts to rush past. "Look alive. Chief Inspector Grant Flett's just arrived."

Orders are being barked before I can even see him. Stand here. Pay attention. Why's this thing here? When are CSI arriving?

"And who let some soft, puking English civilian into my crime scene?"

He rounds the corner and I'm staring right at him.

He's got sharp features and an almost military-grade hairstyle. The greying hair's thinning at the front of his scalp, but elsewhere it's thick and trimmed like a Ken doll. A pair of friendly-looking dirty green, brown eyes stare at me down a Roman nose. It's the mouth and jaw of a suave politician. A handsome, friendly face. Shame about the person it's sitting on.

"The name's DC Flint, Sir. Thank you for allowing me the chance to throw up here. Not on active duty, but I was hired-"

"Yes, I know. By the victim's brother."

He turns to DC Sutherland.

"Is he coming? We need an ID."

DC Sutherland shakes his head. "DC Flint could provide an

ID in his absence?"

DCI Flett lets out a mocking laugh. "Let this guy near the body again? Not bloody likely!"

He turns back to me. "So, English Detective. You got anything helpful to offer us here?"

I'm scrambling around mentally like a dog chasing a ball across a patch of ice. "I guess you'll be aware of her car. Ford. Light blue."

DC Sutherland nods. "We've been running checks on the reg. Car keys are here. Her light blue Ford's parked down the road which they'll likely unlock."

I've known the guy for minutes. Even so, I doubt DCI Flett has ever looked so smug. "Is that it?"

I shrug. "I know the brother's up to something. For one thing, I saw him walking along whistling yesterday. Even after being told about his sister's death."

He turns around and puts on a sarcastic voice. "Well, as you know, whistling is illegal in Scotland, since a few months ago."

He stares right at me. "Get away from my crime scene. Ideally, you'd keep getting away. Keep going until you're back in your wee English home. Sitting in your cartoon character pyjamas and slippers. Console yourself with TV dramas. Wondering what it's like to be a *good* detective."

I look at DC Sutherland. He does nothing to vouch for my presence. Time to head back where I came from.

I don't know what I was expecting to find here, but I haven't found it.

Somewhere there are clues to inform on the killer.

I've just gotta know what they are, and where they are.

If I can find something before they do, I might buy a few minutes of polite cooperation.

I'd go for a couple less death stares and sarcastic comments.

11. WHERE'S THE REMOTE CONTROL?

A momentary lapse.

That's all it was.

But those moments can be costly. Especially when they can be the difference between freedom and captivity.

It was all an unnecessary risk. Could've left Moira like the others. No one had suspected anything with them. Not yet, anyway. They will in time.

What was her brother playing at, anyway? Hiring some detective from the other end of England? There were other, better ways of throwing off suspicion.

Even if the truth came out, he'd say he didn't ask anyone to kill his sister. Folks might believe him. They might not. The guy sitting with the phone in his hand is in the latter camp.

Davie had practically begged for this to happen, even if he hadn't said so in as many words. In any case, you run that kind of a business, there are risks. There's breakage.

Gotta be a moment when you say the wrong thing to the wrong gee. He says she's causing him trouble and she needs to be out of the picture. What else could he have meant by that? As it turns out, she was a nice fit for this particular plan anyway.

But he might get the chance to chew the fat with this man on another day. Educate him on ways to not make stupid choices. Stupidity got people caught, or it got them killed.

He's not immune from poor choices. He's looking at the consequence of one of them. A tiny blue dot on a phone screen. Still there. Right at the farm.

The police would've removed her handbag, phone and all,

already. It would be sitting in their property store. Maybe this was good news. If the remote wipe command had worked, would the location update anymore?

He didn't know enough about any of this to answer that question.

The thing to do would've been to remove the phone. Take the SIM card out. Chuck it in that lake. But he didn't do any of that. He left the thing on, in her bag. Carried away in the moment.

A loose end. They become threads that detectives pull at until things start to unravel.

He was worrying about nothing. Had to be. It's not like the gal knew him. Not like she'd been texting him about meeting for coffee.

But that phone might have something against her brother. Something he could have used if he needed it. He had plenty of evidence of his own anyway, and he could use it if things took a turn for the worse.

Some important people around here have made their own stupid mistakes. Theirs would certainly come back to haunt them. So they should. When you become someone important, someone respected, you've gotta be better. Got to be above reproach.

There was no honour anymore. No one doing the right thing, because it's the right thing to do. Always looking for some benefit. Some way it improves their image or adds dough to their accounts.

Gone are the days of chivalry. Dependability. When people could say something, and they'd do it, regardless of personal sacrifice. The days when people leaned towards mutual respect.

The days when society meant something. When community was about bringing people together. They'd then do something other than stare at their phones.

He could bring back those days. Sure, some people would have to die. Some sacrifices are still needed. Some people need to suffer for their sins.

He looks at the phone again.

A notification.

> Remote wipe successful.

He stops clenching his jaw and lets himself smile.

Things are getting back on track.

All he needs now is for that idiot brother of the dead gal to send that private detective packing. The police here aren't hot on this stuff, but this guy's an unknown. A mad, dancing aunt at a party. A fly in his Martini.

He has to go.

Davie Wallace? Maybe him too. Hard to say at the moment.

Either way, things are more or less where they should be.

No one's gonna be allowed to throw things off course again. Not when there's so much left to do.

12. WHEN THINGS ARE FALLING FLAT

"Anyway, just a quick call to tell you I'm still here. My focus is switching from finding Moira to finding her killer. You don't want me to do that, you just gotta let me know."

I hang up the call.

He hired me out of desperation.

I doubt he's gonna keep me on the payroll for this. The police will keep trying to find their man. Chances are I'll get in their way.

Already been back to my hotel room. My stuff's packed up and sitting there.

There's a good chance I'm heading back to Aberdeen on the morning flight.

Flick won't be able to hide her amazement. I'm not gonna tell her when we talk tonight. Gonna let her think I'm still needed. Surprise her when I walk through the door. Offer her my hat for a snack. No one up here seems to think it's good for anything else.

Davie might be glad to let me go. He's not gonna be as happy to know where I'm calling him from.

I'm in Moira's bedroom. Staring at that pen.

No pad. No paper anywhere near it.

The one detail that keeps bothering me.

She must've been writing on something. Maybe I'm reading too much into it. Maybe there's nothing to find.

When the fuzz show up and tear this place apart, they're probably not gonna find anything more than I have.

Nothing's appeared in the drawers, or the other drawers, or the wardrobe.

Nothing under the bed.

Nothing in the bathroom cabinet.

I've nearly hunted through every bit of standard storage in the joint.

I've gotta start looking where people don't usually put things.

Inside appliances. Nothing.

I pull up a loose corner of carpet. Only insects.

I check down the back and under the sofa. Empty of everything but about thirty pence in change.

Back to the bedroom. I lift the mattress. Nothing under it.

But there's something about the mattress. A deliberate hole cut in the side. I shove my hand in. I find nothing but springs that wanna take my hand off, piece by piece.

I'm on my knees. Arm partway stuck inside the mattress. Not a good time to hear footsteps behind me.

A floorboard creaks.

Another one closer.

Davie's gonna flip his lid if he finds me in here again.

I snap my head around.

It's not him.

It's a girlish face. Dirty blonde hair. It's Bella from the café. Still in the gear she'd wear in there. Black top, tight blue jeggings. A tan satchel bag over her shoulder.

"What are you doing?" she asks.

I manage to pull my arm free without losing any skin. A minor miracle. I get to my feet. "Looking for something."

"What kind of something?" She's got a smirk on her face. Like it's not normal to find a guy in your missing friend's place with their arm half stuck in a mattress.

I point to the pen. "Something to write with, but nothing to write on. That seem odd to you?"

She shrugs. "You think she's hidden something?"

I nod. "And I think that something's gonna help me find who killed her."

She reaches into her bag and pulls out a small black notebook. The tiny kind. She walks towards me.

She holds it out. "If I give you this," she says, "will you promise to use it to find who killed her, and see if you can help the rest of us?"

I nod. Take the book. Look back at her. "Help you with what?"

There's a clattering noise outside. Bella looks like a scared kitten. She backs away a couple of steps. "I've got to go."

She's high-tailing it out the door before I can say another word. I ain't gonna persuade her to come back.

I look down at the little black book. I flip through it. A diary. Names. Phone numbers. Appointments.

Time to head back to the hotel.

Looks like I've got some reading material. Might give me a lead or two.

This could be the first useful thing that's happened since I got here.

13. LITTLE BLACK BOOKS CAN LEAD TO BLACK EYES

The thing about a little black book is you can't fit a hell of a lot inside the damn thing. You ain't gonna fit an epic within that fake leather cover. Even if your writing's so small only six-legged creatures can see it.

But Moira's writing isn't so small. It's got all those girly loops. Rounded, neat lettering that takes up pretty much every bit of white space. At least her handwriting was neat. She hadn't got around to taking a leaf outta that book and applying it elsewhere.

A whole list of names and numbers. Some have dates and times scribbled nearby.

A page at the front has the title 'The Girls'. Bella, Fiona, Jenny, Naomi, Shona. She's even got them alphabetically. A number next to each. All but Jenny's have a number crossed out and a new one written smaller above it. Seems these girls change their numbers like I change duvet covers.

The rest of the book's got a week per double page for the whole year. There's a map of the London Underground too, in case that's any use the opposite end of the UK. The names and numbers could be appointments. Unless she wrote them anywhere there was a space. Not too many have names as the dates move on. Just numbers. Some with initials.

Seems like there might be something important in here. I ain't gonna know it until it hits me between the eyes while I'm doing something else.

I set to work taking a snap of each page with my phone. I've got between forty and fifty pictures that could be useful someday to someone. For me, right now, they're just taking up space.

I walk round to the café again. I ain't gonna breeze in the door. That'll get Davie putting eyes on me again.

He knows more than he's letting on. What's the betting he's told his staff to give me a welcome fit for yesterday's pop star?

The sun's breached the clouds for a couple of minutes. There ain't a lot of warmth in it. If anything, it's a couple of degrees colder than it was a minute ago. It's doing its best to bounce its bright light off every wet surface. Dazzle pedestrians from above and from below.

I keep walking past.

I spot an alley down the left side of the building. Goes somewhere dark. Looks anything but a good idea.

Who am I kidding? I'm gonna wander down there and maybe plead ignorance if someone nabs me. Claim I was trying to find a car park back there somewhere. Could swear I left my car near here.

What little warmth the sun might have been dishing out, none of it's making it down here.

The space opens out a little, but it ain't any brighter or warmer. A little forgotten courtyard. Cheap cement flagstones. A couple of overgrown weeds and a hedge that needed trimming a decade ago. Might be beyond saving now.

Then a door slams somewhere. Loud, like someone forgot to turn the TV down.

A shout. A scream. Some voices getting a little closer. Unless they're just getting louder.

Seems like some domestic dispute. Two folks vying for the crown befitting a drama queen. Something about washing up.

Something about drinking. Something about some gal wishing she was anywhere else.

I step to the side, into the darkest of shadows. It's rude to spy on people. It might even be ruder to do it in plain sight. I've never asked.

This bird's gotta get something off her chest before she sticks something through his.

But this ain't got a thing to do with me. Not as much as a bean to do with Moira or her brother. I've got no business being here.

I look around for some back door into the café.

Nothing. Just a stone wall.

Must be round the other side.

It's time to turn around and to find something else to do with my time.

But my time's run out. I ain't got the freedom to make my own choices just now. On account of someone wrapping something round my neck.

I've been here before. More times than anyone should've visited this exact scenario. Gotta keep my wits about me. Gotta get a hand between my neck and whatever's trying to cut off my air.

I go one better. I get both hands under there and pull an arm free.

Success. I've avoided strangulation again. How many times before you can put that kinda thing on your résumé?

But I ain't got time to celebrate.

Not a chance to count the times I've escaped

unconsciousness. Not even a moment for a delighted whoop.

Not before something crashes down on my head.

Something hard. Something cracking and splintering that was once a solid lump of pottery. A plant pot.

Not that it matters.

Sometimes you hit the floor and your head's shutting down for a beat. When that happens, you don't care about the thing that put you there.

All that matters is that you lost the fight.

You lost it badly.

And now you're at the mercy of some maniacal plant-pot-wielding thug.

There's a lot to be said for avoiding dark alleys.

People don't warn about that kinda crap enough.

14. A PAY-OFF WITHOUT A SET-UP

I get that all-too-familiar swooning feeling as I start to wake up. I'm a little there, then I'm gone. I come back to the world of the living in waves, until I'm lapping at the shore of full consciousness.

My eyes open like the door of an ancient Egyptian tomb. I gotta wonder if it looks like there's any more life in me than in one of those places.

A flat ceiling. A single lightbulb hangs from its fitting without any kind of a shade. A dull light hitting it from small windows.

The walls are bare. Not a picture on them. Not even a coat of paint. Nothing but some misguided attempts at repairing the plaster job laid bare.

I get a whiff of a smell from somewhere underneath. Fried food. Coffee. Filtered through inadequate floorboards, also uncovered.

I'm lying on the only bit of real furniture in the room. A huge brown sofa that was all the rage when a cordless phone was a pipedream.

There's some guy sitting on a small wooden stool beside me, clicking his fingers at me. Most folks might expect a washcloth to the forehead and reassuring words when they wake up from a hit to the head. Not this guy. Not here.

It's Davie Wallace. Waiting for me to wake up so he can ask me how my investigation is going. When am I gonna give up and go home. That sorta thing.

"You took quite the hit," he says.

I croak out something. I clear my throat and try again. "Did they catch the guy?"

"He got away. Nothing anyone could do. I happened to see the whole thing as I walked past."

Sure he did. I'm sure he's got no idea who whacked me. I'm sure he wasn't the one holding the plant pot.

"The good news is that the cuts on your head from the broken plant pot are only small. Should heal in a couple of days."

I'm almost ready to sit up. I give it a go. It works better than I'd hoped.

"It's admirable of you to want to find Moira's killer," he says. "Don't you think it's a job for the police now?"

I touch the top of my head. One of those moments of instant, painful regret. After a good long wince, I say, "I thought you didn't trust them."

He shakes his head. "I never said that. I said they weren't doing anything. That changes now that it's a murder investigation. They're throwing everything at it."

My hand works its way down to my neck and tries to rub out some tension. "Are you telling me you don't want my help?"

He smiles at me. It's as fake as a thirty dollar Rolex from a New York street seller. "I think it's time to call it a day. Don't you?"

"What if I don't?" I ask.

The smile falls off his face like glass falls from a shattered window. "I'm the client. It's up to me. It's over when I say. When I stop employing you."

I nod.

He carries on. "I'm saying it's time to stop. It seems Moira's been dead for a while. Before I even met you, as it happens. You were never gonna win this one."

"What about justice?"

He gets up from the stool and looks out of one of the two windows. "I trust the police to deliver justice, or at least to give it a go. I trust you to get on the next plane home and know when your services are no longer required."

"What if I want to stay?"

He spins around like I set off a firework. "I can't force you to leave, but I can stop paying you. As of now, you're fired."

I nod. "I understand. How are we gonna settle up?"

He shrugs. "You've got the retainer. I already paid for the hotel and the flights and the hire car until today. That seems to cover everything, as far as I can work out."

"You covering the cost of the return flights?" I ask.

He looks at me like I asked him to cut off a foot and put it in a bag for me. I've got as much chance of getting a house on the moon as I have of squeezing any more cash from this guy.

I start to get to my feet. A slight sway, but not too bad at all.

He lets out a sigh. "I'll have another four hundred sent to your account to cover the past couple of days. Can we call that suitable terms for ending this?"

I nod, taking a step towards the door. "Thank you."

He thanks me in return with the sincerity of a child's forced apology.

Time for me to get my things together, it seems.

I can't promise I'm done yet, but anything I do from now ain't on this guy's dime. The longer I stay, the emptier my pockets get.

But it could be that this is about more than money.

And Bella. She asked for my help. How can I cut and run?

Gotta find out the facts before I can catch a plane outta here.

But if I hang around, how long's it gonna be before he tries to run me out of town?

And when you're run out of town here, where else is there to go?

15. MORE THAN ONE WAY TO DIG YOURSELF A HOLE

I've seen a hundred houses like this one since I got here a day and a half ago. Might as well start the day looking at a couple more.

Thick stone walls. Slate roof. Small but new windows. A doorway through which a hobbit might even have to crouch. A row of six of them. These days, they're two-bedroom starter homes. A couple of generations ago, who knows?

This little row is in the village of Stenness. The locals call it a town. They call anything a town when three people stand together and chat for long enough.

A woman answers the door. She's short, plain and more than a little overweight. Small eyes. Crooked nose. Think she shaves more than I do. She asks me who I am through uneven, yellow teeth. Those sweat pants look newer than the sweater. That's only because they don't look like they got dragged out from some nearby hole in the ground.

"The name's Flint. I'm a private detective."

She has a look that suggests it's the strangest occupation in the world. Might as well have said I was a sword swallower, escaped from the circus. Reduced to going door-to-door looking for kids' birthday party gigs.

"Is there a Stanley here? Surname Kerr? He's the only one in the local phone book."

"Stan? Yeah, he lives here, but he's not here right now. What's this about?"

I've gotta come up with a lie quick, or I could be setting off a domestic incident for a little later on.

"He knew someone at work. Someone who's just died. I wanted to see if he knew anything."

"Work?" She smirks and laughs a little. "He hasn't worked in ten years."

I open my mouth to try to dig the guy out of a hole I'm making, but she cuts me off.

"If you mean volunteering, there's loads doing that up at the dig site. The big new one, near the standing stones." She points to some distant spot. I could only see the place from here with a good telescope and X-Ray vision.

I shrug. "I know it's a long shot, but I've gotta work my way through a list. See if anyone's got anything at all to tell me. Is he there now?"

She nods. There's an intake of breath that's a little like she's shocked. Seen a few people do that around here. You get used to it after some time around the locals. I'd assume so, anyway. Seems she's saying 'aye' in agreement whilst breathing in instead of out. No idea who might have started that one, but it's caught on around these islands.

I nod and back away. "Thank you."

She probably wants to ask how her other half knows this chippy who's died. Wants to know if he's in trouble. She doesn't ask any of those questions. Her face settles into some resigned curious look. She closes the door.

I drive out of Stenness and turn right a little way down the road. I'm soon on that land bridge between the two lochs. If I look back and to my left, I'll see the police still hunting for clues at the farm.

I look out at two vast pools of water, one on each side. Someone told me one's fresh water and one's salt water. Strange how these places get put together. How mother nature paints with her brush. Patches of blue sky overhang distant shores. Dull clouds cover others. The rest is some kinda apocalyptic fog and rain combination.

Up ahead is the big talking point of the Orkney Islands. A new discovery of ancient settlements they call the Ness of Brodgar. All I can say about it is it's a couple of big holes full of stones and bones.

At least I make it to the site between a couple of spells of rain.

I make noise until I track down Stan Kerr. He's wearing jeans and some black top, covered by what looks a lot like a bin liner with neck and arm holes cut out.

He's as short and unattractive as the woman who answered the door to his house. Losing his hair as quick as the rain here washes away dirt from a pavement. Somewhere north of forty. Jutting out lower jaw. Eyes of a delicate spaniel. She could have been his wife. More likely his sister, comparing the two. Could be off the hook after all.

I hand him a picture. "You seen this bird?"

He takes a look. He recognises her. Pretends he doesn't, but he does it too late. An over-the-top shake of the head to try and convince himself. Even that ain't working.

"Your phone number end 675?" I ask.

He looks at me, surprised.

"Then you *do* know her. Or at least, you *did*."

He backs off a step. "Who are you?"

"Flint. Private detective." Already getting sick of saying that. "I'm looking into the death of that doll, named Moira. You wanna tell me anything you wouldn't tell the police? Help me out a little?"

He looks at the ground and shakes his head. "It's sad that she's dead, but I only met her once. Months ago."

I swipe a couple of things on my phone for effect. "According to her diary, you saw her a few nights ago. On the night she died, as it turns out."

Sometimes you've gotta chuck out a straight-up guess and hope it gets you somewhere.

He goes pale. He wasn't exactly bronzed to start with. "I didn't have anything to do with that. She was alive when I dropped her off."

"Then care to tell me what happened?"

He grabs my arm and walks me away from everyone else. His voice is as low as a whisper. The distant scraping of sharp metal against dirt and stone almost drowns him out.

"Alright," he says. "I used an escort service. My first time ever, if you can believe that. I arranged it all with the girl's boss, you know? Told me to pick her up outside the cathedral on a little side street, eight o'clock."

I nod. He's got my permission to carry on spilling.

"We head to a wee guest house a little farther south. We... you know."

I look at him confused.

"We... were intimate. That's what I paid for, wasn't it? Anyway, then I dropped her back off outside the cathedral. Same place I picked her up. Must've been about nine. I swear I haven't seen her since. She was walking down the high street. Couldn't tell you where to."

All done in an hour, including travel? Moira must've been a lucky gal, having this guy to herself. I guess she and the other girls do a pretty good job of earning their cash.

"You know anything about Moira?" I ask.

He shakes his head. "Didn't even know that was her name. Pretty shameful, I know."

"You see her with anyone else? You catch sight of her car?"

He shakes his head.

"She tell you anything about herself? Anything at all."

He goes to shake his head. He stops. "Now that you mention it, she said something about not getting used to her. She wasn't gonna be around for much longer. She had plans. Big plans to get away."

I nod. "Thank you. Anything else?"

He pokes out one hell of a lower lip and shakes his head.

"Who was she working for?"

He's dithering now. He doesn't wanna share that.

"I can ask the police to run your phone records and find out," I say. They might have a few more questions for you. In a locked room. After a caution. They could even arrest you."

His eyes get wider. If he wasn't sweating under that plastic sheet he's wearing, he is now.

"No need for that. It's the guy who owns a café on the high street. Davie... something."

I cut the guy loose and thank him for his honesty.

Someday soon the police are gonna find him and ask him some tough questions of their own. He's got time to get his story straight. Or at least a little straighter than the yarn he tried to spin with me.

Police seem to think Moira drove herself out of town. She parked the car herself. Someone grabbed her. A mugging gone wrong. That shoe doesn't fit. When they find out, they're gonna think a client took her out.

I've gotta find out what the elephant ears know. Gotta do something more than chasing my tail.

This time, I've got something to offer them in return.

16. FROM ONE LITTLE BOOK TO THE GOOD BOOK

I'm sitting in an ice cream shop on the corner. It's a kinda bright blue eggshell colour outside. Trying too hard to be relevant inside.

The place calls itself The Daily Scoop. A name that's funnier to the locals, I'm told. Used to be a newspaper store.

I get a table by a big window. I look out at the grand red St Magnus Cathedral. Ornate carved red sandstone smattered with a horizontal dash of yellow sandstone. A big old impressive structure.

But I ain't here for the view, nor for the iron brew ice cream, which might've tasted better when it was warmer outside.

I got DC Sutherland to walk over. He walks through the door. Got the awkward gait of a Mormon in a dive bar. He clocks me. Heads over.

"Hey, Flint. You okay after yesterday morning?"

I shrug, a little plastic ice cream spoon in my hand. "I'm managing to keep my food down a little better now."

I fish the little book from my pocket and drop it on the table.

"You might have some interest in that," I say. "One of Moira's friends was looking after it for her. Seems to hint at something?"

He screws up his face. "We don't go for hints. Anything obvious?"

"An escort service. Run on the hush-hush by Moira's brother."

He leans back in his chair. "Is that all?"

"What do you mean is that all?" I ask.

He leans forward and stares at me. "People sometimes have a funny idea of the law. You say escort. Is that what you mean? Not prostitution?"

I shrug. "Isn't one usually linked to the other?"

He shakes his head again. "Escort services are perfectly legal. You want us to haul him in, give him a hard time, question the girls, all to slap them with something like tax evasion? Sounds like one for the HMRC, if they're even interested."

I pick up the book and open it to the final appointment. "This guy. He saw her the night she died. Picked her up near here at eight, dropped her off again at nine. Worth checking CCTV?"

He's wearing a pained smirk. "We've got two cameras covering the whole area around the cathedral. Put in years ago. Couldn't use them to ID a guy with a giant head in a florescent jumpsuit."

I sigh. "Could still use it to corroborate. If it doesn't add up, you've got a lead?"

He nods. "Makes sense."

"How's the investigation going?" I had to ask.

He scowls a little before his face straightens out. "It's all a wee bit odd. So much doesn't add up."

I nod, but say nothing.

"You know that blue car? Not hers. Belongs to a farmer out there. Seems some gee messed with the plates. One of our DC's got a task to find her car. It's not hit the ferries. No one's seen it driving around. Nothing on our few ANPR cameras."

It adds up. "Were they the only keys on her?"

He nods. "And the thing you noticed with the shoes off to the side. Why do that?"

"Foot fetish?" I ask.

He looks out the window and shakes his head. "Who even knows these days? The world's a messed up kinda place."

"So what's the motive?" I ask.

He shakes his head. "Got no more idea than you."

"What about the handbag? I saw that there."

"Her phone and wallet were still in it. Not a mugging, that's for sure. Forensic results of the phone might take a day or so. Also something else a little strange."

"How strange?" I ask.

"A single page, torn from a pocket bible. A bit of Second Timothy. Someone highlighted chapter two, verse twenty two. No other writing. Nothing. Gotta mean something, but no clue what. Could also mean nothing at all."

"So, you got no motive. You got no witnesses. Not even an M.O. Just a body dumped in some random farm building. And a bible verse?"

He nods. "A bible verse. And a farm building anyone could've gotten into."

"What about Moira saying she was leaving? That any sort of a motive?"

He looks at me, shocked. "How could you possibly know that?"

"Got it from the last guy that saw her. It's all she said."

He's angry now. "For goodness sake, Flint! You sit on something like that?"

"I'm telling you the first chance I got."

His hands are fists. "It's not nearly soon enough. You understand we're talking about a murder here?"

His voice is getting louder. People on other tables are staring. He's interrupting their Friday treat.

"Hell, yeah, this changes a few things. What if the brother doesn't want her to go? What if he's decided to get rid, so she can't tell anyone what he's up to?"

"It's all still guess work," I say.

"Maybe for you," he says. He gets to his feet. He picks up the black book. "This is now evidence. I've got to get a statement from this guy. Get the stuff Moira said in writing. Might just about give me cause to drag Davie Wallace in for an interview."

He's shaking his head in a furious kinda way.

I'm waiting for a thank you, but I'm not gonna get one.

"Flint, maybe the DCI's right. Perhaps you should head on home before you muddy the waters here any more than you've done already."

"Muddy the waters?" I say. "You mean hunt down viable lines of enquiry?"

He points the book at me. "You could cost us at court if you keep poking your nose in. Just be glad I don't arrest you for interfering with a police investigation!" He looks away. Takes a breath. Looks back at me. "I'm not gonna tell anyone where this came from. Anyone asks, I found it at the café."

Now's not the time to point out I've broken into her flat and searched it. Twice. He can find out on his own that there's nothing there. He probably already knows.

One more foot wrong and he'll walk me onto a plane at Kirkwall Airport himself.

I'm gonna head across the street and find a bible in that cathedral. Must be a few in there. See what that verse says.

17. PUSH HIM UNTIL HE JUMPS

What's the deal with this guy?

Are all private detectives as nuts?

Maybe they are. A group of people a little wrong in the head. Could explain why they do the job they do.

If so, Flint's a quick learner. He's only been in business a month.

That was the plan. Get the greenest, most useless nobody of a shamus. He'll wander in, blunder around, screw up some evidence for the police. He's screwed up for the police before. He'll do it again, leave after he gets nowhere pretty quick.

But Davie didn't count on Flint having a history of getting caught up. If he'd have taken any time to look him up before jetting off to Hampshire, he'd have learned of previous heroics. No doubt previous problems too.

He has plenty of contacts who know things. Someone should've told him. Someone must've known about Flint. How could they not?

What to do with a guy that gets in the way?

Simple. You cut him off at the knees.

He picks up the phone. Dials a number.

Kirkwall Harbour Hotel.

"I'm paying for a room for an Enoch Flint until further notice," he says.

"Yes, Mr Wallace. What can I do for you?"

"I'm settling as of right now."

There's a pause.

"Is there a problem, sir?"

Davie paces the room, phone pressed against his ear. "No, no problem. I'm happy to pay the next few days. Let's say the next week. I'm happy to compensate you for the inconvenience."

Another pause.

"But only if he's gone today. Can I leave it with you?"

"Yes, sir. Consider it done."

He hangs up.

He smiles. Hotels like that build their reputation on treating their guests well. But they've got to treat the bill-payer better.

Flint thinks he can hang around, poke into his business? Cause problems? Well, good luck to him.

That was the first call. Time to call the other big hotels. Some of the larger Bed and Breakfast places that are still taking guests this time of year. Get the word out.

Build a picture. A false reputation. This Flint is trouble. If he shows up, asking for a room, tell him you're full. Tell him anything until he goes away.

The car hire's a problem. Davie paid the deposit, but it's in Flint's name. Verified with the guy's license on arrival.

Let him keep the damn car. He can tell the rental company that Flint's gonna pick up the tab, starting tomorrow. They can figure it out.

How long can a man stay in a place when someone with contacts is trying to make his life difficult?

Davie is about to find out.

18. FUNNY HOW I GET TURNED OUT

You know when you go to a place and you get the sense you ain't wanted?

It's a feeling I know well. Too well.

What happens if you ignore it?

What's next if you ignore the stares, the head-shakes, the muttering under their breath? What if you pretend that people aren't going the long way round to keep their distance?

I'll tell you what happens. The stares turn into glares. The muttering turns into vocal, indirect questions. The malcontent keeps on growing until it's got roots, branches and even a damn bird nesting in it.

Before you know it, folks ain't taking the route to avoid you anymore. They're shouting at you. Throwing things at you. Baying for blood.

I reckon it's been a while since there was a proper mob situation on Orkney. If I hang around, what are the chances of causing the next one?

Leaving the hotel. Not by choice. Nothing positive's chugging through my head.

Checked out. Luggage waiting for me downstairs. Key card deactivated.

The man behind the desk tells me the cost of the suite per night. Until he does so, I'm thinking of paying for it myself.

I try calling a couple of other recommendations. No vacancies. Not likely when we're falling towards winter. Whatever.

Seems every guest house has stopped taking people. Seemed

to decide that moments before I get in touch.

Islands are communities like no other. They can work together. They can spread rumour faster than a fresh lava flow. They can come together when it counts. When there's an outsider to keep at arms' length.

Now what?

Late Friday afternoon. Near closing time for a lot of places on the high street.

I carry my two cases, one in each hand.

I wander down Bridge Street to the end, turn the corner.

I clamber through the door of the café. Put my cases on a table on the right. Sit down.

I don't even pick up a menu. I ain't here to pretend I'm eating.

Another girl's serving. Naomi. Straight nose. Dark green eyes. Light brown hair to the shoulders. Mouth scrunched up tight. Brow furrowed. She's heard of me. She's not coming over.

I pull out my trusty notebook. I read over the last thing I put in it. That bible verse, found on Moira.

> 2 Timothy 2:22
>
> Flee also youthful lusts: but follow righteousness, faith, charity, peace, with them that call on the Lord out of a pure heart.

Coincidence? Can't be. No such thing. Not in a murder investigation.

There are puzzle pieces here that almost line up. I'm missing a few.

But right now, I'm burning up inside. Torn up that this

man's turned me out on my ear. Without even the courtesy of a phone call.

I'm only busy trying to find his sister's killer. Should earn me a little time.

No more flights to mainland Scotland today. Already checked. The last thing I did on the hotel Wi-Fi.

No one's even coming up to me. No one's gonna so much as glance in my direction.

I could stand up. Cause a scene. Shout. Throw stuff. It's not gonna do anything but get the police dragging me away.

But at least a night in a cell means a bed and a meal or two.

I get why people at the bottom commit the little crimes they do. When you've got nothing, you're only gaining by getting someone in uniform to cart you in.

I head out the door. I carry the cases a little farther down the high street. I pass Moira's place. Surrounded by yellow police tape.

There goes another possible bed for the night.

Can't keep wandering the streets. Gotta head somewhere.

I packed light, but I haven't got the muscles to carry the cases around for the rest of the night.

Time to head back to the car.

Still got a full tank of fuel. Maybe I should hit the road. See if folks in some other town have escaped Davie's influence. It ain't likely, but could be worth a try.

I smell a couple of food places. Gotta eat first. Then I'll see what this island's got to offer a lone wanderer.

19. THEY WON'T BE ABLE TO KEEP THIS QUIET

Seriously. Halfway through.

No one's even noticed.

Do the police know what they're doing?

How could they not spot them? Any of them?!

Not one clue. Not even two. Three big clues.

Each time.

There's one private detective snooping around. He's done as little as the rest of them.

Maybe another one would help. Some mysterious, alleged do-gooder could put on a suit, act like he knows something. Show up. Point out the things they've missed. Just to get them on the right track. Disappear into the night.

It was always suspected that the police didn't know one extremity from another, but really? Was this the level he was dealing with?

By now, they must have tied together his previous work. The local news should be in a tizzy. Anyone could be next. No one's safe. That sort of thing.

What have we got?

A story about a shed break-in on the front page. The front page!

That should've been his page!

Should be his for the rest of the week.

Why aren't there reporters crawling all over this?

What? They just drive past Stenness, and they see the forensic stuff and think, 'can't be anything serious'?

The police can be so frustrating.

So can the papers.

They can all accidentally get in the way of a good criminal plot.

They can also sit by, being useless, exactly when you don't want them to be so damn ineffective.

There's no other course of action.

This needs ramping up. The dials need turning all the way to the max.

Needs to be someone who's had his photo in the local papers. Someone who thinks of themselves as a minor celebrity.

Needs to get dumped somewhere the public are gonna find him.

Some shopper. Heading down here to check out the furniture store bargains and... massive problem. Tell the police. Tell your fellow shoppers. The crowd will gather. Rumours will start.

Soon, the Orcadian will have to be all over this. There'll be no other option.

The panic will get into their minds. Infect them with fear and mistrust.

Then, the next victims will hit the truth home.

No one's safe.

They won't trust the police.

They won't trust government.

No one's gonna be able to stop this anarchy once it gets going.

That's when he'll have earned his ticket outta here.

But it starts here. Right now.

Here comes the guy. Right on time.

Here goes nothing.

20. NOBODY'S GONNA MAKE ME LEAVE

The guy who hired me, got me here, threw me away when I got close to the wrong kinda truth, he was right about something.

October hits on these islands and it's like they're put in deep freeze, ready for thawing out next spring.

But I ain't on the clock anymore. Davie saw to that.

Kind of him to let me keep the dough he handed over as a retainer. The extra four hundred too. Trouble is, things like this get expensive. By the time I hit my own front door, I ain't gonna do much more than break even.

The wind blasts me with tiny pellets of ice. Not the kinda thing to make a slap in the face hurt any less. But about as warm as the greeting from my former client.

One of two things happen when you're close to the truth. Sometimes you get warned off. Paid off. Told to forget everything you thought you knew about something. You got it wrong, so forget it all. Or bodies start turning up like they're the latest craze and they're on sale.

Still, the girl is dead. The one with the diary. The client list. The one I already handed over to the local law.

If only I'd held my nerve. Seen the crime scene with a more professional, clinical eye. If only my stomach had been up to the task when I was at the farm. I could've seen something they didn't get in one of their official snaps.

But if I'm playing with a bunch of if-onlys, might as well wish that I'd been there on Sunday or Monday. I'd have caught the guy or gal in the act. Could've returned the doll to her determined brother and left this place while I could still feel my ears.

But I couldn't do my job and find her when she was still alive. Never on the cards. The least I can do is find out who's behind it. No brother I ever saw would stop caring when a sibling's heart stops.

But the first thought on my mind is on food. Then it's where I'm gonna stay tonight. The cases are in the car, awaiting a journey to a new destination. They'd be happy going anywhere. Perhaps even nowhere at all.

I got some cash on me. The English kind with the monarch's head all over it. The kind they sneer at when you hand it over up here. But it's a little late for check-in anywhere. No budget motels. No open-all-hours diners.

Some store's still doing a trade in something they allege to be Orkney's Best Kebabs. Maybe I head on in. Grab something close to actual food. Enjoy a little warmth. If my hands can move enough to open that door. Who knows? They might even give me a turn on the spit to help get me feeling like a warm-blooded creature again.

But something moves the other side of a gate to the left. Somewhere in that courtyard beyond. In front of the furniture store, something glass breaks. Is that a torch light?

Definitely some shadowy figure moving around.

I stare for a moment, peering round the edge of the gatepost. They're hunched over something on the ground.

Could be someone scavenging through garbage.

Could be someone needs help.

Could be some local artist. Some nut who gets their kicks outta putting their latest piece together in the dead of night. See the reactions in the morning.

Only one way to find out what it is, and why it caught my eye.

I walk through the gate, pushing it a little.

There's a creak loud enough to wake the dead.

Panicked, wide eyes shoot in my direction from the shadowy figure. Enough neon light from the kebab place has sneaked in here. Lights them up the smallest amount. Not enough to show off the whole face.

They get up from beside the shape on the floor.

They charge outta there like it's gonna blow.

They try to miss me, but bump into me and send my face into the gate.

There's a small thud, a rattle and a roll and light's bouncing around.

The person peering down's scarpered. Gives me the feeling they were up to something I shouldn't wanna know about.

They beat their feet fast enough that they left their torch behind.

I pick it up, still wearing the gloves. Keep my fingerprints off it. At least they're good for that. They don't do enough to stop my fingers from wanting to drop off. I suppose even if they did, they'd be easy to find.

I point the fading beam at the lump on the floor.

Another body.

Something sparkles nearby. Broken glass.

I point the torch up a little. No glass covering the bulb.

Must be what I heard. What I can see chucking some tiny bits of light back at me.

I walk a little closer. Not close enough to screw up a crime scene, but too close to still want that kebab.

He's a big fella. Pale face. Something a little Polynesian about his features. Can't be many from that neck of the woods up here.

Glasses are on the ground almost an arm's reach to the left of his face.

Long, black hair. A peaceful, almost happy expression on their face.

Maybe the dead really do rest in peace.

Maybe I'm beating myself up over folks I knew. Folks who've moved on because they got close to me.

Maybe it's just us left behind who get all upset. Stressed, worried about stuff that ain't gonna matter when we join them.

I set the torch down, beam pointing at the body.

I pull my phone from my pocket.

Time to get reacquainted with the local law.

They eyed me like I was a tourist, too late to the party.

They're gonna wish I hadn't shown up at all.

21. LEAVING IT TO THE POLICE? NO DICE

I'm sitting on a park bench, talking to a dead guy.

Looks pretty good, all things considered. No zombie-like features. No worms eating his eyes out. He's sitting on the bench, looking out over the Brough of Birsay, like me. As if the life-ending event a few months ago hadn't happened.

"I watched you die," I say.

Jasper shrugs. He's still wearing the dark blue beanie hat. A good choice with icy winds that could throw you into the sea if you weren't careful.

He's still under-dressed for black tie and over-dressed for a family gathering. Blue shirt, unbuttoned collar. No tie. Grey woollen cardigan. That's new. Maybe the dress is a metaphor for the scene in front of me.

The place the Atlantic meets the North Sea. A rocky path through the middle when the tide's out. When the tide's in, there's no telling one body of water from another.

"You certainly *watched* me die," he says. "Didn't do a hell of a lot about it, did you?"

I frown. I'm not gonna meet his gaze. Too much bad stuff building up in me to take in the pity-me look in those eyes too.

I close my eyes and shake my head. "I couldn't have saved you."

He throws his hands up. "We'll never know now, Flint, will we?"

I turn to him with fire in my own eyes. I can feel it. "I was your partner. You put us there with your betrayal. You still wanna blame me?"

By the time I hit the last couple of words, I'm not where I was seconds ago.

I'm staring at a car ceiling.

I'm swaying a little. Balanced on the edge of the back seats of the champaign-colour Ford C-Max I'm renting from the airport. The rental agreement was boiler-plate and brief. Not sure if it covered sleeping in the vehicle. They're not gonna know if I don't tell them.

The car's shaking. The wind's doing its best to throw me into some salty water.

I sit up and look out the window. Out there's the bench I was sat on in that weird dream.

Seems I'm not only haunted by my own mistakes now. I'm haunted while I sleep by the guy who fell because of some of mine, some of his own.

It wasn't enough that I saw the guy everywhere I looked back home. That he was the face reflected in every surface of the station I'd worked at for a handful of years. I thought I could get away from my demons. No such luck. The damn things are following me everywhere.

A hell of a way to start my Saturday. A week ago, I could've watched cartoons in my underwear if I'd wanted. If you'd told me then where I'd be, I'd have had you sectioned under the Mental Health Act.

All I've gotta do when I get up is stick my head out the windows for a moment. That wind's enough to wake up someone who's been in a coma for a decade. Wonder if anyone's tried it.

Gonna head back to the station in Kirkwall. Give them a full statement of the stuff last night.

Always seems to be me finding the bodies.

It'd be nice, for once, to find something cheerful.

A trunk of ancient gold coins.

Some rare antique.

Hell, I'd take finding a dropped bag of candy.

***

I keep telling myself on the half-hour drive that I did what I could for Jasper. A bullet in the neck's not the kind of thing your average first-aider has a chance of putting right.

But could I have done more? Should I have taken off my coat, pressed it against the wound? Would it have made a difference? Given him a few more crucial minutes?

Forensics, some other woman who's now in the ground said the same thing. Everyone else possible told me there was nothing I could do. They weren't there.

Spinning those thoughts round my brain gets me all the way to the edge of the city. I still haven't found the answer that's gonna help me sleep next time.

Still haven't got rid of the soreness in my neck and my back from the stupid choice of bed for the night. Turning left's gonna be a challenge all day.

Part of me thinks the pain's deserved. Part of me thinks it ain't enough. There are more folks I've seen buried. More ex-people who could point a finger at me for choices that put them there.

But today's for these new murders. The second one found since I got here. I can tell the police what I saw. I can offer my help, my opinions. Pretty sure I'm gonna do that anyway, even if they'd rather I got on that plane and took my bad luck home with me.

***

DC Sutherland stands near the front desk. Longish brown hair with a hint of red. Kind eyes the colour of mud. A sinister smile stuck on his stubbled, fed-up face.

His tie's already loose and his top button's undone. It's only half nine. It's been that kinda day already.

He leads me through to his desk. It's a big room. Two medium rooms knocked through some years ago.

Twelve desks split in half by a path that leads to another eight desks. Someone's at every one, looking busy. There are enough other bulls waiting to jump in their graves if they leave their desk for a few seconds.

They're in the old, stone bit of the station. Not the big, unsympathetic pre-fab extension out the back.

The rabble are like any group of people you might pass on the street. Nothing special to look at. The kind that blend in. Notice things.

One guy's tall enough to disrupt the false ceiling tiles with his scalp. He never stands up straight, though. Don't blame him.

One gal's wearing glasses that make her eyes twice the size they should be. Another's short and thin enough that the coat hooks on the wall behind could hold her up with ease.

"Want to go somewhere quieter for your statement?" He asks.

I shrug. "I'm used to places like this."

He nods with a slight smirk. A sign of relief. There ain't a good room going spare in this place anyway, judging by the people crammed in here.

I give him the low-down of not very much from the night before. He's nodding. Writing stuff down on some sheets pre-printed with lines. Most places would type these things out these days, hit print, chuck it in front of the witness for a signature. Maybe even go all fancy and paperless. Not this guy.

He's reading it back to me, so I can point out anything I didn't say.

About halfway through, I ain't listening anymore. Crime scene photos showing Moira Wallace and new victim Sam Muriel are up on the wall. It's only when I see them next to each other that I pick up on it. How did I not see it before?

DC Sutherland finishes reading the thing to be polite, but he knows my mind's on something else. You'd have to wonder about the exams they had to pass if they didn't pick up on the glazed eyes of their witnesses.

He sighs as he puts the last sheet face-down on the desk. "Let's have it. What's got your attention?"

I get up and walk to the wall of photos. Moira's on the left, Sam's on the right.

"Moira's crime scene," I say. "The first victim?"

Everyone around me nods.

I point to one specific photo. "You got this photo, looking down on the body, and the area around it."

More nods. Some raised eyebrows. Looks of people who wanna know what some foreign nobody's doing in their incident room.

"I thought the car keys on her stomach were hers. Didn't she drive a Ford Fiesta?

Someone goes to consult a few stapled, printed sheets of paper.

I point right at the keys on the photo. "Those aren't her keys. I found her keys in her flat."

"A spare set?" DC Sutherland says.

I shake my head. "A different shape. Different style. I'm thinking they're for a different model of car. Gotta be a different year."

Some guy finds the serial number from the keys and gets on the blower. It'll take a couple of minutes to get an answer.

I point at the upper right and the lower left corners. "Shoes ain't next to her feet. They're moved to the side. Handbag, not cleaned out by the killer, up past her head."

They stare at me like I've lost the plot.

I point at the newest victim. "This guy, he's not got anything sitting on his stomach."

"He got interrupted," DC Sutherland says, "by you."

I nod. "Yeah, but what if it didn't change his plan too much?"

There's a hat, top left of the picture. A shoe bottom right. A glove top right.

"Three objects near him," I say, pointing at them. "Now imagine there should've been a fourth. That's what I changed by showing up. Got something missing, or in the wrong place"

They're all looking like I've sprung a surprise quiz on US state birds. "You guys seeing what's going on in both these pictures? What message the killer's sending?"

DC Sutherland frowns.

That frown changes.

His eyes widen a little, and then a little more.

"No!" He says. "Moira's got to be the first one. She has to be."

They stare at him like he can share my ride in the van to the looney bin.

"I know we all work a lot," he says, "but you lot must've played Monopoly? Ludo? Snakes and Ladders?"

If they thought he was crazy before, they're now thinking he might be mad enough to run for office.

He walks up to the Moira picture. He puts his arms across the top and bottom, making it a square. "Look at the objects on and around her. Imagine they're dots."

He leaves it and does the same with the other guy.

We're getting gasps and nods. We're getting a couple of people putting hands over mouths.

I nod. "You know what this means? Not only is there a serial killer, but he's struck four times already."

DC Sutherland turns around and walks back to his desk. Shakes his head like it's one of those pens with the ship inside. Coasting from one side to the other and back again. Never reaching where it wanted to go.

"Means we missed the first two..." he says. "Also means that there's gonna be two more."

22. ENOUGH SKELETONS IN A CLOSET FOR A HALLOWEEN PARTY

To some, promotion in the police means you get to the point you work regular weekday shifts. Not a bad gig, all things considered. Weekends to yourself. Home in the evenings.

Some folks struggle adjusting. They like the six-days-straight working life. Four on earlies. Two on lates. A full four days away from the station afterwards.

Grant Flett isn't sad to see the back of that shift pattern. Those ten hour days could be gruelling. It got worse on that last day. Tired and with a near-midnight finish.

No, free evenings and weekends were better. You could get into a pattern of sleeping. You could take the dog for a walk every morning. Could sit down for dinner with the family.

On Saturday morning, you could head out to one of Orkney's beauty spots and let the dog run where it liked. The Golden Retriever, Robert loves exploring. Getting soaked and dirty. Giving his owner something to sort out when they get home.

Today, that spot is Scapa Bay. Cliffs in a horseshoe shape shelter the beach from most of the wind.

The bay draws the eyes out to the very deep water of Scapa Flow. So deep was the water, that you could hide a whole fleet of ships in the water out there, and you wouldn't even know it. Some Germans tried it a few years ago, with some encouragement from the British Navy. It's not uncommon to see teams of divers bobbing around, checking out the wrecks.

It's not the biggest of sandy beaches. It's shallow, and when the tide's out, like it is right now, you see more rocks and seaweed than greyish sand.

The place is a goldmine for gatherers of shellfish. There are enough of them. Rain or shine, hot or cold, they come out and get a few sacksful of whelks and cockles to sell by the kilo.

On the pier to the left, further out to sea, there are a few people with fishing lines. A handful of hooks, spaced out a little, cast into the salty water. Mackerel hauls come pretty easy here too.

Grant could've been a fisherman, if he'd wanted. A whelk gatherer. Would've been a simple life.

None of the stresses of being the area commander for the entire Orkney police service. Anyone who takes on that job's dealt a losing hand from the get-go.

How can you police the whole of these islands when you don't even have an officer on half of them?

Even when you took one of the z-cars on a ferry, they called ahead from the control tower. You'd find everything tidy and squeaky clean by the time you rolled off at the other end.

He smiles. Wonders what the top brass would say if he said he needed a helicopter. See what was really going down on those outer islands.

But living off the land or the sea would've also been dull by comparison to his lot.

They say no two days are the same in the police. Granted, not as true in an island community. You could still find variety when you wanted it.

Like that fleet of submerged ships, retirement wasn't too far away.

He could pack it all in for his police pension in less than five years. If he wanted to gather shellfish, he could do it as often as he liked (tide-permitting, of course).

He could get up early. A small catch of three or four mackerel. Get them home and fry them up for the family for breakfast.

Can't beat sitting down to eat something you caught with your own hands a few minutes before. No feeling like it. You can't get fresher than a fish that was swimming around with its buddies an hour ago.

His phone buzzes in his pocket and lets out some shrill ring. He could've change it, but every ringtone sounded as bad as this one when he tried.

He recognises the number, although it's not saved as a contact. He's being careful.

"I've been trying to run Enoch Flint out of town, in my own way," says Davie Wallace. "What can you do to help me?"

Grant lets out a little laugh. "He stumbled across a body last night. He's been in the station this morning to give a statement. He's a witness of something now."

"What are you saying? I've got to accept the fact he's gonna hang around? Shove his face where it's not wanted? What am I supposed to do?"

"You could trust me to deal with him in my own way," Grant says, "instead of panicking and trying to cut the guy loose. Looks like you're hiding something now."

"Damn right I'm hiding something. If I'm not mistaken, it's something you'd like to stay hidden too."

Grant stands still. He's not watching the dog anymore. This phone conversation shifted underneath him like wet sand.

"If I'm not much mistaken," he says, nervous tremors in his

voice, "that might come across as a threat. But I'm sure you're too smart to say something like that."

"Don't be like that, Grant. I just want rid of this guy before he causes either of us problems."

Grant shakes his head. "You're the one who brought him here. I could've told you it was a bad move."

"I had to do something," Davie says. "It had to look like I cared about Moira. That I was pulling out all the stops."

He's looking down at his old shoes now. Covered in wet sand. The stuff sticks pretty well. Once they dry, it all comes off easy enough. Maybe some other stuff that sticks isn't a problem after some time's passed.

"What is it you want from me?" Grant asks. "I assume you didn't call to vent?"

"Can't you help me get rid of Flint?"

Another shake of the head. "I can't order people off the islands. How much power do you think I have?"

"What about closing down the Moira investigation?"

If you can do an ironic belly laugh, it's what Grant's doing. "You think I can boss around everyone under my command? Order them to forget about every outstanding enquiry? Pretend this didn't happen? You know how quickly I'd get found out?"

"Is it better than some other secrets of yours coming to light?"

No, the comment earlier wasn't a threat. That's what a threat sounds like.

Grant sighs. "I'll see what I can shut down. There'll be some enquiries I can say we're not gonna focus on. Too costly. Lack of budget. That sort of thing."

"And what about Flint?" Davie asks.

"What about him?"

"You got any plans for shutting the guy up? Making his home look more attractive than staying up here?"

"He slept in his car last night. Pretty sure he's not gonna hang around longer than he has to. Could tell him to go home and await further contact if he's needed for court."

"You certainly could, but I think you can do better."

He looks around at the bay. No sign of Robert. He'll turn up.

"I've already had a DC threaten him with arrest if he interferes. If he's where he shouldn't be, talking to someone we haven't spoken to yet, he'll spend a night in custody. By the next morning, we'll suggest he gets on a plane."

"That's better," Davie says. "You know it's for the best."

"Aye. And you now know it's a bad idea to hire some randomer from further south. You never know who you're gonna get."

"Lessons to learn for both of us, then."

"True enough."

Grant hangs up.

How on earth is he gonna force the private investigator to drop this?

A message arrives. DC Sutherland.

Taken DC Flint's statement. He's found something exciting about WALLACE and MURIEL. Might have a few ideas of where to take things. Got to look back over some old files. Will update in person tomorrow, but this is getting bigger.

Damn it.

Just what he needs.

Robert pads up to him. Panting and with something akin to a grin on his face. He's done sniffing around and he wants to go home.

If only the same was true of Enoch Flint.

23. IT'S NO GOOD PRESSING FOR DETAILS

The trouble with a double murder investigation is that you get your rest days canned. You end up fitting into a busy room with a host of other tired, overworked detectives. Your reactions take a nosedive. Your ability to think goes with it. Your very motivation for catching a killer ain't too far behind.

That's the world I'm in right now. For once, I'm not part of the crew who got called in.

I'm the guy standing in front of a room full of sweaty people. I got their waning attention. Now I've gotta explain what I've found out. Not much to see but a sea of tired heads wearing fed-up expressions.

The woman with the bug-eyed glasses hangs up the phone she'd been holding to her ear. "I've got the details about the car key. It belongs to an old Ford Escort. Not a match to Moira's car. Still no hits for hers on ANPR or anywhere else."

I stare at the overhead snap of Moira's crime scene. "Why change her keys out for a different one?"

I turn around. DC Sutherland holds up the little black diary. "Flint... Ford ESCORT."

My eyes are widening. I get it.

I pull the book from my pocket and read them the bible verse highlighted from the torn sheet in her bag.

I'm looking back at the photo. "Ford Escort. Flee youthful lusts. Number three on a die. A strange jumble of stuff to put together."

A woman with an air of authority walks into the room. She's carrying a stack of suspension files. The mood changes quicker than you can say, 'The boss is coming.'

It's DS Inness. Her photo is on a board on a far wall, along with others in the department. She's near the top. Must be important. She's around her late thirties. She's got a face where her eyes, nose and mouth all look a little bigger than they should do. Makes her look like one of those semi-realistic characters from a Disney animation. But she ain't about to launch into some absurd musical number with animals helping her clean up. She's got long, reddish blonde hair. Seems to be fading closer to the scalp and redder the closer you look to the ends.

"What are we all standing around for?" she asks. She's got a perfect mouthful of teeth. She's got a dentist for a parent, or she spends a decent chunk of lettuce on top-notch servicing of those snappers. Maybe she's got nothing or nobody else to spend that salary on. Maybe she prioritises oral hygiene over most other things.

DC Sutherland says, "We've got a couple of clues, sarge."

"One or two of you can look into them. The rest of you..." She jabs a forefinger into the pile as she puts it down on the nearest desk. "Share these out. Based on this dice idea, we're looking for any recent deaths that could be victims one and two. Most are clearly not relevant, but we can't rule anything out right now."

DC Sutherland beckons me over to his desk. He thrusts a photo under my nose. Another torn page from a bible. More dog-eared than Moira's. A single verse highlighted once again. None of the words are easy to make out.

"We found this folded up, under the insole of the guy's right shoe."

They're thorough. I'll give them that.

"What's the verse?" I ask.

He points at one of his computer screens. He's already found it online.

> 1 Corinthians 10:31
>
> Whether therefore ye eat, or drink, or whatsoever ye do, do all to the glory of God.

"What does that mean?" he asks.

I poke out my bottom lip and shrug. "What do we know about the guy?"

"Samuel Muriel. Moved over here as a child with his family a decade and a half ago. They live out in St Margarets Hope. We know he's overweight, and not shy about it. Looked him up. A couple of newspaper articles about eating competitions. A bit of a food fan on social media."

There ain't any time to process this.

DCI Flett walks in, wearing a pale yellow shirt. Navy trousers. No jacket or tie. Must be dress-down Saturday. He looks angry enough to kick a kitten.

"DC Sutherland, Mr Flint." He points at both of us. "Come with me."

***

We're standing near the door inside DCI Flett's office. If this was a long meeting, he'd bark at us to sit down.

"Sir, we've got to organise a press conference or something," DC Sutherland says. "Get the word out. Warn people."

A disapproving look from DCI Flett. "Warn the people about what?"

"A killer being loose on the island."

He shakes his head. "You think it's a good idea, especially when we don't know all the details yet? You don't think it'll get people in a panic, and make it look like we don't know what we're doing?"

"Maybe but-"

"And when the press start firing questions at you. How long have you known about this individual? What do they look like? How many people have they killed? What do the public need to look out for? You think we won't look stupid when we can't answer a single one of those questions? What would it achieve, really?"

DC Sutherland's deflated.

"On to why I called you both in here. DC Sutherland, what do you really know about Mr Flint here?"

He shrugs. "I know he's been helpful. Picked up on some things we hadn't spotted."

DCI Flett holds up a finger like he's making a point. "*Yet*. Things you hadn't spotted *yet*."

He nods. Accepting they might have found those clues in their own time. "He's got us looking for two other murders we didn't even know had happened."

DCI Flett rolls his eyes. "Making more work for us when we're already stretched."

"He's a good private investigator-"

"Who was sacked yesterday. His client doesn't want him, but he's still here. Want me to tell you what I know about him? Why he's a DC but he's not currently on active duty? The kinds of problems he creates? I've been on the phone to his bosses and colleagues down in Cookston."

He looks at me. Eyes burning with a thousand degree fire of hatred. Mouth in a playful smirk. It's like two faces from a magazine. Both torn through the nose on the horizontal. Bits swapped, and they've been stuck back together wrong.

He doesn't wait for DC Sutherland to answer.

"He's on unpaid compassionate leave at his own request. Was gonna pack it in entirely. Instead of recovering, figuring out what he wants, he's made another stupid decision. He's come jetting up here, ready to stick his oar in. Stir up more trouble as a PI."

DC Sutherland looks at me like he ain't' got a clue who I am anymore.

"People approached me for help," I say in defence. "I didn't go looking to do anything."

DCI Flett chirps up again. "You mean you don't have a newly kitted out office for private investigations at home?"

"Well, yes-"

"And you say you have no intention of leaving the police? No desire to investigate things on your own?"

This guy would make a hell of a cross-examiner if he swapped his police uniform for a Barrister's wig and gown.

"It's a temporary arrangement," I say. "I only came here to help."

"We thank you for your *help*, Flint. Now, if you don't mind..." He ushers us out of his office.

"DC Sutherland. Head back to CID. Mr Flint, I've got one more thing to show you."

I follow him down a corridor. Down a flight of stairs.

Through a magnetically locked door.

We're back beside the front desk.

He points at the desk. "I'm about to inform all front desk staff to refuse you entry. No exceptions. I don't even care if someone inside's on fire, and you're the only one with an extinguisher."

He points at the entrance. "That's what I wanted to show you. The way out. Police Scotland thank you for your help. Should you be required at court at a later date, we'll be in touch. For now, there's the front door. Use it one last time."

He moves in closer. His voice lowers to a sinister whisper. "If I hear that you so much as look through the window into here, I'll lift you for interfering. Obstructing. Hell, for fun, I might even plant a few grams of coke on you and arrest you for possession. You get me?"

I nod. I head out into the cold.

It's time to get out of here.

The locals don't want me here. I don't wanna be here.

Yes, one of Moira's colleagues wanted help, but I can't fight against everyone to make a difference for them. DC Sutherland has that black book. He'll have to be the one that helps them now.

As for me, my career as a snooper is finished before it ever got going.

Back to Cookston. Back to the day job.

Back to a place where somebody wants me.

At least, that's how it's shaping up, unless this place throws up a damn good reason for keeping me here.

24. SOMEONE'S GOTTA KNOW SOMETHING

I'm sitting in the driver seat. Psyching myself up for the next few hundred yards.

Already crossed three of the Churchill Barriers. I passed the little hut that became the Italian Chapel. I've passed the Amber Museum off to my left. I managed to come this far unscathed. One more of these to go. This one seems a little riskier.

Before Winston Churchill was the big cheese, he had these things made. They did their job. Protected the British ships from German U-Boats. Since then, they stuck a road on top of each and called them causeways. The only way on and off four islands.

Problem comes at high tide, with strong winds. Waves crash against the giant concrete blocks. A few of those waves don't stop there. They look pretty angry, and they're not done. They're gonna get somewhere and a barrier ain't gonna stop them.

The wind rocks the car as I sit here, hoping I can make it across without a big wave sweeping me out to sea. I know the car's a rental, but I fancy leaving these islands in one piece.

South Ronaldsay beckons. There's a fishing village down there that might give me a final chance of getting answers.

The sea calms a little. Sea water's drained from the road surface. Time to put my foot down and make it as far as I can.

After a couple of hairy moments, I'm on the other side.

Gotta hope the tide's retreated some by the time I head back again.

Doesn't seem to be a lot here, but there's a village here somewhere.

Sure enough, the road takes me to a quaint little bay. More stone houses with slate roofs. But they're not the ones I'm heading for.

On the edge of the place, up a hill, there's a patch of unsympathetic houses. Cheap-built. Semi-detached. Brown pebble dashing finish. Looks like they were council-built. New about the time the road got put in, linking St Margarets Hope to mainland Orkney.

The house I want's the last one before the road seems to take you out of town. By the looks of it, there's nothing out there but fields and a bleak sense of being completely alone.

The chain link fence has seen better days. So has everything else in view. Some folks are house proud wherever they are. Some kinda make do and make excuses.

My guess is that the Muir family are the latter.

I walk up to the front door. Press a doorbell that's not worked since the seventies. Then I knock on the door. The cold wind's doing its best to make me regret doing it.

The door opens just enough for an eye to peek out at me.

It's a wary eye. A suspicious slice of a face is all I can see through the gap. Large, metal rimmed glasses. Hair thinning on the guy's scalp.

"Yeah?"

One word. A greeting, and a question. This ain't a guy for wasted syllables.

"I'm Enoch Flint. Private Investigator."

"So?"

"I've got a couple of questions about Sam. Was he a relative of yours?"

"My son."

I got two words outta him. And I was beginning to wonder if I was making any progress.

"I wonder if you could tell me if Sam had anyone that didn't like him."

"No."

I scowl a little. "You mean No, he didn't have anyone that disliked him, or no you're not talking to me?"

"Both I guess."

"I'm trying to help catch the guy who-"

The door swings open. The man I was speaking to is hunching. Cowering, almost. A woman's standing there, tall and annoyed, in a dressing gown with a towel wrapped around her hair. The look on her face makes me think this is her battle get-up.

"I don't know what you want from us. We told the police what we know. We're not answering any more questions."

The door slams.

What a nice family.

I turn around.

Crisp packets are trying to dance in the breeze, but they're caught in the grass and the weeds of the front garden.

I walk through the gap where there was once a gate.

I look at the village below.

This is where the guy grew up. Someone's gotta know something about him. Someone has to be willing to talk.

I get back in the car while I can still feel my fingers.

Still got a few hours to kill until the next flight outta here.

Time to get some food and ask around about Sam.

***

I'm lucky to find a parking space on any of these streets.

Got the last one, by the looks of it. Gonna annoy some local, no doubt.

Next to a hotel with a restaurant.

It's not long gone through a refit. New grey leather covers the booth seating. I'm on a new dining chair at one of those tables that's new but trying to look old and made of driftwood.

I spin my head around a little. A guy sits at their smallest table. There's a big window looking out on a courtyard. There's a picnic bench out there that no one's using here before at least June. Creeping plants up the walls. Trying to look like some Mediterranean vista. Looks like a painting I saw once. Can't put my finger on where it was, or who painted it.

I order fish and chips and a lemonade. Quiz the waiter about Sam Muriel. Never heard of him.

Someone else brings me my food. Never heard of the guy either.

The food's good. Makes it worth risking my life to get here.

So good that I'm gonna get dessert. Some fudge cheesecake made from the stuff in the local area. It smells pretty damn good.

It's put down by a large guy who looks a little like Sam. Got a name tag on. Joseph.

"You knew Sam Muriel?" I ask.

He nods. "I ought to have known him. He was my brother."

I bow my head a little and say, "Sorry."

He nods in appreciation. He goes to turn around. Head back to the kitchen.

"I was wondering," I blurt out, "if you could tell me something about him."

He's thinking it over. A nod tells me he's happy to speak. He takes a seat opposite me for a minute.

"What was he like?"

He shrugs. "Quiet. Except for the eating contests. He lived for those things."

I nod. "Many friends?"

He shrugs. "We're a quiet family. Keep ourselves to ourselves."

Don't I know it.

"We're all a bit different to the natives. Never really fit in. The food competitions was Sam's way of feeling a part of things, you know?"

"Anyone not like him? I mean enough to hurt him."

He shakes his head. "Sam never hurt anyone. Never was a problem I knew about, anyway, and I'd like to think I would've known."

I've still got the picture of Moira in my pocket. I pull it out and hand it over. "Ever seen this gal before? Would Sam have known her?"

He looks and smirks. He shakes his head. "Never seen her

before. She's a little out of Sam's league."

"Name Moira Wallace mean anything?"

Another shake of the head.

I thank him and let him get back to work. I say the usual hollow words of being sorry for his loss.

I'm not getting anything about this guy. Not seeing any link between the two victims.

I try the cheesecake. Delicious.

I could hang around these islands a little longer with food like this.

I'm about done. Resigned to heading to the airport.

A message arrives on my phone. Unknown number.

> Meet me in an hour at the Peedie Sea on edge of Kirkwall.

Intriguing.

Looks like I've finally got someone willing to talk.

That plane home might have to wait a little longer.

25. A HANDLESS MAN CAN COUNT FLINT'S FRIENDS

Whoever wants to meet here couldn't have picked a spot more exposed to the elements.

I'm stood at the side of a perfectly round bit of sea. A level path follows all the way around it. For all I know, the whole thing's man-made, like the path.

At my usual fast walking speed, I guess I could walk its perimeter in around five minutes and be back where I started. Even with the wind resistance.

A flat patch of land surrounds it. An area highly favoured for local birds, but they're all hiding somewhere today. I'm the only mug out in these conditions.

I'm looking in the direction of Kirkwall cathedral. The green copper spire and red sandstone tower stick out. They've done that for the best part of a thousand years. Back then, the place I'm standing would've been underwater. Times change. Things move on. Even up here.

The sun's had enough. It's setting behind me, the other side of one of those creeping, meandering hills.

A small figure is approaching from the city. A woman, judging by the build. Can't tell much more. They've got a coat on with a huge, furry hood that could get them through an arctic expedition. They're missing the team of huskies, though.

There's a swagger to the way the gal's moving that reminds me of red lights and curb crawlers.

My toes could've fallen off. Gone numb in the cold. I stamp my feet a little to get the feeling back. I only get pins and needles and pain for my trouble.

She walks up and stands beside me. Hood still up.

"You the one that messaged me?" I ask.

"Aye." That weird, breathing in thing again. "Heard you were thinking of leaving." I can't quite place the voice.

"More than thinking. Was heading for the airport until you got in touch."

"You said you'd help. Have you forgotten?" I know the voice now. Bella, from the café.

"I've done what I can do. People here are doing their best to get rid of me. I know when I'm not wanted."

There's a nod, barely discernible under the massive hood. "Thought you'd stick around. You seemed the type to see things through."

I throw my arms out. "What can I do? No one talks to me. I can't even get a night in a hotel anymore."

"You can stay with me. I won't even charge you. You can't just give up when it gets difficult."

I start walking around the little lake. She falls in-step by my side. "When I see through difficult situations, other people seem to pay dearly."

She takes down the hood and stares at me. "I've not got anything worth hanging on to. Neither have the other girls. We've got a lot to say about Davie. We need someone to fight our corner. Is that person gonna be you?"

I look in those arresting blue eyes. Self-pity has invaded them. Taken up lodging and it ain't going anywhere.

"Back home I've got a girlfriend, a son, a job. I've gotta head back sometime."

"Can you spare another week? Even a couple more days? Can you give me that? Just please don't give up." She looks away, out at sea. "If one more person gives up on me, I might be inclined to give up on myself."

I give a frustrated glance heavenward. The dark skies don't hold any answers.

"Alright," I say. "But don't be surprised if life gets unpleasant for you, harbouring me."

She laughs. "Oh, I wonder what that would be like!"

She hands me a slip of paper. "My address. Spare key's under the doormat. Don't have anything worth stealing."

She walks back the way she came.

I'm left to myself in the freezing wind.

At least I ain't gonna be sleeping in my car tonight.

What am I doing, staying here?

Everything inside is screaming that I should cut and run. That things will get worse before they get better. That the getting better ain't gonna happen for a long time yet.

But Flint doesn't turn his back on someone in need.

Damn these morals. Damn my conscience.

Life would be easier if I could end my working day and leave it all behind in the office.

No, that's not the life for me. Never will be.

I'm the guy who puts himself in harm's way for a meagre wage. For the satisfaction of an almost happy ending. At the moment, I'm here for no wage at all.

Deep within me is a sense that this isn't over yet. That I've still got stuff to do.

Let's hope getting bumped off ain't one of those things.

26. KEEP YOUR HANDS OFF MY GIRLS

I get to the address Bella's given me.

The building's newer than a few of the others around it. But small. I can tell that before I've even got in the door. Three little houses in a row. The whole structure's the size of maybe two small semi-detached bungalows.

Small windows. Brown stucco walls, again. The stuff could last longer than bricks around here. Someday, someone's gonna tell me why it's so popular.

Sure enough, the key's under the doormat.

I'm in. There ain't much to be in, if I'm honest.

I'm immediately standing almost in the centre of the lounge. A small, waist-high simple set of shelves squeezes in next to the door. A tired black sofa to my left. To the right, a foldaway beech wood effect table with a small television perched on the corner.

Ahead of me and to the right is an opening to the kitchen. Smaller than the offerings in some hotel suites. But it's got a fridge, an oven and a microwave. Enough counter top for maybe making a sandwich. Not a footlong baguette, though. Even that would be a struggle.

There's a door to the left of the kitchen. It leads to the smallest hallway a guy could possibly build. About enough room to stand there and turn around. Still, there's four doors off it.

Ahead, the door leads to nothing more than a storage cupboard. A pre-pay electricity meter sits about halfway up the shelving on the wall.

The next door to the left is the bathroom, but a bath would

only fit in if you stood it on one end. A shower in the corner. Made for people who don't stick their elbows out when they wash their hair. A toilet and a tiny sink made for people with tiny hands.

I turn around. The final door takes me to the only other room at the front of the property. One double bedroom. Only the smallest of double beds and a tiny side unit.

When she offered me a bed for the night, I kinda figured she had more than one to offer. I ain't the kinda guy to kick a gal out of her own bedroom, make her sleep on the sofa.

Looks like she's thinking one of two things. Either we share the bed (a little presumptuous), or I'm risking neck ache on the furniture in the other room.

The tour didn't take long.

I sit on the sofa and run over what I know in my head. I'm looking down at the world's thinnest carpet. Random streaks of different shades of grey and brown. Designed that way to hide the dirt. Could be that it's already doing it, and that it started out a different colour.

A strange little apartment, but one she's made the best of. She's a gal that keeps things tidy. Organised. She's house proud, even if she ain't got a lot to be proud of.

My mind wanders and then stops for a beat at Davie Wallace. Not so close to Moira as far as I can tell, yet close enough to have a spare key. Not in a single photo of hers, yet he makes a big song and dance of hiring me to investigate when she goes missing.

What do I know about the kid? He owns and runs a café that might make a profit in the summer months if he's lucky.

Might run an escort service from the same place. Lives in the flat above the café.

Might be another flat up there he rents out. Has to be to someone who can keep their mouth shut.

He's got parental debts to clear. No idea how much. Likes to dish out cash to people who'd struggle to keep up repayments. Warns them when they fall short.

Not exactly a good apple. Doesn't mean he killed his sister and chucked her body in a random farm outbuilding.

I couldn't tell you how long I've been sat there thinking, but Bella walks through the door and turns on the light.

I'm one of those guys who's sat in fading light so long I have no clue how darks it had gotten.

"I was starting to wonder if you were here," she says.

I'm starting to wonder why she asked me to stay here.

She heads to the bedroom. Shuts the door. Emerges in a couple of minutes in a sweatshirt and sweatpants. One thing's for sure, she ain't dressing to try to seduce me. At least that's one thing I can clear from my stupid, egocentric brain.

"Nice place you've got here," I say. Nice is one of those words you can use in all sorts of situations. Means different things to different people.

She nods. "It's not the biggest, but I make the best of it, I think."

"Renting?"

She nods. "We all do. All us girls from the café. Same landlord."

It hits me. The spare key. "You all rent from your boss? From Davie?"

She nods. Resigned expression on her face.

"What happens when you... walk away?" I ask.

She shrugs. "Only one girl ever tried it. Far as I know. You know what happened to her."

"He's your boss for the café, he's your boss for the escort business, and he's your landlord? Your lives are entirely in his hands?"

She nods, looking down. "Can't speak for all the girls, but it's getting a little restrictive, to say the least."

I nod. "No kidding."

She's on the verge of tears. She jumps up and heads to the tiny kitchen. Makes herself a drink. I shake my head when she holds out a mug, offering me one too.

"You got any family?" I ask. "Any friends you could stay with?"

The kettle threatens to drown her voice out. "Had a sister. Died when I was little. Never knew my parents."

I knew the answer to the friends question. When, exactly would she have time for friends? She spent every spare moment working for Davie in one capacity or another.

"You given the choice about the escort business?" I ask.

She finishes up making her drink and walks back through. It doesn't take her long. "It's just kind of expected. Once you're in, you're soon kept there. Threats of getting kicked out. Homeless. Jobless. Threats of some photos of you getting paid for sex making their way into the hands of the police."

I sit back. "You ever try to stand up to him? Tell him where you wanna draw the line?"

She shrugs. "Not if I want to eat. Or have somewhere to sleep. He doesn't exactly pay us a great deal in cash."

I look out the glass front door. It's opaque glass, so I only see indistinct shapes. "How'd Moira manage to save enough cash to get away?"

She shakes her head. "Pretty sure she didn't have anything. If I had to guess, she got a client involved. Tried to get them to pay her way off the island. Would've worked, too."

I look right at her. "You think Davie stopped her going?"

She puts the mug down. Gets up. Paces the floor. "Sometimes I think he stopped her. Sometimes I think he killed her. But why would he hire you?"

I raise my eyebrows and look to the ceiling. "That's the question I've been asking myself since I got here."

***

I'm starting to think Orcadians can't sleep if there ain't a gale howling at the windows. It's like being stuck inside the world's biggest white noise generator.

Throw in the rain, sleet and hail. Plus whatever else's beating against the roof and every bit of outside-facing glass. Add it all up, I ain't sure I'm getting enough sleep to qualify for a power nap.

The sofa's comfortable. At least, it would be for someone a foot shorter than me. I try another position in the howling darkness. Hard to move when you're losing the feeling below the ankles.

I doze again for maybe an hour, could've only been a few minutes. Could even be seconds. It all feels the same.

There's movement of a key in a lock. Somewhere miles

distant from where I am. The sound of a door opening. Could be a door to Narnia for all I care.

But these things are happening closer to me. A hell of a lot closer.

My eyes open and a dark shadow's crouching over me. Too big to be Bella.

A light flicks on.

Davie Wallace. Right now, that look on his face, I can believe that he put Moira on ice.

"The hell are you still doing here?" he shouts.

I don't get the courtesy of a chance to reply. He drags me off the sofa by my shirt.

My numb feet give way beneath me.

Pins and needles shoot through my ankles and feet. In a minute, I could stand up again, but it'd still hurt.

"Get up!" he yells. "Face me like a man!"

There's a kinda scream from behind me. "Davie, please, leave him!" Bella's voice sounds more pathetic than I thought possible.

"You should be gone," he says, pointing at me on the floor. "Everyone's telling ya to leave. Why have ya not done it?"

He's asking me a lot of questions for someone who doesn't give a damn about the answer.

I flex my toes. It ain't pleasant, but the sensation will pass. I'll be able to get to my feet. That seems to be what qualifies someone as a man in this guy's eyes.

"I asked him to stay here," Bella says. Got to be a mistake.

Davie steps over me. Before I can roll over, I hear her scream. Someone hits the door. It crashes into the wall.

There's crying.

There's the heavy breathing of the angry and the guilty.

I've gotta try getting to my feet. Works like a charm.

"Davie, I've been helping the police-"

He launches himself at me. Why the hell did he ask the questions?

Hands are around my neck.

Bella pulls at his shoulders. Grabs for his arms. Tries to stop him. Pleads with him.

But he ain't here to kill me. He pushes me as he lets go. Sends me tumbling into the shelves next to the door. They break apart and fall around me as I land.

Bella darts at him. "Leave him alone!"

He turns and shoves her hand against the wall between the kitchen and the hallway. She hits it like a paintball splat and falls to the floor, sobbing.

"The police don't want you here," Davie says.

He pauses to give me a hard kick to the lower ribs.

"I don't want you here," he continues.

Kicks me again. Same place.

I roll over a little. At least try and take the next one in a different spot.

"These girls, if they know what's good for them, don't want you here."

He kicks me a third time. Whatever air's in my lungs runs off like it's terrified. I'm on my front, gasping. Crawling around.

I could wipe the floor with the guy in different circumstances. If I was fully awake, able to stand on my feet, and maybe he was three feet short and built like a girl guide.

I've gotta psych myself up. Get back on my feet. Remember any of my combat training. Put a stop to this guy. Save Bella. Save the rest of them.

"I'm not leaving," I manage to force out.

"Oh, yes you are. If you know what's good for you, you're leaving on the next plane."

He crouches down. "If you don't, your little roommate here might have a couple more things in common with Moira."

He swings an arm at me. I wince. But the fist doesn't make contact. His elbow, hard and sharp, collides with my cheekbone.

I hit the floor.

Bella's still sobbing.

Davie steps over me again and walks out the door. He closes it and locks it behind him.

I ain't got the strength to get up. To even roll over.

I lay there on the floor.

My eyes close.

I'm gonna get a little more sleep now.

Seems all I need when I can't get some shut-eye is some brute to charge in and give me a hell of a beating.

Who needs sleeping pills?

Who needs white noise?

27. TEXTS, LIES AND VIDEO CLIPS

He's one of a declining number in that cavernous space. Sitting on one of many hard wooden chairs.

He's right in the centre. Right between rows of imposing red stone pillars. Each supporting an ornately carved Romanesque arch.

The other arches are very much gothic in style. Unusual to see two different styles from different places, different eras, blended together.

Really, the stonework is sublime. Considering its age, the stuff this building's survived.

All the stone cut locally. That wouldn't happen these days. Would be most likely shipped in from Norway. India or Brazil if they're stretched.

Here, you could take a trip out to a beach not more than a couple of miles from here, near the airport. You could walk along its quiet, white sandy shore. Gaze into crystal clear waters. See veins of yellow and white through the bright red cliffs.

You could bend down and pick up a chunk, if it didn't crumble in your hand from years of weathering. Same stuff surrounding him right now. Expertly extracted and crafted. For what? Someone making a statement about some murdered Earl who hailed from Norway?

There were odes to Norwegians everywhere you looked around here. Plenty of relics of the Scottish too. A weird combination of heritages. An island community of mixed loyalties.

What did it say in the bible? A house divided against itself cannot stand?

Seems to have stayed standing a while. Maybe *he* just couldn't stand the division. Scottish folk, even English folk retiring up here. Genuine Orcadian people. They look back with longing for subjection to anyone other than the British.

When he looks up. He sees the gothic-style ceiling. The sandstone blocks at each edge making a spiderweb-like pattern.

There's a lot he knows about this building. From the dungeon beneath to the hangman's ladder hidden above their heads. From the writer's corner to the gravestones all built into and around the walls.

He's not sitting here for some recital, some concert, some poetry reading event. He's had to endure enough subpar cultural events. How things are, apparently. They can't keep the people of Kirkwall out of *their* cathedral.

Today, it's a garden-variety Church of Scotland service.

The minister's going on about something. In all honesty, it's hard to pay attention to this one. Monotone voice. Always stumbling over his words. Nothing insightful. Plenty of things that could incite him in the wrong way.

Still, it gave him plenty of time to let his eyes wander. See what other fascinating detail he could pick out from the walls.

Today, he's eyeing up the symbols of death carved into those tombstones. The accompanying bones are outside now.

The carved depictions of Memento mori are still in here, protected from the elements for all to see. Skulls and crossbones. Coffins. Hour glasses to show one's time running out. Clocks and candles hinting at very much the same message.

Death comes to us all in our time. He knows that as well as anyone.

His phone buzzes in his pocket. A good thing, really. Nice to have a new distraction. He was getting bored of the weekly wandering of the eyeballs.

Something new from the encrypted messaging service.

Please indicate progress. Inform of any further expenses.

They weren't the kind for pleasantries. Not like the guy that befriended him. Recruited him. Got him buried in trouble with this group so deep that his only option was to pay off the debt by working for them.

The promise of a huge payday was the real draw. Come to think of it, he hadn't been much of a friend at all. Also, what had happened to him? It was like he'd just disappeared.

The minister's still droning on. Something about the Good Samaritan. Obvious. Clichéd as always.

He glances around. No one's even sitting near him. Not close enough to see his phone screen, anyway.

He's safe to open up a few photos and videos of Moira and Sam and to send them. The final photo of Sam needed a little modification. He'd not been able to finish that off that scene as he'd wanted. They didn't need to know about such an insignificant detail.

The Moira one looked good. Had the police stumped. They still had the farm blocked off. All their forensic efforts concentrated there. Yet, the girl was dead before she got there.

They would scavenge around, find a couple of clues, develop some ideas. The dice thing had popped into his head late on with victim one. Another layer of symbolism to baffle them.

It was disappointing that even now, the first two bodies had not even caused a bit of a stir. Even now, up to victim four, they'd kept a lid on this.

Where were the press these days? Didn't the people of Orkney have a right to know that they had a serial killer in their midst?

Maybe he'd need to take things into his own hands. Give it a couple of days. If it didn't break, he'd email one of these photos to the Orcadian, the local newspaper. Watch all hell break loose.

He's ready to send the Moira details. A short video. The best of the photos. Say police are aware of the murder.

Are they happy with that? Should he anonymously break the story?

And what about Sam? People knew him for one thing. His body was left in the city centre, for goodness sake. How could they keep that quiet, and still keep that furniture store in business?

He sends them the modified photo of Sam.

His phone buzzes again.

> Messages received. Photos secured. Please delete.

He presses a couple of things. They start to disappear.

Still saved on his phone. Kept securely locked away.

He types out another message.

> Alert the press?

He waits.

The minister is now talking about good deeds in the community.

Why can't he be on the list of future victims?

Might eventually get a replacement. Someone capable of not

boring their congregation to death. Could outdo his achievement in one sermon, if that was possible.

He sends another message. Forgot about one expense. The thing was a bit like a dentist's drill, but different. Plus the cost of the ink. That wasn't cheap these days.

Anyway, back to the plans for five and six.

Did they need to know yet?

Maybe alert local media to the kills first. Then deal with kill number five.

The minister's closing his remarks. Be like Jesus. Do good. The usual sort of thing.

His phone buzzes again.

> Leak to press needs to happen ASAP.

The message disappears as soon as he's read it.

Things on Orkney are about to get a little crazy.

That's the whole point.

28. BEATS A STORY ABOUT A SICK COW

Maybe people shouldn't seek a career in journalism. Not off the back of watching Superman and Spiderman, anyway.

News rooms, in the imagination, are places full of life. Full of fantastic stories and the sounds of people hammering at keyboards.

For the intern, the novelty wore off within fifteen minutes. You could set a timer for anyone walking through the door of The Orcadian the first time. See if they keep their dreams a little longer. Probably not.

Not a lot of excitement here.

We're getting a few extra cruise ships next year. Someone's signed something. Locals have got to elbow more ignorant old folks out of the way to get to the places they need to be. Wonderful.

The mackerel fishing haul's down a bit. Plenty of shellfish still around, though.

They've narrowed a list down for the best fish and chip place on Orkney. There'll be an article, detailing the top three.

Every few minutes he's asked to make another round of teas and coffees for people. It's a break from something close to interesting. How much of the stuff did these people drink? Can't be healthy.

If he's not doing that, he's emptying bins. He's refilling the vending machine. He's hunting around for more copier paper. Should be easier, but someone didn't say they'd used up the last of the previous lot. Never anyone's fault, though.

They even had him watering the plants the other day.

He's pretty sure half of them are artificial, but it was

something to do.

Today, the intern gets the fun job of sorting through the random emails.

They come through to a central address. They're sent by some boring people, and some whackos in near-equal measure.

Did you know my neighbour has a sick cow? Just stands in a field all day, complaining. What do cows usually do? How does that look any different?

Someone thinks aliens are behind the Ring of Brodgar. Only slightly crazier than the mythical story of its creation. Giants dancing until the sun came up. Much more believable.

Another person's sure that the Ness of Brodgar's a hoax. The stuff being dug up wasn't there ten years ago when he lived in that house, so they say. Some conspiracy to get more money from UNESCO.

On and on they go. Utter nonsense.

Until this one.

This is different.

A photo of a dead body.

Dumped in a farm, out past Stenness a few days ago. Some dice motif. There's a fourth body too. Another picture. This one left off Bridge Street.

Police have even got a private investigator on the go. Helping them out. Looking into things. He used to work for some big national task force.

There was that big white tent just off the main road last week. There were some places next to the high street taped off. Is that what's been going on?

He needs to get this into the hands of the boss.

This could be big. Could be the biggest story of the past few years. Maybe ever.

He smiles.

Maybe, just maybe, life in a news office is every bit as exciting as it is on the TV.

29. YOU HAVE MY WORD

"This kinda thing's happened before," I say through a fat lip. Pressing the ice pack against my right cheek.

DC Sutherland smirks and shakes his head a little. "Why does that not surprise me?"

"At least this time I didn't wake up in the baggage section of a plane to Glasgow."

He laughs. "That really happened?"

I nod. Things hurt, so I stop.

"You should write a book on how to make friends, Flint."

I shrug. That also hurts. I've just gotta stop moving altogether. "They say the author always learns more than they can put in their books."

DC Sutherland's back to the paper and pen. "That so? Who's they?"

I wanna shrug but decide against it. "No idea."

He's writing away. He says, "That Bella Johnson's a smart cookie, isn't she?"

I give him a puzzled look.

"She's done with her statement. Turns out, when she heard the door, she set her phone recording. Got the audio of the whole thing. No video. She hid it down next to the sofa."

Maybe she was ready for this kinda thing. Could be it's happened before. She vowed that next time she'd get something on him.

"We've got Davie Wallace out as wanted. Shouldn't take long to track him down. We're gonna go for remand in a cell here until his initial hearing. Make sure he doesn't harm anyone else."

"You think he killed Moira?" I ask.

He stops and looks at me. "We can't rule it out, that's for sure. But..."

"But what?"

"But that's not the only murder. We've found the first two. Why's he gonna kill her in some crime of passion when he's already got some scheme going in getting rid of others? Leaving clues? Doesn't fit with a guy like Davie."

We're in a different room this time. It's possible the rest of CID will mercilessly mock me for getting beaten up. Or maybe DCI Flett ain't gonna let me in any other room.

This is a smaller room. Nothing in it but a desk, a computer and a couple of chairs.

Could be in a worse place.

Some neighbour had called the police with the noise Davie made. The police had called in the paramedics. They'd treated our injuries. Done an on-scene triage and said we didn't need to go to 'The Balfour' whatever that was. I'm assuming it's the local hospital, and not the morgue.

A hell of a lot of bruises on the both of us. Nothing broken.

"Flint," he says, still working on a bit of my statement, "why exactly *are* you still here?"

"Bella asked me to stay and help."

He raises an eyebrow. "Help with what, exactly?"

I frown in small doses. "Not with whatever you're thinking."

He carries on writing. Trying to repress a smirk.

"They're trapped, these gals. Did you know that?"

"Who?" He carries on writing. Only half-listening.

"The birds who work at the café during the day. They're forced into working as call girls at night. The places they live. They're owned by the boss. Bella's no doubt gonna get evicted because I agreed to try to help her."

He stops writing. He's thinking. "We got a women's refuge some place. I'll look up the details."

We sit with spells of me flapping my gums about the night before. Other spells of awkward silence.

We get towards the end of statement number two of my stay here. Two statements more than I'd have liked to have given during my stay.

"Can I ask something?" I get DC Sutherland's attention. "You said you knew about victims one and two now?"

He nods. "Not supposed to talk about it."

I give him a slow deliberate nod. "Any cameras in here? Any listening devices?"

He shakes his head.

I stare at him.

He smiles.

"Found them not long after DCI Flett threw you out," he says. "First one, Sean Drever. Unemployed his whole life. Looked like a washed out Paul McCartney from a few years back. One single glove over his midriff. A bible verse again in his personal effects. Proverbs six, verse six. I remember that reference. Nice and easy."

He pulls a slip of paper from his pocket and reads out a bit at the top. "Go to the ant, thou sluggard; consider her ways, and be wise."

I can't stop him telling me about victim number two.

"Second's a wealthy guy. Blair Miller. Sold a dairy here a while back. Missed him at first. Thought it was a suicide. Looked that way, anyway. A note and everything. Though the note was where one of the dots on the die should be. Was a clue we missed. Bible verse was Hebrews 13:5."

He's back to the slip of paper. Prepared, like he knew I'd be asking.

"Let your conversation be without covetousness; and be content with such things as ye have: for he hath said, I will never leave thee, nor forsake thee."

I nod like it means something.

"So, does having four victims make any difference from having two?" I ask.

He shrugs. "Not a hell of a lot. Still a serial killer running loose. No idea when he's gonna hit someone next. You've gotta assume he's not done."

I nod. "No one starts with a dice motif and stops at four, I'd guess. We're looking at two more."

He leans back in the chair. "Trouble is, we've not joined the dots on the first four. Even if we warned anyone, we wouldn't know who to warn."

I clear my throat. "What about Davie?"

He shakes his head. "We're going for remand. He's violent. He's a threat to those girls. He ain't getting to them any time soon."

"If he gets himself lawyered up? You think what you've got will stick long enough?"

He looks over the sheets of my statement. "I hope so, for your sake, and for the sake of those other girls. Who knows where he'll turn up next if we're ordered to cut him loose."

He has a wistful glance out of the window. "We've just got to find him before we can do any of that."

***

"You know about this Flint?"

DC Sutherland stands in the middle of the small, dark office. He nods. "I know the headlines," he says. "That enough?"

DS Inness shakes her head. She closes the door. Turns to look at him. "You've let this man into our investigation. I hope you know what you're doing."

DC Sutherland shakes his head. "First Flett, now you? What have you got against the guy?"

She walks past him. Opens a drawer. Pulls out a small stack of paper. "I'm not holding anything against the guy that didn't come from his personnel file. You know some of the stuff that's in here? You talk to him about any of this?"

He shrugs. "I feel like I've got the measure of him."

She puts on a sarcastic laugh. "You've got the measure of him? Really? Like how he was accused of killing his own wife?"

His eyes widen a little.

"Like his suspensions for being drunk on the job?"

He still says nothing.

"Or do you mean his going against every order? What about

causing a national emergency where people could've died?"

DC Sutherland is at a loss for words for a moment. "But he was cleared of a lot of wrongdoing," he finally says. "Otherwise he wouldn't still be a DC."

DS Inness sits down in her chair. Lets out a sigh. "Maybe this is some kind of bro-code thing, I don't know."

DC Sutherland sits in the other chair alongside her. Says nothing.

"Maybe you think you've got things in common, so he's got to be okay. But you should know you're more different than you are similar. You're not gonna get some divorced DCs Club off the ground with the two of you as founding members."

He laughs a little. Shakes his head. "You think you know me, don't you?"

She's not smiling. "He cheated, many times. He split with her to shack up with a witness from a previous investigation. He tell you that? Yeah, their marriage was doomed, but he's not sitting around, pining for his ex. Hoping she'll change her mind and come running back."

He closes his eyes. Shakes his head. Says in a low voice, "I'm not pining. I know it's over."

She leans back in her chair. "There's another thing that concerns me. I wonder if it's crossed your mind."

He looks at her. Intrigued.

"Death follows this guy like paparazzi followed Diana. Victims. Partners. Suspects. Fellow officers. Others caught in the crossfire. You thought about what that might mean for you?"

He's looking serious now. A grave nod. "Policing can be a

risky business."

She looks him square in the eyes. "There are things you can do to minimise that risk."

He smirks. "He makes a hell of a news article, though. Fascinating stuff."

She raises an eyebrow. "The press love a failing hero in our country. There are a lot of others who would make a better hero than Flint. You should acquaint yourself with a couple of them. Your career could go places if you made better choices."

He gets up. "The only aspirations I have involve catching criminals. It's my belief that Flint can help me do that."

She starts to stand up too. "I hope you're right," she says. "Otherwise DCI Flett's gonna come down on us hard. He'll have us both working some horrible inner city spot in uniform for our sins."

DC Sutherland gets up. Leaves the office. Pulls the door to.

Those last three words echo in that head of his.

For our sins.

It's gonna line up with something at some point.

For now, it's back to the powder keg that's DC Enoch Flint, down the corridor.

Let's hope the guy's gonna turn out to be worth all this grief.

30. WHAT'S THE POINT IN BAD NEWS WHEN YOU CAN'T DO A THING?

Almost free to go after giving my statement.

Not a great time for the phone to ring.

It's Flick.

I didn't call her last night.

She might not have appreciated my sleeping arrangements. Spending the night sleeping on a twenty-something escort's sofa could take some explaining.

She cuts right to the chase when I pick up.

"Toby's gone," she says.

I frown. "Gone where?"

"I don't know." Her voice is reaching hysterical tones.

I've got a heap of questions wanting to pour outta me all at once.

Gotta take a breath.

Got to be the calm one right now.

"Tell me what happened," I say in the calmest voice I can manage.

"We were at the park. Right next to the house. I turn around for a second, and he's not there."

Okay, not so bad. He'll be hiding. Playing with some new friend. The way toddlers are.

"How long ago was this?"

She's gonna say about five minutes ago.

"Two hours."

That answer doesn't compute. Two hours? What's she been doing? Why am I only now hearing about it?

"Police are here," she says. "They've got a picture I took of him yesterday. They've already searched through the whole park. The streets nearby too."

I can't be a whole lotta help from the other end of a phone.

The thought comes to mind. I've already failed to find one missing person this week. What good can come from me looking for another one?

How bad can this get if I wade in?

I'm staring at a wall. Doing nothing.

Two hours. A hell of a time for a kid to be gone. Would seem like an eternity to him. Could be anywhere.

But how far can a kid of about three wander?

"What have the police done so far?" I ask.

"Looked around the park. Door-to-door on the streets around it. They're checking hospitals now."

She's getting teary now. I can hear it.

We've got different ways of dealing with difficult things, Flick and me. She heads for tears, I head for a tantrum.

"They checked CCTV yet?" I ask. "The park have any?"

"I don't know," she says. "Flint, I'm terrified. What if they don't find him?"

I've got nothing to offer but hollow promises.

"The police are good at stuff like this. They'll know what to do."

There's a pause.

"What about you?" she asks.

"What about me?"

"Are you coming home?"

Well, that's the question. Most folks up here want rid of me. But I leave now, Bella and the others are still in the hands of Davie. Can I let that happen?

"I'll try to get home as soon as I can."

"That's not a promise of anything, Flint. Are you coming home, or not?"

"I'm not done up here. There are people relying on me to fix something."

"What? Your own son's missing and you're staying there? Putting a client ahead of us?"

I shake my head. "What I mean is I can't just drop everything. It's a delicate situation here."

"I don't know if it's escaped your attention," she says, "but it's a pretty delicate situation here too."

The anger's rising within me. What the hell am I supposed to do?

"I'll get the message out on social media from here," I say, "and I'll try to get a flight back in the next day or so."

"Flint," I can tell she's building to something, the way she says my name. "You know if the roles were reversed, I'd swim from there if I had to. What are you prepared to do for your own flesh and blood?"

"I'll leave what I can with the police up here, and I'll call the airline now about getting back."

"Better," she says.

"But I'll be honest, I don't know what I can do that the police there ain't already doing."

No answer.

I listen. Nothing.

I move the phone from my ear.

She's hung up the call.

I look over at DC Sutherland. I guess he heard a lot of that.

"You need to get home?" he says.

I nod. "Gotta leave all this in your hands."

He looks out the window. "I wouldn't be too sure."

I look out that same window. What's he seen?

A mild winter storm. Nothing to be too concerned about, surely.

"Last time the weather was like this, planes didn't take off."

He had to be kidding. In this?

"I'm gonna make a call," he says leaving the room, "before you clear outta here. Might not be as simple as you'd think."

***

"You checked the weather forecast since you've been here?" DC Sutherland asks as he walks in and closes the door again.

I shake my head. "Had other stuff on my mind."

He has a pained look on his face. "The thing about a place like this, the weather makes a hell of a difference."

I give him a narrow look. "What are you telling me?"

He shakes his head. "Weather's not great, but it's gonna get worse. Gales. Blizzard conditions. The works."

"But I guess the pilots, the ferry operators, they're used to that?"

He shakes his head with a smile. "They know when to cancel their plans."

I look out the window. Is it that bad out there?

"It's only fairly recently that they've been able to land at the airport in fog. We're not as well equipped as airports further south."

I keep staring out at the weather. "That's it?" I ask. Can't help the angry tone. "I'm stranded?"

He sighs. Sits down. "The planes we use are mostly small. Easily blown about. Plus they're usually propeller-powered. One bit of ice gets in one..."

I can see where he's heading with that when he trails off. I've no reason to doubt him. I got to experience those planes in reasonable weather. The landing was pretty spotty, even then.

"What about the ferries?" I ask.

Another shake of the head. "The Pentland Firth's difficult at the best of times. When the wind gets above safe limits, they're not gonna sale past all those rocky shores and cliffs. Too much of a risk of getting beached. Maybe smashing into something they can't steer away from."

I sit back in my seat. "That's it then?"

He nods.

"What am I gonna tell Flick?"

He shrugs. "Try the truth."

Tried that a couple of times before.

Hasn't always worked out well.

31. NOBODY'S GOT A BIRTHMARK LIKE THAT

Screw the weather.

Everyone here wants me to leave. Hell, I wanna leave. That doesn't seem to be happening.

I call the airport. The ferry company. I try a couple of private boat hires, even. Nothing. Not today. Maybe not tomorrow, either.

Even if they got the planes going tomorrow, there's not a chance of me getting a seat. Couple more days, they tell me. Maybe more.

Who's bright idea was it to come here anyway?

I jumped into it too quickly.

Should've asked the guy hiring me if he was a nutter with a secret criminal enterprise. If I was heading somewhere I might get stuck. Didn't occur to me to ask in that coffee shop.

I've walked down a blind alley. Now I'm trapped at the end with nothing for company but a pack of wolves.

A call comes in. DC Sutherland answers. "I'll be there shortly," he says. Hangs up. Gets up to leave the room.

"Gimme a minute," DC Sutherland says. Gets to his feet and disappears outta the room.

He's gone for more than a minute. The weather's turned full-blown apocalyptic in that time. Clouds have gotta be some kind of purple colour. Wind's picking up even more. Wouldn't be surprised if the whole building's shifted when I step outside. Picked up and dropped on some green witch in a strange land. Tiny people looking on, delighted.

He comes back. Carrying a load of papers. The DS is with

him. She's carrying a newspaper.

She holds out a hand to me. "DS Fiona Inness. We haven't been properly introduced."

I shake her hand. "Flint."

She chucks the newspaper on the desk. "I guess you haven't seen this?" She looks right at me.

I give it a glance.

That headline can't be right.

> ORKNEY POLICE INVESTIGATING MULTIPLE MURDERS. PRIVATE DETECTIVE BROUGHT IN TO HELP.

I pick it up and speed read through the first few paragraphs.

It's all there, in print. No photos.

Bigs me up like I'm some all-conquering hero. Enoch Flint, the man who stopped the Heathrow Heist. Seems I'm gonna sweep in and solve everyone's problems. The hero without the cape. Catch this guy by lunchtime.

I put the paper back on the desk.

I've gotta sit down.

DC Sutherland looks at me like I've sold his house for magic beans. "You talked to the press?"

I shake my head. "Wouldn't even know who to talk to. This hasn't come from me."

DS Inness smirks. "Certainly reads like it came from you. It's like they think the sun shines out of your-"

"I had nothing to do with this!" I shout. "I wouldn't. I don't work like this."

DS Inness raises an eyebrow. Her voice is getting louder.

"You don't leak stuff to the media? Hope it changes things? Isn't that exactly what happened at Heathrow?"

I shake my head and I look at the coffee-stains on the floor. "That wasn't my idea then. It ain't what I'm doing now."

She picks up the paper and heads for the door. "I've got to try and sort this. Don't go anywhere, Flint. We can't have anyone see us letting our knight in shining armour disappear now, can we?"

The door slams after she leaves.

A moment of silence.

"You know," DC Sutherland is looking at me, all serious, "Fiona Inness. She's always been the most patient, understanding, level-headed Sergeant. More than anyone I've seen in my years in the force."

I let him get where he's going with this.

A smile breaks out. "That was until maybe five minutes ago."

I try to put on an innocent look. Not sure I've pulled one of those off for a couple of decades.

DC Sutherland puts the papers he's holding down on the desk. "Truth is, we're on our knees a little with investigating four murders. Might as well kill some time looking over these?"

I nod. I pick up an autopsy report.

Sam Muriel.

Starts with piercings, unusual markings, that sort of thing. Something in this section. A small tattoo. Not a whole lot worth much ink and paper.

Cause of death is strangulation. Quite the neck to grapple

with.

Not a lot on here to write home about.

I pick up the next one.

Sean Drever. The first victim.

No piercings. A tattoo, though. Very recent at time of death. A series of lines. Described as being like something from a tally chart.

"Strange," I say, putting the second report down.

"What?" DC Sutherland picks it up again.

"Similar tattoos on both of these."

He stares at the page I was just reading. "Seems to be the only link of any kind any of us have found."

He picks up the remaining two reports.

"Well, that's interesting," he says.

He lays them all out on the desk.

He points at each of them in turn. "Every one of them has a very recent tattoo. In each case, the body's not had a chance to heal."

I look through the rest of the pages. "Any photos of the tattoos?"

He shakes his head. "They make a note of them, but they don't photograph everything in an autopsy unless we ask."

I look at him. "Any way we can ask now?"

He purses his lips and stares at a wall.

I look down again.

The door opens, and he's gone again.

Another few minutes. Hail starts beating against the window.

Every time he clears outta here, the weather gets worse. He keeps doing it, I'll be leaving in eight feet of snow.

The door opens. He's standing there, looking like he's missed his own birthday party. "Got an issue. The first victim's body's already released for burial."

He walks to the window and stares out. "Wasn't a murder victim at the time."

He didn't need to explain it to me.

"Got them to get a picture of each of the other tattoos. Give a bit more detail about them. As much as they can."

Got nothing to do but sift through the rest of this paper.

Maybe stare out at the weather, getting worse by the minute.

***

I brave the weather and venture out for a sandwich. Nothing special.

Not even anything average.

Might as well have eaten some weeds, mixed with a little mayonnaise, folded in a wash cloth.

Wasn't worth the trip. I'd rather have been hungry and been able to feel my face.

More like a metaphor of my life since I set foot on this island.

"A birthmark indeed!" DC Sutherland is saying to himself when I walk back in the room. He looks at me. "That's what he thought on the first autopsy. Didn't think to mention it by number four, did he? Could've linked these much sooner."

I give him a can't-get-the-staff kinda shrug.

"He's had another look. He's emailing photos." He's glued to the computer screen, hitting the send/receive button every few seconds.

Nothing makes time drag like waiting for an email. Five minutes? More like thirty seconds.

"DS Inness came back a few minutes ago," he says. "She's cleared you to work on this. Got the go-ahead from your bosses down south. Said you're integral to our investigation."

I nod. "Nice of her."

He smiles. "Got her arm twisted into it by the newspaper article, really. Bad PR saying it's all codswallop."

A grovelling apology arrives by email. Three photos attached.

A paragraph with a few technical words chucked in. Make it sound like you're indispensable. Like you haven't just screwed the pooch. A final sentence.

Tattoos in each case are consistent with application immediately before death, or post-mortem.

We look at each of the photos.

ᚷᚾᛚᚠ

Not a lot like a tally chart.

Not really like anything I've seen before.

They're like a series of scratches. Like some kid trying to draw trees by scratching flint into a cave wall.

"Why would someone go to the trouble?" I ask.

"There's a chance they were already dead." He looks at me. "Some way of tagging them?"

I look back at the screen. "But they're all different. You ever seen markings like this?"

He gets closer to the screen. "They look a little familiar, but I've no idea why."

I get out my notebook. I do my best job of recreating the strange markings.

Applied close to death. That's gotta mean something.

Maybe the killer put the marks on each of them. Could be something less sinister. Like they all visited the same tattoo parlour.

Time to hit the streets and ask around.

"Any tattoo places around?" I ask.

He nods. "One or two. Never visited the places myself."

It'd be unusual for none of the police to know about them. Might as well be part of the ritual of becoming a cop in most forces.

"We've gotta find out about them. Especially the back-room jobs. Someone put these on the victims. There's a guy out there who knows something about that."

32. SCREW DOING NOTHING

It's just like Flint.

It's more like Flint than any other thing he could possibly do.

Sure, take on a job without asking anyone else. Without even some basic fact-checking first.

Disappear to some island miles away.

It's like the guy to be nowhere near when things go wrong. Either that, or he's usually up to his neck in whatever's going wrong.

No middle ground. Ever.

Where is he now, when Flick needs him?

He's stuck on the Orkney Islands. Couldn't get home if he wanted. Hardly a mess he created, but it's just so like the guy.

Leaves her on her own. Staring out the window. Calling every friend she has. Getting them to call everyone they know.

No one's seen Toby. No one's heard from him.

A lot of sympathetic calls. Well-wishes galore. Nothing that gets anything done, though.

The police checked with the hospitals. No sign.

They checked with the coastguard. Nothing there either, which is a good thing.

Checked every children's home. Every homeless shelter. Every women's refuge. Every school, nursery, everywhere any kid might go.

But a kid doesn't just disappear.

A week away from his third birthday. He's all alone.

Somewhere.

How could that be?

He was there one moment. Not there the next.

She replays the moment in her head. Can't help herself.

He was climbing up to use the slide again. Maybe the tenth time in a row. She heard her phone go. A message from her friend.

A quick check. Asking to borrow that new book when she's finished. That was all. She didn't even reply.

She just looked at her watch. Nearly lunchtime.

"Toby, time to go," she said. She turned around. No Toby.

Rewind.

Look again.

Really pay attention to the details.

Was anyone near him before she turned around?

Another kid. Younger. Bright blond hair.

Where did he go? Was he still there? Was it his dad who was watching on?

They didn't come over when she started screaming out Toby's name.

Some other mums, dog walkers came rushing over. People scattered. The kid was nowhere.

Police had shown up. Took their time, but they got there.

Everyone else who had been in the park, the ones that might have seen something, had already gone.

They told her later on that there was a camera. One

mounted atop a pole for the whole park. Spins around every few seconds.

When it last points at the play park, Toby's there, on his own. Next time the thing's done its circuit, a minute or so later, he's gone.

She walks up to Toby's room. The only fully finished room in the house.

What does he like? Where might he go? What's he drawn pictures of recently?

Okay, so there are dinosaurs. He likes those.

Superheroes. Not gonna see many of them at a park.

She shakes her head. Not gonna see many dinosaurs either. Not for the past few million years, anyway.

His drawings have mostly been of the house. Mum. Dad. Him with or without a balloon.

This is driving her mad.

She kneels on his bedroom floor and cries again. Lets everything out when there's no one to hear.

But crying's not gonna find Toby.

She puts on a new, steely resolve. She's gonna find him.

Forget Flint and his uselessness, all that distance away.

The police can do their checks.

She's his mother. If anyone can get in his head, find out where he went, it's her.

Start at the park. Look out for adverts. Banners. Anything that might appeal to a child. Anything colourful. Take it from there.

She puts on her coat. Grabs a hat. Closes the door behind her and turns the key in the lock.

She's gonna find Toby.

She's certainly not giving up on him easily.

She's not giving up on him ever.

Toby's out there somewhere, and it's time he came home.

33. ONLY ONE TATTOO IN SCOTLAND WORTH TALKING ABOUT

Some of these places should come with a health warning.

Gotta check when I last had a tetanus shot. Might have to get a booster or something. I haven't even touched anything.

Already hit the official tattoo and piercing places around the high street.

The first one. A guy behind the counter. Looks too thin to be human. Got a nose ring, an eyebrow ring. Every shape and style of tattoo you could fit on those skinny, sleeveless arms.

Black top with a skull on it. Buzz cut. Couldn't be any better a fit for working in such an establishment. As welcoming as a stale, hot-cross bun found underneath a kitchen unit in November.

I get a lot of shakes of the head from that guy. Never seen those kinda tattoos before. Very small. Tricky. Usually the work of someone who knows what they're doing. I ask for a list of his staff. He says sure, if I come back with an order from the judge.

Second place is all neon lighting. Dark as midnight inside. Not sure how the person doing the tattoo off to the right sees anything. Whatever works for them, I guess.

Same deal from the unimpressed woman who comes up to me. She's got everything possible covered in ink or pierced, at least as far as I can make out.

"We get a lot of people wander in, asking for this and that," she says. "Can't be expected to remember every single request from every single weirdo.

I say, "I'm not asking about every single one. Just asking if you think you've seen anything like these."

A shake of the head. Still a whole lotta nothing.

The gal in this next place is wearing more rings than I've seen in a jewellery store. About six in her nose. Maybe twice that in her left ear. Tongue stud. Who knows where the piercing stops. If it does.

If all that metal's taken out of her, it could melt down and make a decent statue. She might look about sixteen without it. Could be why she does it.

Same deal as the first two. Never seen it. Never heard of anyone doing it.

I'm off the high street now. An upstairs flat not far from the hospital. Might be a good thing, in case of infection. Wonder if they thought about that.

The place is neat, but it ain't clean.

There's a reclining chair with a footstool. A hand-held tattoo machine resting to the side.

No one's adding permanent markings to their body at this very moment. Not here, anyway.

I show her the photos. First, of victim faces.

"Ever seen any of these?"

A shake of the head.

I break out the tattoo photos.

"You seen ink like this before?"

She shrugs. "Maybe. I see a lot of things. Very small, though."

I nod. "Quite intricate? Requires someone to know what they're doing?"

She shrugs. "Maybe. Maybe not. Seen some people do a pretty good job with a biro and a needle."

She shakes her head. "Not seen anything like this for a couple of weeks at least, and they look pretty recent."

"You think these are the work of an amateur?" I ask.

She looks again. Closer. She shakes her head again. "No. Done with a decent injector-style machine."

She keeps looking at the photos.

"Quite neat lines." She points at the one from Blair Miller. "Except maybe this one. Not as neat. Might be they were getting used to what they were using, or they were in a hurry."

"You ever seen markings like this before?"

She shakes her head. "Vaguely familiar, but so's a lot of stuff."

I take the photos back. "You ever hear of anyone tattooing someone after they've died?"

She gives me a disgusted look. "Why would someone go and do something like that?"

I shrug. "Not sure yet. You think it would work?"

She nods. "You can tattoo a lot of things. Could do it to an orange skin if you wanted. I guess you could do it after someone dies."

She smiles. "They aren't gonna move around much and screw it up, that's for sure."

I give a polite smirk and a nod.

"Wouldn't heal, though. Would be red and blotchy. Would stay that way forever."

I thank her.

I turn to go.

I'm heading for the door when another guy walks in. Glasses. Short but greasy hair. Thin face. Got half a tattoo on the side of his neck.

But the thing that gets my attention is the t-shirt.

It's a specked grey. Got ORKNEY on the front in large letters.

Right above the letters, the same kinda marks as those tattoos.

"What's on the t-shirt?" I ask.

He shrugs. Looks down. Hasn't given it much thought.

"Just Orkney, isn't it? Got it in a charity shop."

I point at the markings. "Yeah, but what are these?"

He shrugs again. "Some cave markings round here, aren't they? Some ancient thing from a tomb or something."

I rush past him. "Thank you," I say.

I look back at the girl who's picking up her tattoo gadget. "Thank you too. You've both been helpful."

I'm heading out the door as I hear the guy ask, "Who's that?"

Last thing I hear on the way out the door, she says, "No idea."

***

The car sways while I'm sitting in it.

The near constant rocking shakes me enough to make typing on the phone screen difficult.

A search for 'ancient cave carvings Orkney'. It shows me pictures of random circle patterns in rock.

I see some stone thing called the Orkney Wife. A vague similarity to a person if you squint and tilt your head.

Lots of circles, jagged triangle shapes.

Some detailed animal and hunting pictures.

I keep going.

I see something.

The side of some upright chunk of stone.

Neolithic carvings.

That's as close as I can get on here.

I turn the car around and head for the high street.

The tourist shops have hundreds of books about their old caves and tombs. One of them's gotta give me a clue.

34. TURN OFF THE ENGINES. LET THIS DRIFT

It's a bland office. As vanilla as they come. Dull walls. Dull carpet. Not so much as an interesting desk ornament.

They're distractions. He doesn't need any of that.

Besides, senior police officers don't tend to make themselves too comfortable. They don't ever plan on staying in that office for longer than a minute or two.

Some go as far as a couple of framed photos of family on desks. They don't go choosing artwork. They have no say in the furniture. They don't usually get to even suggest a repainting.

The life of senior police personnel is one of transience. Moving from place to place. Following that next promotion.

It's been four and a half years since first accepting the DCI post. On Orkney, that came with the title of local area commander.

He's still sitting in that same chair. It creaks more than it used to. The padding's gone a little. Have the arm rests always been this uneven?

A gentle tap on the door.

He's expecting her.

Detective Sergeant Fiona Inness continues to be a nuisance. She's a direct threat to everything about his life. She doesn't even know it.

She's standing there. Neat trouser suit. Some paper in one hand. Calm look on her face.

"Take a seat," says DCI Flett. He leans forward and puts his elbows on the edge of the desk.

"Thank you for sparing a few minutes," she says as she sits

opposite. "I'd like to catch you up on some of the enquiries we're looking at for these four murders."

She looks like a woman in a hurry. Always has. The best leaders always find ways to be busy. Some are pretty good at faking it. She's the real deal.

He sits up a bit straighter. "We can get to the murders."

She looks right at him. This is the biggest police investigation on these islands in decades. What could be more important?

"First, I want to have a brief chat about your future. You've been a DS for what, three years?"

She's puzzled. She nods.

"Are you looking to advance? Have the opportunity to act as Inspector? Do it a few times, you'll be in a position to take the exam. Get that promotion you deserve."

She sits straighter in her own chair. "Sorry, but this doesn't seem like the time-"

"When ever do we have the time? Police are always busy. We've got to make time for these conversations. Otherwise, they don't happen."

She nods, but not in a way that's believable. "Yes, I would like to further my career, but we've got a killer-"

"You have a team handling that. A few minutes isn't going to make or break this entire investigation." Now he leans back. Puts his arms on those arm rests. They're not both the same height. Not even close. No manner of adjusting's gonna fix it.

He looks a little like he should have a cat in his lap to stroke as he talks.

She looks down at the desk and nods. "I'd like to advance my career, but it's not as easy as that."

He puts on a compassionate nod. He's quite good at looking like he cares when he doesn't give a damn. Another key skill for the upper management in the police. "Your family. They're settled. I get it. It's easy to stay as you are."

She nods.

"Police Scotland are always looking for ambitious women. There's a shortage of them as Inspectors. I can recommend you for an opportunity."

She nods. Stops. Looks at him. "Why now?"

Feels like it's got a little warmer in here.

"Another email." He rolls his eyes. "Reminding me again about the shortage of Inspectors elsewhere. You know the structure here, our numbers, they don't allow for it. I thought I'd collar you while I had the chance to discuss."

"It feels like a distraction. Now, there are some enquiries that need Inspector-level authorisation." She leans forward with the forms she's been holding since she walked in. "If you could-"

"I need you to make sure you're not over-reaching with your enquiries about our victims," he says.

She looks around for a moment. Might be looking for a hidden camera. The meeting's going that way.

He picks up the forms. "You want network billing data for Moira Wallace?"

She nods. "We're led to believe that she might have been involved in-"

"She was involved in nothing. I've spoken with her brother."

She clenches her jaw. She wants to say he's wrong. That the evidence points elsewhere.

"We have to be very careful when it comes to surviving family. We can't risk complaints. They might flood in if we start heading down the road of intrusive techniques for everyone."

She's quiet. Stewing on that, by the looks of that clenched jaw. Angry eyes.

"He's a small business owner. Respected in the community. We can't just go intruding. You know he was paying her phone bill? It's in his name, so we need him to be okay with it."

She's getting visibly annoyed now. "Sir, have you even seen the intel we've got on Wallace over the past couple of years?"

He gives her a nod, like a caring patriarch. "I know there have been accusations."

She tilts her head and has that 'oh, really?' expression.

"If you look closer," he continues, "you'll see he's been cleared of any wrongdoing on every occasion. You run a customer-facing business. You rent out a few properties. You're gonna attract negative attention."

An attempt at a patient nod from DS Inness. "Yes, but this goes deeper. There are suggestions of human trafficking. Those girls at the café. Do we even know where they came from? They just showed up on the islands one day. Living in his properties. Working for him. It's all got a whiff of modern-day slavery to me."

DCI Flett puts his angry face back on. It's had enough of a rest. "So someone giving young girls a chance to work. Opportunities to start out on their own. That makes someone some kind of criminal exploiter now? Is that the world we're living in?"

"I can't ignore what the public are telling us about him," she says.

He looks out the window and sighs. "It's all unproven. All of it." He looks back at her. "Without some genuine belief in wrongdoing, and I mean with evidence, you're not to launch into such intrusive enquiries."

She sits back in her chair. She's clutching the forms to her like they're the opening pages of a screenplay she wrote. Something that means a lot to her, even if no one else is interested. "This is pretty standard. And I told you about the small black book-"

"That has mysteriously shown up. We can't even hope to provide that as evidence of anything in court."

She sighs through her nose. Lip buttoned. Eyes closed. "We're not talking about court."

"We're always talking about court," he says. "We've got to think about evidence, disclosure, legal process from day one. We've got nothing from that point of view to justify further enquiries for Wallace. Not a thing."

She sits. Stares out of the window. It frames a view of another stone building over the road. Nothing to grab the attention for very long.

"What's really going on with Moira Wallace, sir?"

He recoils. "You'd best not be insinuating anything, DS Inness. Think very carefully about any accusations you might make against a senior officer."

She shakes her head and looks at her feet. "A moment ago, we were talking about my future career prospects. Now, we're into threats?"

He stares her in the eyes. "Same conversation. Different ends of the scale. So many possible outcomes."

She lifts her head up. Looks at him again. "What I mean is, has Mr Wallace complained? What grounds would he have for a gripe with us?"

He shrugs. "He hasn't yet. But he's concerned about his own right to privacy."

"Surely a dead body trumps privacy," she says.

She's got a fire inside her. She'd make a hell of an Inspector. One willing to fight hard for her staff. Put a few noses out of joint to get things done. For now, that flame needs dousing with realism.

He shakes his head. "I'll have to pay close attention to the enquiries your team is conducting," he says. "You seem very willing to set the rights of members of the public to one side to get a result. A little too rogue, if you ask me."

She starts to get up from her seat. "I don't know what it is you think I'm doing wrong, sir," she's struggling to stay polite. "We're following standard lines of enquiry for a serious incident. In fact, several of the *most* serious incidents."

"You'll be following those lines of enquiry I happen to agree with now. If you disagree, I can arrange for you to have a change of scenery. It'll give you that chance to step up as well."

She walks towards the door. "I'm not going to say yes to an opportunity when it's dangled in this manner. Especially not when I have four murders to investigate."

He's riled up now. Fists are clenched. No one's gonna talk to him the way she is. "If you'd prefer to be a uniformed officer on a beat in a city farther south, that can also be arranged."

She's ready to storm out. "Those girls are being forced into things, and they're trapped. I'm not seeking promotion so the same injustices can happen to women that have happened for years." She closes the door behind her. Harsh, but not quite a slam.

He pulls out a form for transfer. Signs it. He'll get around to sending it away.

She can cut her teeth as an Inspector somewhere around Glasgow. Maybe inner city Edinburgh. She can spend her days dealing with HR issues for beaten-up officers who need to be on restrictive duties.

Anything to draw her attention away from the mess up here.

A mess that no one can be allowed to fully clean up.

If they do, he's gonna come out of it worse than Davie Wallace.

He's known about his less-than-legal side business.

He's used it before.

Hell, he's spent a night with a girl who's turned up dead when she wanted to leave him. He was ready to help her get away. Ready to send some money from the overseas account no one knows about.

Even Davie doesn't know everything.

But if people go digging, they're gonna find more dirt than anyone wants or needs.

But there are still people he can't control.

There are those who set the truth up on some pedestal, like it's some amazing, cure-all outcome.

It's not.

The truth hurts more than it helps.

It certainly does in this case.

No one can be allowed to get to the core of all of this.

They'll find it's rotten.

They'll find fragments of DCI Flett's lies intermingled with it all.

That wouldn't be good for anyone.

35. A WATCH THAT AIN'T WORTH MUCH

Turns out, the pubs north of the border (and I'm way north of the border) ain't a lot different to the rest of the UK.

Not if this one's anything to go by.

Same long, badly lit bar.

Same smell of spilled beer. Same occasional whiff of salty food. The sting of the nostrils brought on by a strong wine.

Same floors and tables that feel sticky, even if they're cleaned a hundred times over.

The difference is in the accents of its regulars. Changes from town to town across this country of ours. Funny how a few miles in one direction or another, it can seem like some folk are speaking a new language. Even more the case here.

To me, those local to Orkney (Orcadians is their term of choice), sound pretty much the same. They've got voices that hit high notes and low. You learn to talk in the local dialect, you might be a shoo-in for a role in a choir. You can talk like that, you can sing.

For the locals, they can tell a Stromness from a Kirkwall. A Finstown from an Evie. Pushed, I might be able to find differences, but it's like asking me which brand of cheddar I prefer. You've tried one, you've pretty much tried them all.

DC Stephen Sutherland's sitting opposite. Kind of him to invite me out.

Tells me his story. A wife he still loves. Even now, she's given up on him and shacked up with someone else. He'd take her back in a heartbeat. Poor guy. He's got it bad.

Someone ought to tell him there are other fish in the sea. Maybe not in the paddling pool of choice that is the Orkney islands. If he broadened his horizons, got on a plane or a ferry to some other place, he could find the next Mrs Sutherland.

But he's done looking. At least for now.

Gonna focus on his career. Seems to have stalled at the Detective Constable stage. That's a thing I know a little about. When I find the way out, I'll let him know.

They say more than half of weddings end in divorce. That's one hundred percent of our party. But from what I see, that ratio hasn't made it this far north. I see older couples everywhere. Bitter. Sometimes resentful. But together. Still.

He gets the next round in. We're on straight beers tonight. No messing with anything fancy. A slower route to getting drunk than tall glasses of wine and little glasses of stuff that can burn a hole in your gut. Gives the men a chance to talk. Commiserate. Empathise.

Women share intimate details in bathrooms and coffee mornings. Guys don't dish the details, but they hint at them in places like this over frothy amber liquids. Maybe we all ain't so different after all.

Seems Stephen Sutherland feels like the social pariah. The guy with all the good dirty jokes, but only wholesome churchgoers to share them with. The guy who lost the friends in the separation.

I spin the yarn of my own trip here. The wife who loved me. Who stopped somewhere along the way. A husband who wandered, strayed. A marriage we both realised had gone on too long not many days after I saved her from a thief and a killer. How I still managed to land a pretty dame like Flick. Sure, it was all sympathy and tears at first. A few drunken episodes later, a dash of near-death experience, we've settled on a life that just about works.

Two DCs in a bar. Divorced. Career cancelled.

We could get on to talking shop, but that ain't the purpose of tonight. Never was. Forget it all. Spend some time away from the near-endless string of thoughts, theories, ideas, what-ifs.

Time to just be two men. Some shared interests. Some shared pain. Chewing the fat. Letting the local drinks drag us a little further away from a consciousness of our own petty failures.

***

I make it back when I've still got plenty of my faculties. Awareness to spare.

Bella ain't shy about throwing the door open to a guy who's visited the local establishments. Doesn't mean she's gotta hang around and smell the result.

She's glad, right now, of someone else to keep the abusive boss away. Or at least to fend the guy off if he turns up.

I know a little about stuff that stops you getting to sleep.

When some guy's determined to hurt you, knows where you live and they've got a key, that ain't any kind of a nightcap.

The police haven't found him yet. They're a little tied up with the quadruple murder I just keep making bigger.

But Bella's not got anywhere else to go. Neither have I.

"You head to the other room. See if you can get some sleep," I say. She was already by the door. Didn't need a second invitation.

I'm dragging the sofa in front of the front door. It opens inwards. The key's turned and left in the lock. That gee ain't gonna sneak in on me again.

"I'll keep watch," I say.

She appears in the doorway in a high-riding nightdress. Some sorta bright flamingo pink colour. Got the word goodnight sprawled across the front in some black graffiti-like writing.

The thing rides high enough when she moves. If she bent over, I'd know what she had for breakfast.

I've gotta force myself to think about Flick. She's pretty. She's kind. She's put up with me longer than most women have. Seems to think she can take some more. Can't go thinking too much about a pretty girl in a short nightdress. However good those bare pipestems of hers look right now.

"You sure you don't mind?" she asks.

I shrug, sitting down. "Done this kinda thing a few times before."

She's got on a slight disapproving look. "You've stayed in an escort's place and barricaded the door?"

I shake my head with a smile. "That bit's new. I ain't one for getting a lot of sleep anyway."

She spins around. Says goodnight. I'm trying to look at the back of her head. Not the hem of the nightdress, flying out. The thing threatens to show whatever she's got on underneath, if anything.

I manage to look away before I get an answer.

Flick would be proud. Well, sort of. There's no way she would agree to my even being here.

Knowing I've managed two nights keeping my distance,

she'd feel I deserve a medal. Or just a slap for getting myself in this situation. Most likely the slap.

I'm left in the company of a book about ancient Norse runes I found in a store on the high street. Managed to avoid the tourist-heavy ones. The ones with the big, colourful photos of neolithic landmarks. Geared at getting you into caves and cairns.

This one's got a huge spiel about where these carvings came from. I ain't interested in that. I had looked at a couple of photos and diagrams in the store. They were a match for a few of the symbols.

I get my notebook and flip to the page with the tattoos. Set it to the side.

I flick through the book. I find a chart near the back. Lays out every symbol. Tells me the letter it corresponds with.

This spy, code-cracking stuff's easy as pie.

What they don't tell you is you need to do a good job of staying awake to get this kinda work done.

I'm on Moira's tattoo.

ᛚᚾᛦᚾᚱᛁᚨ

First one's a little like a lowercase R. Next one's like an N. There's one looking like a badly drawn Y.

I start checking them against the chart.

First one's called a LAGUZ. Then it's a URUZ. Then an ALGIZ. What kinda word is this? Still not gonna be English when I'm through with it.

I get as far as the last letter when there's some sorta noise outside.

I go to the window. Nothing I can see that means a hell of a lot. Maybe a trash can down the road falling over.

Should I head out that door? Have a quick look around? Make sure Davie's not lurking somewhere in the shadows?

I shake my head.

All I'm gonna do is get myself strangled or hit over the conk again. People seem to wanna keep doing that to me. Like there's a bullseye shaved into what's left of my hair.

I flop back onto that sofa.

Was more comfortable yesterday, somehow. Maybe getting dragged off some furniture, beaten-up, it affects your enjoyment of it.

Maybe it's the bruised rib that the first-aider said no one could do anything with. Gotta smile through the pain for a few days. Well, the smiling's optional.

Back to the book and the notepad.

We got a capital R-type letter that's a RAIDO. A straight line they call an ISA, which ain't a savings account. An F-looking thing that's an ANSUZ.

In real money, that all spells out LUXURIA.

At some point, I'm gonna fire that into Google on my phone. See what it tells me about the word.

But my eyelids ain't in the mood for letting my hands do anything that requires looking.

My head's gaining weight like someone's dropping sandbags on it.

It ain't long at all until my looking out's only me looking at the inside of my eyelids.

Still, even if Davie shows up, he's not getting in.

Stupid sleep only seems to come on when it ain't convenient.

I've gotta let it happen. Who knows what tomorrow's gonna have in store.

Gotta get this brain of mine in puzzle solving mode. That ain't gonna happen if I don't get some shut-eye.

Hopefully they'll stay shut until the morning without some brute interrupting me.

Gotta get this puzzle solved. Find the guy. Get home to Flick. By then, Toby's gonna have turned up.

With any luck, I'll get a week of a peaceful home life, without someone trying to kill me.

It's the kind of la-la land thinking that finally pushes me over the edge and into a pile of Zs.

36. YOU'LL RUNE EVERYTHING

LUXURIA. Not a clue, staring at it in the cool light of morning.

Cool isn't the word. Freezing morning.

This is a small place, but with only a couple of old storage heaters, it's far from cosy.

My fingers could be losing feeling whilst holding my phone. Shouldn't be cold enough inside for that to happen.

I touch the storage heater. Stone cold. The thing's been off overnight, so it's gonna be useless all day. If anything, it's gonna suck out what's left of the body heat.

Bella must keep costs down for that pre-pay meter. Keep just the one heater running.

She emerges through the door. She's got a white towelled dressing gown over that nightshirt. Gotta be grateful for small mercies.

"Sorry it's so cold," she says. "I usually cook breakfast. Heats up the space pretty well."

She has a cooked breakfast? Where does she put it? She doesn't look big enough. Even if you include the robe.

She proves me wrong. Gets out porridge oats. She gets it heating up. I wanna walk over and hold out my hands like it's a campfire.

I sit in my freezing corner. Back to the phone.

A search for Luxuria. I get a holiday thing. Some kinda alcohol. Jewellery. Every Internet search becomes an invitation to go shopping. Less like the world's biggest library, more like the world's virtual strip mall.

I put the phone down and get to work on the other two words.

I already recognise a couple of the symbols. A few more of these and I could pass myself off as an expert. Would be nice to have people think I'm an expert in anything.

Sam Muriel's tattoo is short at four letters. Gula. Could be a type of chewing gum. Maybe some hit new TV show. Got me thinking it could be one of those biopics about some bird who worked and died in the fashion industry.

Next word. Blair Miller. There's an I or two. A is in there twice. The word is Avaritia. Maybe a bus company. A vacation company for those of retirement age.

Got the three words next to each other.

Luxuria

Gula

Avaritia

Other than all sounding pretty old and all ending in A, I've got nothing.

Bella's done with the porridge. Didn't ask me if I was okay with it. Could be my only choice is breakfast or no breakfast.

We sit at a couple of folding chairs at the table.

She stops a couple of times. Gonna maybe make polite conversation, but she stops herself.

I try some of the food. Pretty good. She sweetens it. Not like the alleged Scottish way of adding salt instead. Nothing like starting the day with something to harden the arteries.

I say the words I've just written down in the book. "They mean anything to you?"

She shrugs and shakes her head and keeps eating her porridge.

She's not one used to company for breakfast. Either that, or she's not a morning person.

"Supposed to be working at the café today," she says. "You think I should still turn up?"

"No idea," I say.

She shrugs again. "I'll show up. See if anyone's there, I guess."

It ain't long until the painfully quiet breakfast's done. She disappears to go shower and get ready.

I'm left puzzling over those three words.

They all sound like they could be boutique shops. Places that sell high fashion items at obscene prices.

I send a message to DC Sutherland. Tell him I've got the tattoos translated. It's at least a form of English. He should drop by and see what he thinks.

He replies. He's gonna come over. Best to keep me away from the station where possible. Some people there still ain't a fan.

At least they haven't run me out of town yet.

They haven't thrown me in a cell, either. Even though I suspect I might've been warmer in one.

Might have had just as much conversation over breakfast too.

**

Bella's ready to high-tail it out the door when DC Sutherland arrives.

He gives me a look I can't quite figure out.

Does he think I'm some sorta lucky guy for sleeping here?

He wondering what we've been getting up to?

Thinks I'm sweet on the girl.

He might be disappointed at the details. Not gonna burst that bubble just yet.

He's got a thick coat on. Doesn't take it off when he gets inside the door. He reaches for something and stops. Maybe he was wondering whether it was colder indoors than out. Like he needs his gloves as well.

Before he can reach for the gloves again, I hand him my pocket book.

"Mean anything to you?" I ask.

He stares at it and shrugs. "Went to a Grammar school here. No real choice, as it's the only big school on the islands, but still."

I figure he's going somewhere with this.

"It's changed now, but when I was younger, they'd push you towards some language study. I can't say for sure, because I didn't pick it, but it looks a little like Latin."

He goes to the table. Gets his phone out. Lays it down. Gets my runes book.

He's pointing at things with a pen and muttering to himself for a couple of minutes.

I wanna ask what's going on in that head of his, but I'm not gonna break his concentration.

I could ask if he wants a drink. Hell, I could ask him about the weather. Anything. Everything I can say sounds kinda stupid in my head. For some reason, this apartment's where conversations go to die.

I make myself useful and go hunting in the kitchen for some stuff to make coffee. It's in the last cabinet I look in, but it didn't take me long to get there when there's only five.

By the time I've filled and boiled the kettle, he's looking at me with a smile on his face.

"Luxuria, Gula and Avaritia are all Latin," he says.

I'll be honest, I was hoping for more. Unless he's not done.

"They mean lust, gluttony and greed."

I'm still staring at him. He's looking at me like he's told me something vital.

"Three of the deadly sins." He's now desperate for some feedback from me.

I nod. "So are we thinking that's what he's doing?"

He returns to the notebook where he's written one more thing in runes. Hands it to me.

$$ᚠ<ᛗᛉᛁᚠ$$

"This is the runes translation of Acedia. Sloth in Latin. Another one."

Seems he's making stuff up now.

He points at it with wide eyes. "This is the fourth tattoo.

From the body we don't have."

I get that he thinks this is a lightbulb moment. I'm not so sure. "The seven deadly sins? That's what the killer's targeting?"

He nods.

"What are the others?"

He looks at the ceiling. He looks at the walls. He looks everywhere else but at me. "Not sure."

He brings up a list on his phone. "We're missing envy, pride and wrath."

I give up on the coffee. I'd only got as far as boiling the kettle anyway. At least it's providing a little more heat.

He thrusts the pocket book back at me. "I've got to get to the station. Share this with the others."

I don't move.

"You coming?" he asks.

I frown. "Thought I wasn't welcome."

He does a dismissive wave. "No one will even care. Not when there's some new information to act on."

I find the spare key. Follow him out the door. Lock it and walk to the passenger side of his car.

He's more worked up than I've seen him.

Last time I saw him animated, he was complaining about his divorce again. But this is more of a child-like, happy excitement.

We start moving.

"One thing doesn't add up," I say.

He glances over, but he's keeping his focus on the road.

"Seven deadly sins. Six-sided die. Why the difference?"

He shrugs. "Don't know. Interesting though, isn't it?"

He comes alive when a puzzle unveils some glimmer of light. Hints of an answer. Detectives exist for moments like this.

I translated Norse runes into Latin, he translated them into English. An interesting team.

Police love their little clubs and organisations. Got them for singles, LGBTQ+ community, parents, mental health issues. Many, many more.

They might have a multi-lingual divorcee group.

Might be a little niche.

But everyone in the car could sign up.

37. THAT'S GOTTA BE A SIGN

There's something to be said for being a passenger every once in a while.

You get to sit and watch the world go by. You ain't the one who's gotta deal with every idiot on the road.

You get to see things you miss when you're looking in mirrors or looking ahead.

Turns out, this is one of those times.

I'm looking at the Earl's Palace, a wreck of a building, back behind some trees.

There's a Watergate next door. Nothing to do with Nixon, as it turns out. Predates all that by something like a hundred and fifty years. Another broken down stone building. Both buildings were important, back in the day for some rebellion against oppression.

Around the time we drive past the Daily Scoop on the left, we round a corner.

I could've been looking at the stonework. The colours. The stained glass window. The rare patch of blue sky.

But I'm looking at a couple of pieces of wood, hinged together. Makes one of those free-standing boards. The kind you used to see outside of newsagents.

This one's got something to do with the Church of Scotland.

One of those bible verse things that's supposed to get people thinking. Get them penitent, I suppose. Get them thinking a little about religion and why it might be useful to them.

This one's wearing a verse I recognise.

> Whether therefore ye eat, or drink, or whatsoever ye do, do all to the glory of God.

1 Corinthians 10:31 underneath.

"Stop the car!" I shout.

He looks at me when he figures he's not about to run someone over.

"Stop!" I say again.

He pulls over to the side of the road like he's on a driving test.

He's looking around. "Pretty sure we're not supposed to stop here," he says.

I tap him on the shoulder. "I wouldn't worry about that right now."

I point at the board. "What do you make of that?"

He stares at the thing. Keeps right on staring.

He looks back at me. Eyes as wide as his mouth.

"Could be a coincidence," I say, "but we've got to find out who put that there."

***

It's a daunting space to be in.

People talk about God being all powerful. How it's humbling being near the guy. I can believe it.

This place screams all that when you walk through the door.

Polished sandstone, some marble echoes every footstep around the cavernous space. Huge columns and arches lean over me. Like I'm some sorta sinner, and I'm in the wrong place.

There's an information desk to the far left when I walk in. No one stood near it to give out anything.

There's gotta be a hundred people wandering around. Looking at gravestones stuck on the walls. Pointing at stuff. Some with headphones. Listening to some local tell them stuff they'll never remember. They're taking pictures they'll forget about. A hundred people in a place this huge don't amount to much.

A few women of retirement age dot the place. They're wearing dark blue sweatshirts. Gotta be a uniform.

"Need any help with anything?"

A woman with a pale blonde bob of thin hair is looking at me through bright blue plastic-framed glasses.

I nod. DC Sutherland stands next to me, silent.

"The board outside. Could you tell me who picks the bible verse?"

She's got a suspicious, curious kinda look. If I'd have asked about a stone column or a window, she'd have been all over it. This one's come out of left field.

She looks around. Looks back at me. "I don't know if I can tell you."

DC Sutherland pipes up. Steps forward a little. Gets his police ID badge out. "It's the police that are asking. Can you still not tell us?"

She looks like someone just told her a scary story, and she ain't used to them. She excuses herself and disappears.

She comes back with a determined speed walk. "I'm told there are data protection issues with handing out a name and contact details."

I wanna go all Jack Bauer on the broad. Find some new torture technique using stuff nearby. Something involving pamphlets and candles. Push her until she gives the person up.

"But he's an Elder in the Church of Scotland. He often volunteers around the cathedral."

She looks around.

"Can't see him. Might be giving someone a tour of the upper levels."

The torture may not be necessary. If it'd come to it, she'd have squealed before I even got going. Doesn't look like the stubborn type.

She beckons us to follow her on a quick walk around the cathedral.

Certainly is a quick walk.

Never seen anyone close to her age moving at that speed. Almost had to run to keep up.

The ground floor's clear. No sign of the guy. Not that we have a clue who we're even looking for yet.

She walks towards some medieval-looking door. Checks her watch. "A tour started about twenty minutes ago. Can't be long until they head back down."

There are several rows of hard wooden seats.

We only just warm up two of them when the big, solid wooden door swings open. Two middle-aged men walk out, smiling. They're followed down spiral stone steps by two teenage boys. They look like they've been deprived of their Xbox for a few days. This tour wasn't an adequate replacement.

They're followed by a man who looks more suited to rugby

than informative church tours. He's got blond hair. A face I could only describe as solid. Ears that could double up as radar equipment at the local airport.

The woman who'd greeted us gets his attention. "Graham! Graham! Some people here to see you."

We walk over.

"Graham, is it?"

He holds out a hand. "It is indeed. Are you here for the next tour?" He looks at his watch. "You're a little early-"

DC Sutherland cuts him off. "I'm DC Sutherland. We had a question for you, about the bible verse on the board outside."

He doesn't get any further.

Graham's turning around and charging back up those stairs.

Looks like we've got a runner.

But it seems to be he's only heading towards blind alleys.

***

The stone steps don't stay wide for long. They get narrower by the step.

People must've been smaller back then.

We take enough spiral stairs at speed to make an average Joe a little dizzy.

There's a patch of light. An opening.

An archway leads out to two routes at ninety degrees to each other.

I turn left. DC Sutherland goes straight on.

I squeeze down some rough stone corridors. A far cry from

the polished stone on public view elsewhere.

It's hard to run down such a narrow hall at speed. It ain't easy chasing a guy whilst doing your best not to sheer an arm open. You don't spot the massive amounts of sharp flint sticking out of the walls until it can hurt you.

The space opens out.

I'm on a big, upper level section. Archways to my right look out on the rest of the church.

To the left as I run are an assortment of old wooden and stone artefacts. Graham's no doubt just spent a few minutes boring someone about them.

On the inside of each stone pillar is an old stained glass window, mounted in something with a fluorescent light behind it. Looks like they replaced them every once in a while and left the old ones on view up here.

Graham's ahead of me. Stopped. Looking around.

He's out of room to run.

"Graham..."

I'm so out of breath it's all I can manage.

"We just..."

I walk the last few steps towards him.

"...want to talk about the bible verse..."

I don't get a chance to finish my elongated sentence.

Graham charges at me. Sends me into an old stained glass window.

He's making a break for the exit, the way we came in.

Stuff breaks, but the lead strips hold a little better than

you'd have thought.

I recover enough to run after him again.

"Sutherland!" I cry.

I hear some echoed shout that might as well be from a mile away.

He's flinging ancient items as he runs. Tries to block my path.

He grabs a huge wooden ladder. Like two ladders stuck together.

A small printed card with HANGMAN'S LADDER flies up and flicks off me.

The ladder itself blocks my way. I can't stop. Can't get out of its way.

I trip over the thing, and I smack into the stone floor.

I've got to hope that my colleague's got him. By the time I get up, he'll be out of sight.

I turn my head to see Graham heading up again.

What's wrong with the guy? There's surely nowhere down from the tower, unless he knows another route we can't see.

DC Sutherland's got to be hot on his heels somewhere up the forever narrowing staircase.

I've managed to free myself from the ladder. I do my best to scramble to my feet.

I get to my knees when stuff starts spinning.

A ref would count to ten, no problem before I'm on my feet again. No chance he'd let me carry on.

Shouts from both men echo down through every gap in the

stonework.

Loud steps from a wooden platform above. Two sets of feet, close together. Goes quiet again.

No more shouts.

Not much of anything.

Then a tuneless, out-of-rhythm ringing of church bells. Loud as anything at a rock concert. If my head wasn't already spinning, that would've done the trick.

They're too far up those steps for me to provide any help.

I crawl and get myself to the stone stairwell.

"Flint!" DC Sutherland's calling down. "Get on the phone and get some officers here. Tell them we've got a man beaten up and tangled in some bell ropes.

There's more noise.

He's tied up. He's struggling. All he's managing to do is ring those damn bells.

38. WHEN NOTHING STICKS

Gotta love it when some second-rate lawyer puts on that smug look.

The one that makes you wanna find something, anything to charge them with.

The suit looks like it came from a charity shop at least twenty years ago. Something that could almost pass for brown tweed.

How long's the guy been wearing it? How'd he find a tie that matched?

Got a balding head and an obvious comb-over. Not good for such a windy place, surely. Got a hook nose and chubby cheeks. Looks old enough to have bought it new. Old enough to have one technique for dealing with a police interview.

Two words. They get repeated again and again. No comment.

I'm starting to wonder why we bother with suspect interviews. They never say anything anymore.

Lawyers all have the same idea. Keep quiet. Admit nothing (not even your name) and find out what they've got on you down the road. Don't give the police an inch. They can take it and run with it.

All the police have done so far is come up with clever questions for the world's worst chat show.

I can picture it now. The latest Hollywood heartthrob. Granted an exclusive interview. One of those people who've made a name for themselves for asking questions someone else wrote. Out they come. Cheers of applause. First question. What was it like filming that latest blockbuster? No comment. Did you feel you captured the director's vision? No comment. What are you working on now? No comment.

They would jeer the guy as he left the stage. The audience would be as likely to throw stuff at him.

Maybe we should start doing that for police interviews. One of those sound machines. Canned laughter when they say something absurd. A chorus of booing when they say those two most frustrating words in the English language.

Could certainly liven up an otherwise dull morning.

Police arrest a guy, people think that's it. End of the story. Must be guilty. They've dropped the arm on the guy.

It's what TV would have you believe.

Utter nonsense.

Nabbing the suspect is stage one. It gives you the power to search for evidence. That's the key. That PACE Section 8 warrant.

You get a team of people together. They poke their nose into every crevice of someone's home and life. The arresting officer's gotta go and sit in a police building. All the while a team of people, one after the other, take details of the suspect. Get fingerprints and DNA. Check their welfare. Psychological assessment. Determine whether they're capable of answering questions. Check their welfare again. Feed them maybe once, possibly twice while all that goes on.

It's only then that you can think about getting some legal-aid lawyer through the door. They sit with the client. Listen to their fantastical version of events. Tell them to say nothing to the police, and then we sit in a room. Take down the time. Go through the formalities. All for what?

In this case, not much of anything.

We've got the guy's full name now. That's about it.

Graham Craigie.

Has been an Elder with the church here for twenty years. Fine, upstanding citizen. A quiet fellow. Keeps himself to himself.

That's it.

DC Sutherland gives me the lowdown as the guy's carted back off to a cell.

"We've got to let him go," he says.

I look up to the ceiling and sigh.

He shakes his head. "I know, but we've got nothing. We've got a bible verse that the solicitor says could easily be coincidence. Other than that? Just the fact that he ran off when the police came asking questions. What self-respecting Scot would do anything other than that?"

He doesn't really want me to answer that question.

DS Inness and DCI Flett are on-hand to make DC Sutherland feel even worse.

A waste of their day. A waste of the days of another five officers searching his home.

"Find anything at all?" DC Sutherland asks.

DS Inness shakes her head. "We've looked everywhere, hoping we'd at least find the pocket bible the pages were torn from. Not even that."

"His phone?" I ask.

She shakes her head. "PIN locked, and he's not giving us the code. Doesn't even own a computer."

So here we are. Suspect number one, in the door and out again before it even gets dark. That takes some doing here.

The solicitor's done for the day. He's taking his cheap suit, his stupid, smug expression, and he's heading home.

He practically jumps and clicks his heels together on his way out the door.

Maybe they go home. Have a good laugh about how they pocketed a few hundred pounds by getting someone to say only two words on repeat. One day, I'll ask one of them.

There's a heated conversation developing the other side of the magnetically locked door.

DCI Flett says, "We have no cause for keeping his phone. I'm not authorising it."

DC Sutherland's dumbfounded. "Cause? It was seized following arrest for a murder investigation. Lawfully. We have the powers to look at everything if we wanted to."

DCI Flett shakes his head. "Not today. I'm not gonna field the latest grift for you. You arrested the man over a bible verse, for goodness' sake."

"And him running off, assaulting DC Flint means nothing to you?"

"Firstly EVERYONE runs. We're the damned police! Second, I believe Flint tripped over something. What does he want to do? Press charges against the ladder?"

He storms off down the corridor. "It's me with final say. The phone gets returned. Today."

If we're all being honest, it doesn't make any difference.

We're getting one big thing from that phone, and it's nothing.

"Serve him the notice about divulging his PIN?" I ask.

He shakes his head. "Never gonna fly on its own. Every lawyer knows that."

"So we're back where we started?"

He shakes his head again. "Worse. Now, if Craigie's the guy, he knows we're on to him. What chance have we got of a mistake now?"

If he slips up, leaves DNA somewhere, has a mishap with a glove and leaves a fingerprint, we've got him.

I ask the question no one wants to ask. A question I don't even want answered. "What about Davie Wallace? Any sign?"

Another shake of the head. "I've seen louder church mice."

So there you have it.

One possible murderer, released without charge.

One human trafficker, exploiter and downright dangerous individual still out there somewhere.

Orkney's not the biggest place. A few miles, one side to the other.

Trouble is, there are still plenty of places to hide.

39. COMPANY BRINGS TROUBLE

It's the kinda night built for being outside. A rare thing in these parts. Just enough cloud cover to keep in some of the warmth in the air. Not that there was much to start with.

Perfect for the end of October. Candy-hungry ankle biters are heading out, dressed as witches, skeletons, vampires. Parents who read the local papers ain't gonna let a thing like a serial killer on the loose get in the way of free confectionery.

No rain to soak them. No wind to deprive young pretend witches of their hats forevermore. Gotta be the first time since I set foot here that the weather's taken the night off. Maybe they could've managed a flight out tonight. From what they'd told me, even if they had, I wasn't gonna be on it.

But a walk along one of the beaches here is still out of the question. Not when there's a guy on the loose who might want me dead. Throw in the murder suspect, and there could well be another one.

It's back to the small, cold apartment and the sofa.

I walk through the door. Turn the key in the lock behind me.

Something's different.

There's soft music playing through the TV.

Bella's in the kitchen. She's in a dark red velvet dress. First, I make sure I'm in the right place. Second, I wonder whether she's got a different idea of dressing up for Halloween.

Not the best outfit for cooking, nonetheless. Get one spill, one splatter of something, and that crushed velvet might never be the same.

I ain't seen her cooking yet. For all I know, she does this a lot. That dress could be her version of an apron. If it is, it's one hell of an apron. Hugs her figure around her waist. Shows off a thin, delicate stomach, and a sensual curve in her lower back. Hangs a little looser around her chest. Straps wrap to the back and cross over where the material stops halfway up her back.

The scent of sweetened salmon and sharp herbs fills the air.

She looks over at me. I wanna turn around and make sure there's no one else there. That look, full of temptation, full of seduction, can't be meant for me.

But I'm the only one here.

"Welcome home, Flint," she says. "Hope you like salmon."

It ain't my favourite, but I'm gonna nod and pretend it is.

A couple of days ago she was a little lost soul. She looked like a girl fresh outta high school. Now she's a woman who knows what she wants out of life. For some reason, she wants me.

She walks over with a swagger and a bottle of white wine. Fills two glasses already on the table.

It's a minute later she comes over with plates. Puts them down. Retreats to the kitchen. Re-emerges with salmon, herb potatoes and root vegetables, all perfectly roasted. Dishes them out on the two plates.

Her dress has got that bunch of material that hangs a little loose when she bends over. Must've been designed to make a man look. Make him wonder, just for a second, what she looks like underneath. What dress hasn't been?

She sits next to me. "I heard you've had a tough day."

I pick up my knife and fork. "Where'd you hear a thing like that?"

She shrugs. "Small place. People talk."

She cuts off the smallest piece of salmon fillet. She acts like it's the most amazing thing she's ever eaten.

I've gotta try this fish. I do the same. Salmon with a hint of maple in the roasted-on glaze. It's good, but her expression's a little much.

Not sure what's gotten into her to treat me like this. She's forgotten about her lack of freedom. Her feelings of being trapped here, unable to get away. Maybe she's accepted her fate. She doesn't wanna waste my time with this thing any longer.

But that look I keep catching her giving me's telling me something else entirely.

I try talking about tattoos on dead bodies and the hangman's ladder.

She smiles and laughs. I could be saying anything, and I'm not gonna kill the mood.

This girl's got a switch in her head. She flicks that on, she's the perfect companion to someone wanting a pretty girl. Doesn't matter if it's for their night out, or for the next couple of hours. I wouldn't have believed she could be so seductive. Was she like this naturally? Was she trained, polished, until she was ready to take down any red-blooded male with an interest in the ladies?

Dinner's done. She clears the plates away. Says she's gonna wash up in the morning.

Brings out one of those little tubs of chocolate ice cream and two spoons. "Wanna sit on the sofa and maybe watch something with this?"

It's her home. Sometimes I've gotta do what the head of the

house wants to do.

She gets the remote and in a few seconds, some movie's playing. No idea what it is. Not one I've seen before. Probably not one I'm gonna see much of, if I'm reading the situation correctly.

I have a couple of spoons full of ice cream to be polite. The cold stuff, like the atmosphere in here, is a little overly sweet. Like I'm being set up for bad news.

It's one of those flicks about a man and a woman who loathe each other. No guesses for where it's going.

She gives up on the ice cream before that first on-screen tiff between the two of them. Gets up and stashes it back in the tiny ice compartment of that smaller than ideal refrigerator.

She's back on the sofa next to me. Gets closer than she was before.

"My hands are cold now," she says, putting her left on my arm.

She looks at my face as I pull away a little. She laughs.

"Told you they were cold."

In truth, that's not why I was backing off.

Flick's in my head. She's still worried, looking for our son. I'm stuck up here.

Bella pulls out a blanket from behind the sofa. Puts it across both of us. She might as well have poured a jar of ants on me.

I'm on my feet in a shot.

"Bella," I say, cutting an uncomfortable figure, standing by the door, "I can't get too close to you."

She looks at me with a pout. She expecting me to tell her I've got the plague or something?

"I've got a girlfriend. And a son. I can't just-"

"Can't just what?" she asks, getting to her feet. The blanket falls to the floor. "Can't watch a movie?"

I shake my head. "Seems like this is shaping up to be more than just putting eyeballs on a screen to me."

She smirks and shakes her head. "What is it about men? As soon as some girl is friendly to them, they start thinking with the wrong organ. Get this idea in their head that the gal's only interested in one thing."

I glance at the TV. The bird's gone home. Miles away. They'll never see each other again. Yeah right.

She takes a step closer to me. Then another.

I'm stuck in a corner. Nowhere to go.

With me cornered, she leans in. Gives me a long, soft kiss.

I kiss back a little more than I should.

She stops.

I take in lungs full of air.

She reaches for the straps of her dress. It takes very little persuasion to fall to the floor. She ain't wearing a thing underneath.

I reach down, scoop up the blanket and go to cover her.

She tries to kiss me again.

I turn my head away.

"We can't do this," I say.

She giggles. "What? You never sat and watched a movie with a naked friend before?"

I give her a serious look.

Suddenly, she's every inch the lost little girl I first saw. Vulnerable. Confused.

She grabs for the blanket and holds it against her chest. "See something you didn't like?"

I ain't answering that one. A clear trap.

She spins around. Starts to storm out of the room.

The blanket's not covering her back at all. I see every curve of that back. Perfect buttocks and legs for a second or two.

The doors slams.

I look back at the TV. The girl's at a loss at her parent's place. She realises she's thinking of that boy she hates. How many more of these things are they gonna make?

The door opens again. I'm afraid to look.

I glance over. She's back in the nightshirt.

"I'm going to bed. Goodnight."

The door closes again. Hard. Then the bedroom door.

One hell of an evening.

Flick would be amazed at me.

She would wanna kill Bella, but I think I'd come out of it pretty well.

Except for maybe sharing an ice cream and being under a blanket with the girl.

I've got a chance to clean it up before I tell her.

If I ever tell her.

Seems like however I tell her the story, I ain't gonna come out of it like the gallant knight I think I am.

I turn off the TV.

Move the sofa back in front of the front door.

Flick on the storage heater. Put it on low.

Some brave, honourable knight.

Lying there in a shirt I've been wearing for a few days now. Maybe head to a store tomorrow. Buy a new one.

Maybe this is what the honourable get. Nights alone in uncomfortable sleeping quarters.

My prize for respecting the woman too much. For not piling anything else on Flick.

But Bella's out of my head now.

How is Flick getting on?

What's she thinking about?

How's she holding up, Toby missing, and no one around her for comfort?

Is she wondering what tonight could've been? What if she'd been able to head out with him, wear some daft outfit, get some sweets from the neighbours?

What does she think of me, stranded up here?

Not a whole lot, by all impressions.

Otherwise she'd have answered me any of the twelve times I've tried calling her today.

40. PINCH, PUNCH, POUND THE PAVEMENT BEFORE LUNCH

I wake up to the smell of porridge again.

A little warmer.

A little darker outside.

Raining. Again. Windy. Nothing new there.

Check my phone. First of November. If someone had said I'd still be here when things ticked over into another month, I'd have called them daffy.

But here I am, on the sofa of the beautiful escort I rejected last night.

She's in jeans and a t-shirt. Not dressing to impress this morning.

Not a hint of upset about last night. In fact, thus far, not a hint of anything at all.

She puts two bowls of porridge on the table. Does it with all the grace of a waitress who's being fired at the end of her shift.

Says nothing to me. Just stares at that bland oat mixture.

"Hey," I ask, "You got a book like Moira's? Details of clients?"

She looks at me, stone-faced, like I just said I've got her missing pet under armed guard.

"I'm about to head out. Ask around. See if anyone knows anything about where Davie might be hiding. Wondered if I could add any new names to the list."

She looks like she's gotta solve a puzzle on live TV. Spotlight melting her, inch by inch.

I eat my porridge. Let her mull it over.

Must've eaten it a little too quickly. The stuff was still hot enough to scorch my mouth, and a little of my throat.

She picks up the bowls and walks them to the kitchen sink. She pauses. "You washed up last night? Didn't notice before."

She looks back at me. I shrug. "Couldn't sleep."

She turns back. "I know the feeling."

She does her usual morning trick of disappearing to get ready. Emerges with a notebook. The kind that are handed out in school classrooms.

She hands it to me. "I've written down a few of them in here. Can't give you all of them. These are the ones I trust you asking. Not gonna stir up too much trouble with them."

I nod and thank her.

Time to see what I can find out.

***

I'm paying for the mild conditions last night. No doubt about it. I didn't even go out in it.

I'm the only one out in this fierce wind this morning. Everyone else is keen to avoid being pelted in the face by freezing rain.

The first stop's only a street away. Most of them are within a short walk of each other.

First up is a simple terraced house. No answer.

Second, another of the same type. The wife's at home. Had to think on my feet. Going door to door. Helping police with routine enquiries. Ever heard of this girl? She shakes her head at the picture. Any chance I can ask your husband? Where is he?

Turns out, he was only in the shower. He comes down. Insists on words on the doorstep. Closes the door behind him.

"I haven't seen her in weeks. Only spoke to Davie once, just to set up the first meet."

Not getting much outta him. I thank him and move on.

He's gonna head back inside. Tell his wife that he wanted me to understand he can't just go knocking on doors and doing what he likes.

I strike out a couple more times at the next few.

Until I start hitting some streets up the hill, not far from the centre of Kirkwall.

Some big houses. Fancy places. Some of those places have a view of the sea out back, and a sweeping view of the city out the front.

These are the folks with some money. The kind who might have another place or two around the island they rent out to holidaymakers. Empty in the winter. Perfect kinda places for someone like Davie to hide.

The first one's the home of a single guy with grey hair. Short. Looks like he'd rather not be bothered.

"Used to have another place. Out by Stromness. Sold it a few years ago. Used to drop in the café and see Davie. Used to know his parents. A terrible thing, what happened to them."

I thank him and I make like a tree. Seems when you get some of these folks talking, you've gotta not have plans. However much they don't wanna be disturbed, they just keep on talking until you've gotta get out of there.

Next place is only a couple down.

A thinner, younger version of the man I just spoke to. Turns out they're related. When you think about it, probably not a coincidence on islands like these.

Has a beach view cottage on the isle of Sanday. Got a caravan out near Evie.

I recoil a little at the name. I hope I've hidden it well.

He trusts my police story and gives me both addresses. This time, without a story.

As I work my way outta town, the houses get newer and bigger.

It's also getting to be a longer walk back to Bella's place. Could maybe have planned the route better.

Some new houses, set off a side road. A perfect view out to sea.

Hidden away kinda places, in case you wanna get up to anything you don't want people seeing.

Still stucco walls and slate roofs. Just newer. Cleaner edges. Bigger windows.

By the time I'm done, I've got six addresses of places that are empty over the winter. Davie's had a cut-price stay in three of them in the past couple of years. No changes of locks. Gotta start with those.

No one is admitting to having been in touch with Davie.

With any luck, one of these places will turn into something.

But luck's never been my strong suit.

***

First place is out in a town called Evie. A large stone and wood house. Got a gateway like a castle and a mini forest all of its own. Fair-ish weather. Not raining or snowing at least.

I get a little closer. The place has seen better days. A load of land. A great view out to sea, but who hasn't got that around here?

White paint's peeling from old wooden window frames. The front door isn't straight in the frame. Roof looks patched up.

No cars. No signs of any activity at all.

I head down the gravel road, weeds thrashing against the underside of the car as I do.

I get back to the road and I head out a few more miles. Birsay's the next destination. Weather's a touch worse. Wind's picking up. Slight drizzle in the air. All these coastal places up here are starting to look the same. Beautiful valleys dropping down into clear bays of sometimes blue, sometimes green water. A sandy beach every now and then.

This place is an old cottage. Got a dry stone wall around it. If it wasn't an Airbnb, the local kids might think a witch lives here. Maybe she does, but only when it ain't let out. Gotta mix enough potions in off-season to keep her menacing children the whole year round.

The gate creaks as I open it. No car in the driveway.

There's a thin dusting of either snow or hail still on the ground. Not a footprint in it. I'm leaving plenty.

I peek through the letter box. Mail piled up on the doormat. The door hasn't been opened in some time. I walk round back. No other doors. No garden to the rear at all.

Third place, and the rest, are back in Kirkwall.

The locals talk about this being a long drive. Sure, it's a little over half an hour, but it ain't exactly London to Newcastle.

But the difference in weather makes you think otherwise. Could be snowing one side and sunny the other.

I maybe encounter seven or eight cars coming the other way. None of them happen to have Davie Wallace behind the steering wheel.

I get to a street not far from the edge of the city.

Doesn't look like any other street round here.

None of these look like holiday rentals, either.

In fact, the miracle of this street is that every house is still standing. They look like they're made of sheets of wood, stuck together and painted. Each of the weird panelled houses are a different colour. Some brighter than others. All semi-detached. All have a steep pitched roof. Could be an Ikea project that didn't take.

One house has a Reliant Robin parked outside. One of those old three-wheeler contraptions. The things that wanted to tip over to the right when you took a corner too hard to the left. This one's in perfect condition. There ain't gonna be any rust on them with a fibreglass body. Doesn't make them indestructible though. This one certainly isn't, judging by the patches and the sheet of cardboard in a footwell that might be covering a hole.

If I was short of a parking spot, I could pick it up and shift it anywhere I liked. They probably weigh less than your average wardrobe.

But I ain't looking at that house.

I'm looking at one over the road. The right-hand semi of this particular grouping. A dull, greeny-brown colour. About the worst colour you could paint a house. Looks like it was built by an upset stomach.

No car outside.

Garden's overgrown.

Gate's open.

I walk through it and try closing it. It's not gonna stay shut. That explains why it ain't closed.

I walk up the four concrete steps to the front door.

Something moves inside.

Before I go any further, I send a message to DC Sutherland. Let him know where I am, what I might be hearing.

I do a gentle tap on the door. No answer. Maybe I was wrong.

I step to the left. Peer in through the window.

An empty lounge. Looks undisturbed.

But then I spot it.

A curtain's still moving a little. Couldn't do that from outside. I check the window frame in case there's any clear draft that could be to blame. Not finding anything.

Someone's in there. They watched me walk up.

I stay at the window for a moment. The curtain stops. The thing definitely doesn't move on its own.

They've retreated to the back of the house.

I walk around the side. No gate, but a space where there was one, once. Quite a while back, looking at the post and half a leftover hinge.

No windows at the side. All at the front or the back. Stops the planners from having to waste space between. No folks overlooked by someone next door.

These types of houses all have a couple of common layouts. Most put the stairs by the outer wall. Cuts down on noise when you charge up and down them like you're stomping on weasels.

Lounge at the front. Kitchen to the back. Family bathroom and one bedroom to the rear, two more bedrooms at the front.

For all I know, whoever's in there's gone upstairs for a better view of the street.

But if you're Davie, and you think someone's coming for you, you stay on the ground floor. Near an exit.

Two windows on the ground floor at the back. A door between them. Net curtains don't make it easy to see anything. Only empty spaces.

Maybe I was wrong. I wanted him to be here so bad that my mind's writing scripts for my imagination to act out.

The back door.

It's closed, but not all the way. I put a gloved hand on the handle and give it a weak tug. The thing clicks.

Maybe the noise I heard wasn't inside. He could have been on his way out.

A handy bit of advice for gumshoes, keyhole peepers like me, would've been useful here. Covered something like it back in police training. Before you go anywhere, check your surroundings.

If you're gonna wander into a back garden on your own, you've gotta look at the garden before you look at the house. Gotta see if someone's got a place to hide out there. Maybe a pile of rocks or bricks to chuck in your direction. Possibly a spade to bring into hard contact with your thinker.

I turn around. Overgrown shrubbery in at least half of the garden.

No frost or hailstones to map out any footprints here. The ground's wet, and any footprints could've been there for days.

But a couple on a muddy edge of some paving stones, partly reclaimed by the lawn, look pretty fresh. I follow the line they were heading.

Back there, nestled behind some bushes, is a shed. Small, dark brown, and no doubt as ugly as every other garden shed in existence.

Something creaks by it. Might've been the door.

Let's see who's there.

41. WAS IT SOMETHING I SHED?

I walk on light feet towards the back of the garden.

The shed could be a ruse.

I'm watching the bushes as I go. Still a chance he could leap out from one of those and surprise me.

The soaked ground can't take any more rain. Nowhere for it to go but to sit on the surface.

I stick to concrete flags until they stop.

I try to step on bits of grass with no footprints showing. Preserve the heavy footprints heading nowhere but the shed.

The dark brown stain on the wood's worn away in places. Looks grey underneath, where the thing's not rotting.

The cheap boarded roof's felt covering has seen better days. Not that it's doing much covering. Most of it's hanging down the right side of the unsteady structure.

I'm not so sure I'd trust the thing to stay up long enough for me to hide inside. This person's braver than me.

The door's facing me. In the middle of the side that looks a little like an old, brown envelope before someone seals it up. It's not locked. The door's not even closed all the way.

I stand, back to the old wooden wall. The side where the lock would've been.

He could come swinging at me with some rusty implement. If he does, I've got nothing to counter. No way of defending myself.

I should retreat to the car. Find a tyre iron. Something.

Who comes to a place like this, ready for a fight but without a single weapon? An idiot. That's who. Looks like I've nailed my colours to the mast in that regard.

The door flings open.

A sledgehammer, of all things, swings at me.

An insecure shed. The perfect place for bone-breaking tools. Old, rusting garden supplies too, according to this owner.

I duck and shuffle right. The hammer makes light work of the door. The thing goes part of the way through and sticks there, like someone hit a pause button on an action sequence. Splinters fall around me.

I grab the hammer before he can pull it free

I get both hands on the long handle. Gives me a moment to get my bearings again.

He lets go and charges at me. I let go with my right hand and point and push an elbow in the direction of his oncoming face.

He yelps and falls back a step.

I turn to face him. It's Davie Wallace, alright. Been hiding here in scruffy hoodie and sweat pants. Unshaven. Hair's a mess. Looks as threatening as Saddam Hussein when they found him down that hole in Iraq.

The hammer's gonna stay stuck where it landed. I won't be needing it. Plenty of other things chucked either side of the door.

He picks up a trowel and throws it at me. Misses. How bad is this guy's aim?

He's got another one. Matching handle. The keen gardener bought a set. How helpful.

The second one's heading for my face. I get my left arm up

in time. The thing strikes bone. It hurts like hell.

He grabs at the space around him like he's falling off a cliff. The smaller tools are down my end. He's got a lawnmower. It ain't exactly a car, but he ain't exactly a world's strongest man contestant.

Tucked down by the side of that, a strimmer.

He grabs the handle and swishes it through the air like a sword. I swear he's making a humming sound like a kid with a fake lightsabre.

I've gotta duck to avoid it.

He's coming at me now with the least dangerous of weapons.

Shoves it into my stomach. It knocks the wind outta me.

He retracts and goes again.

Sends me backwards. Out of the shed. Into a bush.

I hit my head on the damn sledgehammer handle on the way out, still there.

He throws the strimmer at me lying in a hedge and bursts through the door.

He makes a break for the gap down the side of the house.

I scramble out of the bush. Grab the first long-handled tool I get my hands on. A three metal-pronged garden fork. An old thing. Judging by the state of it. Could've belonged to Poseidon, a while ago and turned into a garden implement with little effort.

I turn and chase him down. He hasn't even reached the end of the grass yet.

Holding the handle, I use it like a claw-grabber in an arcade. See if I can get any of the assailant. Win myself a prize.

I miss his head, but I catch his hood flapping around behind him.

His top half jerks back while his legs keep trying to get some place.

He slams down into the wet ground beneath. His head just misses hard contact with the fork.

The prongs sink in about halfway. Puts holes in the cotton like it's a dictator's speech. I've got his hood pinned against the sodden ground.

He's flailing around, lying on his back.

He reaches towards me and grabs the bottom of my coat. Pulls it hard towards him.

My head jerks down, smacks off the fork handle.

Through the stars I'm seeing, the fork's dislodged. He's scrambled and ripped himself free. Covered in mud. Getting outta there like an in-progress home run.

I pull the fork free and go after him again.

He's clearing the side of the house.

I get right up behind him when he's next to the steps. I throw the fork on the patch of grass and in the same movement launch myself at Davie from a near-sideways angle.

We both end up in the front garden.

I've got hold of him. He's got hold of me.

He gets a couple of punches in.

I return the favour.

His feet and legs are moving like he's a disco dancer on Speed, but he's getting nowhere.

I wrestle him. Pin him to the turf.

He's reaching for the fork, the only thing like a weapon that's nearby. He's about a foot short of it.

I reach out and grab it.

I jab him in the face with the handle. See how he likes it.

He's dazed. Stops wriggling around so much.

I realise the spread of the prongs of the fork are perfect for something.

I raise the thing above his head.

I see panic in his eyes.

I bring it down so the left and middle prongs go either side of his skinny neck and sink just a little into the turf.

I push the thing in until he's got just enough clearance to breathe.

I sit on him.

We're both out of breath. Both hurting.

I'm done with chasing people.

I go to get my phone from my pocket. It ain't there. Must've fallen out somewhere.

I reach into his trouser pockets. He's still got his.

I hit the emergency call button and I get through to the police.

"I've got Davie Wallace," I get out before my jagged breath runs out. "He's wanted... been... on the run... from the police...

I've got him pinned down... by a garden fork."

"Excuse me?" says a man on the other end.

What part of that was unclear?

I say the address.

"Send DC Sutherland here. Please. Needs something to restrain the man."

Davie's trying to say something.

I push down a little harder with the fork for a second.

He soon gives up.

I've just got to sit here and wait for backup to arrive.

Then I can find my phone. Leave this guy to face the many charges mounting against him.

42. A BAD SPOT FOR THE GOOD BOOK

They've gotta be sick of seeing me here.

I'll be honest. I'm sick of being here.

I could go the rest of my life without seeing the inside of this police station again. Wouldn't upset me at all.

Still, a little more comfortable than being out in freezing rain. Keeping an irate man pinned to the ground with a garden fork ain't a simple task.

Someone found my phone in the garden before I could get to it. It got a little messy, but it's cleaned up okay. Same could be said of me.

Police officers made sure I had nothing broken. A hell of a lot of scrapes sustained along the way are barely worth anyone's time. Gotta get them cleaned up when I'm done.

"You were lucky I was already on my way," DC Sutherland says. "I'm not sure you could've held him for more than a couple minutes longer."

I nod. Then I smile. "What do you think of my methods?"

He smirks and shakes his head. "Well, you're unorthodox, but you seem to get results."

"What's gonna happen now?" I ask.

He lets out a laboured breath. "You know the drill. He's gonna get an interview. Let out with bail conditions to stay away from the girls, stay away from the café, that kinda thing."

I shrug. "It'll be tough enforcing that when he lives above it."

He looks back at another pile of pre-printed statement paper. Can't believe I'm doing yet another one of these.

"He owns other places," he says. "We've already checked a couple. Some are empty. He can stay in one of those for a few weeks."

I nod. "He needs to stay away from the girls. Give them a chance to sort their lives out."

He nods. "You can keep an eye on Bella, I'd imagine."

There's that smirk again. Did I miss a wink? If he's gonna suggest something, he should come out and do it.

He's about done, and ready to read it back to me. His phone rings.

He leaves the room. Stands the other side of the door. I can hear every word he says.

"You're kidding me," he says. "Where?"

He's back in, a minute later. Confused. Ashen-faced.

"Don't think he's getting out on bail," he says to me.

Curious.

"Why?" I ask.

"Because we've found that pocket bible at the address where he was hiding. The pages torn out are gonna be an exact match."

I lean back in my chair. Quite a turn up for the books.

But something's not right. Can't say what it is.

I look at DC Sutherland's face. He's got the same expression.

We're both staring at the floor for a minute.

"They think they're gonna find more stuff too," he says. "About the tattoos."

I shake my head. "It's not Davie Wallace. Doesn't fit at all, does it?"

He's got a look like someone just stopped him on the street and gave him a grand in cash, no strings attached.

"I don't know what to tell you, Flint. We follow the evidence." He looks away. "This guy's fallen in our laps with some stuff that's gonna make it hard for him to get free."

"Why hire me? Why kill his own sister? What's with the elaborate set-up? Why'd he do all that? Is he even clever enough, or dumb enough for all that?"

He shrugs. "If he didn't do it, he's even stupider than we ever thought."

I look at him, puzzled.

"He sat in a house with evidence of four murders. Waited for the police to show up and chase him out. I mean, if he didn't do it, hell, even if he did, how stupid can you be?"

***

I get a seat at the table this time.

Thanks, really to the local press.

They started speaking about me as some amazing hero-type. Someone who the police brought in to solve things. If they hadn't, I wouldn't be here now.

I'm next to DC Sutherland.

A desk between us and Davie Wallace. No solicitor. He declined. Says he doesn't need one. Heard that one before. Often just a few minutes before someone says something they regret.

That's why we're here. Push buttons. Get a reaction. Get

him to admit something.

A confession ain't worth much on its own these days. Someone can change their mind about what they wanted to say later down the line. They claim they got scared. Told the police what they thought they wanted to hear. But when you've got evidence to back it up, it's a different ball game.

Maybe he *does* deserve all this. Hell, maybe he did it.

We've got a few things that look nailed-on to belong to the murderer of our four victims.

The recording's started. DC Sutherland has gone through the standard introductions. Names. Who we are. Another offer of a free solicitor. Free legal advice. He's refused it all. Why's he refused? Nothing to hide.

We'll see about that.

"You own a café in Kirkwall. Tell us how business is going."

He looks at DC Sutherland like he's asked what two plus two equals.

He shrugs. "Okay. We make enough to keep it profitable. Keeps us going."

"Keeps servicing the family debt?"

Something in his neck tightens. "It's all under control."

"What about your other business interests?"

Another shrug. "About the same. Renting a few properties I bought at a good time a few years back."

DC Sutherland nods. "We'll get to those."

It's shaping up to be one hell of an interview.

He slaps a photo on the desk. "Bella Johnson. She work for

you?"

He nods.

It's being video recorded. We're not gonna force verbal answers these days.

"As a waitress, and as what else?"

A fake look of confusion.

"What else does she do, Mr Wallace, besides waitressing at your café?"

He opens his mouth. Closes it again. Mentally chides himself for being about to say something. Opens his mouth to try again.

There's a knock at the door.

DC Sutherland goes to answer it. Steps outside for a minute. Gotta be something good to interrupt an interview.

Unless he planned it. Wants to unnerve the guy. Make him think we've found new evidence this minute and it ain't even gonna throw us off course.

He steps back in. He looks like someone's just burned down his house.

"You don't have to answer the previous question."

I look at him. What happened outside?

"Unless there's anything else you want to tell us? Your business interests? The females who work for you?"

Silence.

He moves straight on to his tale. Hiding away in that house. Running from me. The fight that I won.

He asks about bibles in general. What does he know? Is he a keen student?

A shake of the head. Never read the thing.

Funny. We found one in that house.

"Well, it's nothing to do with me," Davie says. "Not my house."

"Anyone ever teach you how to give someone a tattoo?"

Now he looks *really* confused. Sure, the bible question was a little random. What's this all got to do with anything?

He ain't answering.

"Tell us about Moira. Was she a good sister?"

He nods. "Same as most, I guess."

"She ever cause problems? You ever think she wanted to run away?"

He shrugs. "If she wanted to go anywhere else, all she had to do was speak to me. I had no problem letting her go."

DC Sutherland nods. "Indeed you didn't. In fact, it became necessary to make sure she was gone, didn't it?"

He's angry now. "What are you accusing me of, detective? I tried to find my sister. You all tried. I reported her missing."

He shakes his head. Then he points at me like he's trying to stab me with his finger. "I even hired this man, for Pete's sake. What do you want from me?"

"How badly did you want her out of the picture, Mr Wallace?"

He's breathing out like a bull getting ready to charge. "I did not want her *out of the picture.* She was my *sister!*"

"Did you hire Detective Flint, here, as a front to make it seem like you wanted her to be found?"

A shake of the head.

He's shutting down.

He starts asking about the other victims.

Did he know them? Ever heard of them?

Does he know a Graham Craigie?

He even caught me off guard with that one.

"What about the seven deadly sins?" DC Sutherland asks.

"The what?"

"You know, gluttony, sloth, lust, all that lot."

He looks genuinely baffled.

"How's your Latin?"

He's shaking his head. If he wasn't under arrest, he'd be outta here by now.

"My Latin's as good as my Chinese, my Swahili and my Arabic. Don't speak a word."

So much for the fireworks of the interview.

It all started out so promising.

Whoever interrupted, cut him off at the knees. Stopped the only line of questioning that might've got something.

The thing fizzles out and the recording stops.

Davie's taken away.

I turn to DC Sutherland. "What's the deal? What about the trafficking? The Coercive Control? Modern-Day Slavery?"

He shakes his head. "Not a force priority up here right now, I'm told. We don't have a problem with that on Orkney, so I need to drop it."

I throw my hands up and let them fall by themselves.

"I've been *told* there's a problem," I say. "Bella gave a *statement* about it being a problem. He broke into her place and assaulted me over the very same problem!"

He nods. "I know. It's out of my hands."

So there it is.

Something's getting swept under the rug by the DCI. What does he know? What are the rest of us being kept from finding out?

We've got nothing to pin on Davie Wallace.

Murder's not gonna hold. Might be grounds for speaking to the guy who owns the house. That's gonna happen next.

We're not even gonna get bail conditions on him.

He can do what he likes. He's untouchable.

And the way he looked at me a couple of times during that interview, he's damn sure I'm not.

If looks could kill, his was at least a sharp poke in the eye.

***

Same pub as before. Same arrangement.

Here we both are, doing our best to pretend that the investigation's still worth something.

Trying to put it all out of our minds for an hour or two.

There are folks who think the police shouldn't switch off. That they should obsess over everything. Keep gnawing away at the problem until they find the solution.

Here's what they don't know. Their heads are still full of the stuff. They can't switch off. Not even when they're back home. Watching TV. Eating dinner. Larking around with the kids. Cheating on their wives. Whatever they get up to. Today's investigation. Yesterday's too. The one that didn't have the good ending. The one that whispers unsolvable puzzles in their ear in the dead of night.

Some folks wonder about the culture in the police. They seem to think it's all sitting around eating donuts before heading out for drinks. You wanna look at the surface, any job can seem as simple and fruitless.

Truth is, people like DC Stephen Sutherland, people like me, need some help turning off that part of the brain. Gotta relax, sleep somehow.

Gotta suppress the guilt of the past. Gotta shut off that tap. It can't keep dripping relentless, often pointless thoughts about stuff you could try. Stuff you could never get away with. Stuff that could get you or someone else in hot water or worse.

Drives a man insane if you let it.

Everyone needs a little downtime. Even that couple of minutes with a pastry can be like an hour with a therapist to some of the boys in blue.

The drinks are the same. Place smells the same. Table feels just as tacky.

Same people at the same tables. Someone ought to shake things up a little. Show up early. Take someone else's spot. See what happens.

Maybe there's a reason they all stick to their own usual spots. Like a kinda unspoken truce after some ancient bloodshed.

He tells me a little of his journey to being a cop. Father was a failed flatfoot. Sacked for taking a little something from evidence that should've stayed where it was. Too long ago for him to know what. Turned out to be the catalyst for change in the man. Not in a good way.

Stephen grew up thinking he could do better. He could stick it out. Stay honest. Keep his integrity. Make something of himself.

Me? I tried on the life of a cop a few years back. It fit like a custom-made sweater. I kept at it. Come hell or high water, I've got blue running through my veins.

Sure, right now I ain't exactly knocking on the door of a police commendation. Some folks need their breaks in small doses with alcohol in stuffy little bars. For others like me, you need something a little more drastic every once in a while.

Trouble is, where I ended up is pretty much the same thing I left behind.

Two sessions of drinks at a pub's what it takes to be on first-name terms. Except no one calls me Enoch. I can call him Stephen. He keeps calling me Flint.

Glad we got that settled.

Time to get some rest. Something we can manage, now that we've dulled our collective, stupid sleep-shattering imaginations.

Hit this thing again tomorrow.

Hope for some good news. Some mistake. Some oversight.

We sure as hell gotta do something.

Can't expect a serial killer to wander these parts forever. Sooner or later, we're gonna catch him. Stop him.

Get this place back to being the sleepy set of islands it's hell-bent on being.

43. FIVE FINGER DEATH COUNT

He keeps getting messages.

> Progress update on number five please.
>
> Please respond to confirm receipt.

He's been too busy running from the police. Then getting arrested and questioned. Hadn't replied in time.

> One more chance. Please reply or we may need to cancel.

Here it is. Time for number five.

The police, by now, must have an idea of the targets. They've figured out the bible verses. Well done to them. Took them long enough.

What else did they know?

The tattoos weren't too obscure. Surely they've got somewhere with those.

The amazing thing was the newspaper. They printed that story. Front page. Some psycho killer, out there somewhere. Police have no idea. Brought in some special detective.

But the articles got smaller, day by day. No significant breaks in the case.

The newspaper, would, of course, run with it.

The public? They went about life without a care. Sure, there's some madman on the loose. No one even knows who he might come for next. Want anything from the shops while I'm passing?

How thick-skinned are these people up in Orkney? Does anything faze them? Why are they not in freefall?

Well, the next one's gonna need to be something terrifying

and obvious. Really put fear into people.

He knows the person. Pretty well, actually.

That's gonna make this one a little more difficult than the others.

This bird fought his corner, once upon a time. That was a lifetime ago.

They seemed to get on well during those meetings.

But things didn't keep on in that direction.

He got turfed out. She flourished. Strength to strength. Taking on the role of union rep added some to her pay cheque. Where the rest of the pot of union money went is anyone's guess.

Don't ask the woman who can afford to keep a boat moored in Kirkwall harbour. She won't have a clue.

He's got the scrap of paper he's been using to practice the tattoo. He's got a new tattoo machine. An upgrade on the last one, according to online reviews.

Got the torn page from the bible. Highlighted them and tore them out all at once. Then stashed the book.

Only one thing left. The doll.

This one's simple.

She lives alone. She was left the house by her significantly older husband. Not much of a house to leave, a mid-terraced feeble thing, but it's something. The guy spent all his dough on his young, pretty Filipino bride.

He was maybe sixty when they met. She might've been twenty, if you're going by her documentation. He's seen the pictures. Most likely you could knock another five years off.

Maybe more.

She never remarried after he bit the big old inevitable. She got a job. Took on union responsibilities. Managed to look after herself.

Didn't do much looking after anyone else that he ever saw.

She would have an idea of something she wanted. Not long later, she'd found a way to get it. But it was all about her.

When it came time to decide on the theme for his grand plan, she had been the start of it all. She was the inspiration.

She embodied Invidia. Envy.

He knocks on the door.

She lets him in. An old friend, she thinks. No danger here.

They'll sit down. Have a few drinks. Catch up.

One will leave with their heart still beating.

The other will leave in the back of his car, ready to be dumped somewhere. Has to be somewhere people will notice.

Where better than smack-dab in the middle of the high street? What place is a better symbol of envy? Where else do people go chasing stuff they might never afford?

Just gotta distract her. Sneak an extra little something into her drink. Wait for her to keel over.

Should be plenty dark enough by then to take a drive down that cobbled street. No one will be out late on a Wednesday.

Wait until the takeaways close up this time. No semi-drunk patrons to disturb him.

Then get home. Send another anonymous email to the newspaper. Give them advanced warning this time.

Might even get a picture on the front page of her decorated body. The dice symbol, photographed from above.

Beautiful.

Before he even reaches her digs, there's another message to send.

> Number five on the way tonight after unavoidable delays.

They see the message.

He deletes it.

He knocks on the woman's door.

44. IT'S HARD TO KEEP QUIET WHEN THE BODY COUNT RISES

A howling gale had dragged me from my remaining sleep. Dark as midnight outside. How I'd managed to sleep at all in the build-up is a mystery.

There are times when you're rudely awakened, that you can roll over and get back to getting some shut-eye. There are others where you see the time, and the idea of more sleep is as absurd as a hat made of trifle.

You've got no choice but to give in. Get up. Greet the morning with a cheerfulness not earned by its relentlessness.

I'm done showering, dressing in a new shirt but the same suit, when Bella goes through her typical routine.

I wonder if she ever tires of porridge. Is it something she's gotten used to?

Has she never reached the dizzy heights of today's sugar-laden carbohydrate monstrosities? Plenty on offer these days.

Could be that she finds comfort in it. Or maybe the stuff's just cheap, and she ain't throwing good dough at a poor excuse for breakfast.

My phone starts ringing. I haven't even pretended to like this morning's breakfast stuff yet.

"Flint? You need to get down to the high street."

It's DC Stephen Sutherland. He ain't hanging around.

"Whereabouts?" I ask.

He laughs. "You get down here some place, you'll soon find out which is the right place."

I get up and pick up my hat and coat. Head out the door.

The last time he invited me out, breakfast had been a bad idea.

I've got the feeling that this is gonna be another one of those mornings.

***

A walk seemed a good idea.

The weather wasn't so keen on it.

Wind was doing its best to pick me up and chuck me around like a dog toy let loose from some joyful jowls.

Had to hold on to the hat to make sure it didn't end up somewhere in Norway by lunchtime.

Kirkwall's not a noisy place. Traffic is a once-in-a-while thing. So rare, folks can still stop, side-by-side and have a catch up without bothering anyone else.

Aside from occasional church bells, there wasn't a lot of sound generated in these hours of the day.

But today, I can hear something. Like a distant, low rumble of discontent, growing with every step along the cobbled street.

People standing around. Walking excitedly, if folks can walk that way.

More people, the farther along I get.

Pieces of paper are blowing around. Dancing in the air like leaves in autumn.

I pass the cathedral. The streets are filled with people. Could be the king's stopped by with no prior warning. Someone spied some celeb and kicked up a fuss.

I get a little farther through the crowd. No celebrities. No one with an HRH in their name.

Just another body.

Where the street narrows. The wind's mostly cut out of this spot.

Outside the Bank of Scotland. Yellow tape's marked it off with a perfect square. It's like someone decided they needed a little more space, so set up a bunch more a few metres back from the first lot.

A woman, not native to these islands, is lying there. She's close to retirement age, but not that close. She'll never get any closer.

She's got a Polynesian look about her. A one-of-a-few-million kinda cream blouse and a knee-length, straight skirt.

Her shoes are in one corner. Her purse in another. Gloves in a third. The fourth marked out by a jacket of some kind. House keys on her stomach.

Number five.

The runic tattoo ain't even covered up. It's there on her right cheek.

ᛁᛉᛙᛁᛪᛁᚠ

"Name's Maisie Rendell," Stephen says. He's got a knack of sneaking up on someone when there's a body nearby. "Mid-fifties. Widowed. Lived alone. Worked as senior staff at the Royal Mail. Was the local union rep."

I point at her cheek. "Anyone deciphered the rune tattoo

yet?"

He nods. He's pointing to the ground beneath our feet. "Before they saw her cheek."

I look down. This spot is clear of the paper that's doing its best to dance on the breeze. The same runes. Scratched into the paving stones. All big and obvious.

"Invidia," he says. "Envy."

I take a step back, get a better look at what I'm standing on. Someone put a lot of effort into this.

"That's just the start of it," he says. Points at the square of yellow tape. "That wasn't even us."

He points at the bank's bolted-closed wooden door. "See that?"

I walk up to get a closer look.

Something's nailed to it.

A few steps away, I can make it out. A page torn from that same pocket bible. Highlighted verse is Proverbs 14:30.

> A sound heart is the life of the flesh: but envy the rottenness of the bones.

Well, I didn't need to ask about the rune translation, after all.

But nailed to the bank's door? Something a little over-the-top and Martin Luther about this. Could be someone's looking to launch their own reforms in this little community.

Could see the institution with the damaged door as a symbol of envy. Give people credit they can't afford. Keep offering it to them. Feed their wants, their desires. They can have everything they see that they want. They can have it right now. But they're sure as hell gonna make them pay for it later.

"Plenty more to see," Stephen says a step or so behind me. "The killer's gone to town here, quite literally."

I spin around. Look at the nearby store fronts. In all the commotion, the crowds, I hadn't seen them on the walk up.

Different colours of badly applied spray paint all over the ones nearby.

One in red, directly opposite.

> You could be next

The place next door's got green lettering all over the closed shutters.

> One more to go

The other side's an art gallery-type store. Right on the glass, in equally rushed words.

> No one is safe

Two more store fronts opposite. A little further down, towards the cathedral. They've got the same message graffitied on them: Stay inside!

"This guy was gonna make damn sure everyone noticed this time," he says.

I pick up one of the sheets blowing nearby. Simple block letters. Written by hand. Mass-produced on something like a photocopier.

THE POLICE ARE LYING. TRUST NO ONE.

I nod down at it. "Managed to whip up a crowd this early, too."

He nods. "The newspaper were already down here. Before we even got a call."

I look at him. "I guess we're not gonna be able to keep a lid on any of this any longer."

He shakes his head. "Not much of a lid anyway. Was already falling off before this."

I cast my eyes around. "It's like someone's gone round Town-Cryer-style to get folks out here."

He looks to the ground and shakes his head just a little. "Doesn't take long for word to spread here. Goes door to door as fast as a greyhound after a rabbit."

A reporter comes up to me. A thin, young man in a puffer jacket, unzipped, pale yellow polo shirt and smart-ish trousers. "Are you Detective Flint?"

I back away a step. He moves a step closer. Not one for personal space, I guess.

"How are you aiding the police with their investigations? Are you any closer to catching the killer? What do you make of the messages written all over the shops?"

Stephen steps between us. "You know the drill. The police will be gathering evidence. We'll get the information the public need to know out, as soon as we can. We're not gonna comment right now."

"Is it murder?" a woman in the crowd shouts.

"Of course it is!" Someone else yells out an answer.

"You see what it says over there? We're not safe!"

Voices of panic and discontent are chirping up all over the place. Panic is setting in. We're about to have a whole different problem on our hands.

More shouted comments about murder. Not being safe.

Needing to get away. All the stuff you'd expect. Starts to blend into a swell of disparate dramatics. Before long, it's a murky, indecipherable mob-like sound.

There's some movement. The crowd sways one way, then another.

Could break out into a full-blown street brawl.

DCI Flett stands on a raised step outside the bank.

"Everyone!" He's got a hell of a voice to bellow out.

Ears are still ringing as everyone stops dead.

Maybe a poor choice of words for the time. They quit moving, anyway.

"Return to your homes! This is a police investigation, not a matter of gossip and fear-mongering!"

More murmurs.

He shouts again. "We'll hold a press conference later today. Please give us the time to gather evidence and do what we can!"

The crowd starts to disperse. Some are still shouting about how useless the police are.

There are people crying.

There are people who'd run scared right now, if they could move very far in any direction.

It's a minute or two later when the crowds have vanished like pigeons after a gunshot.

Police are still everywhere. Trying and failing to secure the scene.

A couple of reporters from The Orcadian are there. They ain't gonna wait until later to start putting words and pictures together.

I look at Stephen.

"The killer's certainly made us look like fools," I say.

He nods. "What makes it all worse, is we might've had them in custody in the past couple of days."

"Keep your voice down!" shouts DCI Flett. He storms over. Nearly down to a whisper now. "You want reporters to get wind of what you're saying? Don't be such a damned fool."

"At this point," I say, "I think everything's gotta be in the public domain. We can't keep any of this quiet now."

He looks down and nods. Something more in his mind than he's letting on. He looks morose, Almost human. "You might be right."

First time he's agreed with me. Should get that in writing.

Stephen turns to me as DCI Flett walks off like a man about to walk into the sea and end it all.

"Flint, just got word from the station. That page on the door was already gone from the pocket bible before we seized it."

I look at him. "One more to go."

He nods.

"We've got to go through that book, page by page. See what the last one is that's missing. Might give us a clue."

He nods. Looks down at his shoes. "There are only two of the seven deadly sins left. Pride and wrath."

"Who's he gonna target for at least one of those?"

He shrugs. "That's what we've got to find out."

He looks around and sighs. "Something we really could do

with sussing out before we lay this all out for the public."

I look around. "Quite a peaceful place again. When you ignore the body, of course."

He looks back at Maisie. "If we want it to stay that way, we've got to catch the guy that did it."

45. SAY SOMETHING STUPID. ANYTHING

I'm only just getting warm again after that eventful early start.

The feeling in my fingers comes back like a sloth's run when I've gotta answer the phone again.

"You'll never guess what's happened," he says.

I don't have a chance to even throw out theories.

"We've got Graham Craigie back in for interview."

Again, he doesn't give me a second to ask what's going on.

"We looked back at his financials. Got details from his bank. A transaction at a bookstore on the high street. Bought months ago."

"Let me guess," I say. "You asked a guy at the store, and he knows what he bought."

"A pocket bible. Identical to the one we've got in evidence."

He asks if I'm coming back in for the interview.

I guess I'm heading back out into the cold.

***

Same room. Same setup. Same lawyer.

A pre-prepared statement this time.

He was nowhere near the high street last night. He was at the cathedral. A back room, studying something. Some others are gonna vouch for him. Subtext is they ain't happy with the police and that arrest. He wants to be left alone, and a load of other nonsense.

First, DC Stephen Sutherland launches straight into the bible verse.

The lawyer chimes in. Already discussed with the detective that it was coincidence.

Anything new to offer, he asks, or was that it?

A couple more things.

He puts the pocket Bible in its evidence bag on the desk.

A shake of the head. A fake puzzled look.

Never seen that before.

Really?

The bank statement.

The record of sale from the bookstore.

"You still saying you've never seen it?"

Graham smiles. "I'm an Elder with the Church of Scotland. You think I don't buy a bible every once in a while?"

'What did you do with it?"

He laughs. "Probably gave it away to someone in the congregation.'

The lawyer smiles. This is going nowhere again. He's collecting his papers already.

"You know," Stephen says in a casual tone, "we interviewed another guy, under suspicion of this. We found that bible."

Graham's face drops.

"A house, let out by a guy he knows."

He's looking nervous.

"You've rented that house, haven't you? We've got the records."

He looks at his lawyer. His lawyer looks at him.

"No comment."

Back to that again.

"We've already had it tested for fingerprints."

He's trying to act cool. Failing. Badly.

"We've also had a tattoo machine, found at the address looked at."

The lawyer now looks uncomfortable.

"The ink used in tattoo machines. The stuff used in different places. It has a kind of chemical footprint, if you will, but I'm no forensics expert."

Graham and lawyer are seeing what's coming. They can't get out of the way. The questions are coming like a runaway truck down a hill, and it's only heading one place.

"It matches the ink used in the tattoos of our first four murder victims."

All still circumstantial. I ain't even sure that last part's true. Where's the link?

"You care to guess what else we found in your financial records?" Stephen asks. He leans back as he finishes speaking.

"The tattoo machine?" says Graham Craigie.

The lawyer might as well have headbutted the desk.

He won't be skipping on his way out today.

Stephen's doing his best to hide a smile.

They haven't found any record of a tattoo machine in his bank records yet. Pretty sure, now they're gonna keep looking until they find one.

The lawyer's gonna earn his money a little harder today. Even if it's only in stress and frustration.

Stephen starts laying out the five pictures of the victims. The aerial shots.

As he puts each one down, he's saying the Latin name of the sin. His tone becomes friendly. Conversational. Like he's looking for the guy's advice on all of this.

"First victim. Sean Drever. Acedia."

"Second. Blair Miller. Avaritia."

"Third. Moira Wallace. Luxuria."

"Fourth. Sam Muriel. Gula."

He pauses. "The fifth from this morning. Maisie Rendell. Invidia."

He looks up at Graham Craigie. Looks down at the photos again.

Pulls out a thick, red marker. From the first to the last, he circles the objects on and around each body.

"The number dots on a die was a nice touch. Clever. Took us a while to spot it."

Graham's got a flicker of a look of pride written on his face. When his brain kicks in, he wipes it off again.

"Here's what I don't get," Stephen says. He looks at the photos with an exaggerated puzzled look. "Six sides of a die, but seven deadly sins."

He looks at Graham. "What do you think's going on there? Someone forget to count before they started?"

He shrugs. Smiles. "Maybe it's intentional," he says.

The confused look from Stephen's directed at him now. "What do you mean?"

Graham says, "Maybe he wanted the other one to be some kind of... metaphor."

Stephen looks back at the pictures. He scratches his head. "A metaphor?"

Graham looks at him. Confident. "Yeah. Like there's pride, and wrath is the killer himself."

Graham leans back in his chair. "That would be my guess, anyway."

His lawyer won't even look at him now. Might as well not be there.

"The killer... *himself*. Not *herself*." Stephen sits back in his own chair. "And... you know Latin?"

Graham looks like someone's asked him his date of birth, but it's eluded him. "No."

Stephen points at the photos. "I said the Latin names for each of these victims earlier. The names tattooed onto them following their death."

Graham's got the face of a deer in the road, seeing the bright headlights too late.

"I didn't say which sins they were in English, but you knew which ones were missing, didn't you?"

The lawyer earns his money a little more. Leans forward and chimes in. "So he knows Latin. Is that an offence? I suspect there are a few people here who were taught some at school, whether they wanted it or not."

We've got a link between him and the bible. Not a great one, but it's there. We've got a tenuous link to the bible verses. Might be a match in the financials about the tattoos. The guy knows about the seven deadly sins. He knows Latin.

But is all of that enough?

"Who's next?" Stephen asks. "Who's got an issue with pride? Who needs humbling, Mr Craigie?"

He looks at the desk. "No comment."

"Who are you gonna subject to your wrath... if we let you outta here?"

Same response. Same way.

He can fire questions at him for the rest of the day. He's only getting that two-word answer now.

Time to put an end to the interview. We got somewhere, but we're nowhere near the destination just yet.

Stephen's reading out the time.

He'll get Graham Craigie back in a cell for a little while. Speak to some know-it-all CPS guy, who's gonna poke holes in the narrative. Let's hope there's enough left over to keep this guy in a cell.

Prevent that victim of pride from being a victim of something else.

Stop Graham's wrath in its tracks.

Somehow, though, I've got a bad feeling.

When you boil all this evidence down, you're left with nothing but a sticky residue.

46. THE BIG FISH THINK THEY CAN'T BE HOOKED

The café is still open.

Davie is nowhere in sight.

The girls keep working like nothing's changed. Like their entire world, livelihood, homes ain't about to be ripped away.

I've got another steak sandwich. Tastes better than the last one. Something comfortable in this type of food. Familiarity amongst the chaos.

But chaos seems to be good for businesses. The place doesn't have a spare seat. They move me on quick, to make way for the next customer.

I'm halfway back to the station. Graham Craigie smiles and waves from the other side of the street. I nod back. How'd he wriggle free?

I don't get time to think up an answer. Stephen's almost bumping in to me.

"He's out?" I ask.

He looks at some random rooftop nearby. Puffs out his cheeks. "CPS aren't gonna give us this one. They say come back when we can prove something. Put that Bible in his hand. Prove he bought and kept the tattoo machine. Some forensic evidence. Something that'll stick. Plus, we got calls from three people who volunteer in the cathedral. They say he was there late last night. He's got himself an alibi."

"So they're happy to let him walk?"

He nods. "We haven't got the evidence, Flint."

"Easy for them to say if they're in some office in Glasgow or something."

We walk side-by-side to the station.

"We have a list of possible targets for number six," he says. We're heading in through the entrance. "We need to narrow it down. Contact the ones we can, before we hold a press conference at the end of today."

Down the corridor.

We're back in the CID office, and back at Stephen's desk.

He hands me a single sheet of A4 with a printed list of twelve names with their numbers and job titles.

"This all of them?" I ask.

He nods. "Not too many we'd put in the pride bracket up here."

I don't get far down the list before I find a likely victim.

"Allastair Tait. Mayor. Anyone contacted him yet?"

He shakes his head. "Only just finished the list when I came to get you."

"He's looking for a symbol of pride. Wants to disrupt the community. If that's your goal, you're gonna strike big, aren't you?"

He nods.

"Who's bigger than the mayor of Kirkwall?"

***

People's eyes on Broad Street fix on the big, red cathedral that dominates the skyline.

This place, directly opposite, is a hell of a building to miss.

Back in the day, to stand right here, I'd need a boat. Failing that, a snorkel. The church went up right next to the sea wall. Gotta be the reason for the name, I suppose.

They ended up reclaiming the land and a whole lotta land behind it. Stuck this huge building on it.

It's also sandstone, but the duller, greyish-brown kind. Maybe the boring stone they didn't wanna use for the cathedral.

They made the best of it though. Huge coat of arms carved out of stone above a big slab showing the year 1884. It's when they first swung open the big, wooden doors of the Kirkwall and St Ola Town Hall. Small, stone people stand on top of roman pillars either side of the entrance. They haven't moved in nearly a hundred and forty years.

Cast your eyes upwards, you see big windows. Stained glass at the top of some of them. Spires and turrets.

A hell of a building. Would be, anywhere else but here, opposite that thing. Forever casting a shadow, regardless of where the sun's at.

My phone rings.

Stephen.

"Where are you?"

I look around me. No sign of him. "Outside the town hall."

He laughs at me. A little mocking. A little rude. It ain't like I know any better.

"Stopped using that as the actual town hall a long while ago. Walk up the hill, past the cathedral. Turn left on School Lane and it's a little way down on the right.

Thankfully, the council offices aren't far away. Looks like a dull, brownish-grey stone façade on a typical old Victorian era school. Big, sash windows. A small tower that used to have a bell inside. It'd ring for class time. If I keep looking at the street, I might see a kid walking a hoop with a stick. It's got that sorta vibe. A whole load of ivy stuck to it. Dead plants in two matching stone risers out front. Looks like they claimed it once when the Grammar School moved. Thought it would make a handy set of offices.

"Town hall's all commercial now," he says. We're walking through a maze of corridors. "Restaurant. Weddings. Jewellery shop. That sort of thing."

We get to a large room. Simple style. Functional and not at all elegant. Worn carpet. At one end, a reception desk. Chairs around the edge of the rest of the room.

"He's out for lunch," says a blonde broad as we look in her direction. Round face. Could've been the victim of a shovel to the face and never quite recovered. Short hair. A look that might kill mice.

I nod. "But you understand what we're saying, here?"

She nods. Rolls her eyes.

Stephen says, "We just said his life is most likely in danger."

She puffs out her cheeks. Not the thing for her to do to make herself look any more attractive. "Most likely? How likely is that?"

"Is that not enough? I ask. "You need a number? Okay, eighty percent."

She shrugs. "Typical Thursday."

"For the mayor of London," I say, "not the mayor of a place

like Kirkwall."

She shakes her head. "You think we're too small a place for death threats? Had three this morning. Don't even bother telling the police anymore."

We stare at her. Gotta hope the reality of the situation sinks in.

She rolls her eyes again, sighs, and picks up the phone.

A minute or so later, she's done.

"He'll see you at two, today."

She says it like it's a goodbye.

Stephen nods and turns to go.

I guess it was a goodbye, after all.

***

He breezes in, his Hollywood face looking like it's never worn a care nor a worry.

Perfect, side-parted hair, greying the slightest amount around the temple. Almost like it's designed to reflect a little age and wisdom, but not too much to stop him being relevant.

Piercing brown eyes that are close to black. A nose, mouth and ears on that squarish face. Whole thing looks like it was ordered from a catalogue. Fitted on arrival by an excellent plastic surgeon.

Maybe he naturally looks like that. Some folks look more like a computer-generated character than your average Joe off the street. Maybe it's the way the light shines off his forehead. Could be the Cheshire cat smile.

If it ain't his face, there's something fake about him.

He smiles and nods at us. Disappears straight through another door into his office.

"He'll be with you in a couple of minutes," says the callous blondie at the desk.

It gives Stephen time to catch me up since lunch.

"We worked through the rest of the list. Called every one. Got bosses of cheese companies and distilleries, a couple of councillors. I'm more certain than ever that this is the guy."

He's back out again. Shoulders riding high. Chest puffed out. Smile stuck on. Comes to shake our hands like a photographer's nearby. I'm surprised he's not looking in another direction, smiling for some non-existent camera.

"You're the two from the police? Word is, you've got wind of a threat?"

His accent's different to the locals. Not quite as sing-songy. A few more of the tongue rolls you might find in one of the bigger Scottish cities. Got enough of the local twang to just about fit in.

We follow him into a big room where every ornate carved bit of dark mahogany seems to go to die.

He sits behind the desk. We sit in chairs nearer the door. I swear they're set a little lower. Someone's hacked a bit off the legs. He's looking down at us.

"Funny. Since Mr Flint here showed up, we've had more suspicious deaths than we've had in nearly five hundred years."

"You make it seem like it's my fault," I say.

He glares at me. "Must be coincidence, I suppose."

Stephen says, "I'm sure you're aware of the body we found

this morning, and the ramifications?"

He nods. "Aye. Quite the scene, by all accounts."

Stephen nods.

"I was sure we'd have another Battle of Bigswell on our hands if things got any worse."

More nods. "We're here because we believe that was victim number five," Stephen says. "You, sir, are the most likely target for victim number six."

You'd have thought that my colleague was an amateur stand-up. Working every opportunity for his first tight ten. Mayor Tait, his latest audience.

He's still laughing pretty hard.

He's finding this far too funny.

He reaches for a ring binder. Almost throws it down on the desk near us.

"Just about every one of these sounds like more of a credible threat."

"We're here to let you know," says Stephen, "that we're taking this very seriously-"

"As seriously as you took the threat before? Does it take five bodies?"

"We didn't know what he was doing before," I add. "Now, we do."

He leans forward. Puts his elbows on the desk. Rests his chin on his hands. "What do you suggest we do about it?"

We look at each other. We'd thought as far as this. No further.

"Police protection," Stephen says.

That's almost as funny to the mayor as his last apparent joke.

We've gotta come up with something.

The killer's out there.

The Mayor's a dead-cert to be targeted.

The trouble is, there's a chance we've got the tea leaves, and we've read them all wrong.

47. THE SKELETONS IN THE CLOSET WANNA GET OUT AND DANCE

You get this image in your head.

A press conference. Rows of seats.

Reporters. Cameras. All kinds of media outlets are there. Ready to squawk and howl until they get their questions answered.

The spokesperson behind the desk. Illuminated by the flashes of a hundred cameras, pointed at them at once.

Like a lotta things here, it's a little less of an event.

Once upon a time, Orkney was a key strategic place. A place that people fought for. Now, it's out-of-the-way. Beautiful scenery. Impressive historic artefacts. Cold weather. Dark nights. A slower way of life.

We got a function room at the town hall. It was available and offered free of charge. Might as well.

Long table at the end. Twelve rows of seats.

The press maybe occupy the first two rows and a bit. The rest of the room is full of local residents who have wandered in. They want to hear. They wanna know someone's listening when they talk too.

The Orcadian. A local radio station. A load of people with their phones out. Folks are live streaming for various news outlets around Scotland and the UK. Some are doing it to try to get a boost to their follower numbers.

Serial killers are big news. This news has travelled. They'll be onto something else by Sunday, but the spotlight is on this island community right now.

"Thank you for coming," DCI Flett starts up. He sits in the middle of the table. Full uniform.

"I have quite a lot to get through. There will be an opportunity for questions, so please hold them until the right time.

"You'll be aware that a killer struck again overnight. Very publicly. There is a person we have been investigating. There were claims made about peoples' safety, and about the service the police can provide. I want to assure you that the police are here to protect you. I also want to assure you that we are aware of the killer's final target. We have spoken to them personally to offer them protection."

There are murmurs. He ignores them.

"We also want you all to know that we're closing in on that individual. We know what they're doing. We know how they're planning on doing it. We plan on stopping them. Aside from that, everyone else on these islands can be sure that they are safe from harm."

A louder murmur. He waits for a minute before continuing.

"Regarding secrets and an inability to trust the police, I believe I know what that is about."

He's getting to something else, but he's interrupted.

A door opens. In walks the Mayor with an entourage of people in black suits. Earpieces. Looks ridiculous. Over the top.

He sits down right next to DCI Flett.

"I hope you don't mind me joining you, officer," he says with his sickly, charming smile.

"The person who is the target of this killer, I'm sorry to say appears to be me."

There are gasps. Too much of a reaction for his liking. What were they expecting was gonna happen?

"I have my own private security, as you can see. I trust the police to do their investigation, and add to the protection my team can provide.

"But I will not be hiding in some hole for the next few days."

He holds up an index finger. He's got a point to make.

"In fact, our island community needs a little cheering up, while the police do their thing. I've made some calls. It might be a little early, but I plan on personally unveiling our winter season and Christmas lights. The ones that cover Broad Street, anyway. This Friday evening. Seven o'clock, directly in front of St Magnus Cathedral. The rest of the lights will be added at a later date. We invite the media and all residents to join with us to bring some much needed cheer back into our little city."

Those sat in the hall are like a trapped herd of cattle hunting for food. Each one has a question to ask.

There goes the big moment for DCI Flett. It's not coming back round to him now.

***

It was supposed to be his last day. Go out on his own terms.

Hasn't happened.

Instead, he's been upstaged by that limelight-hogging pretender.

Well, he can still go out on his own terms.

Davie Wallace has kept his secret. He won't need to keep it anymore.

In truth, it's been eating away at him for years. He's less of the man, the husband, the father and the Detective Chief Inspector that he should've been.

There's only one reason for that. One reason for the sleeping pills. The bouts of depression and anxiety. The putting on his game face when he felt like jumping from a high spot and ending it all.

It had been worse from the moment Moira had shown up dead. Looking back, he hadn't handled it well.

But she was the first victim he'd seen in twenty five years that he'd had a personal connection with.

Not that there had been many other victims. Not here.

He's changed out of his uniform. That tight-uncomfortable fit will never again be a problem.

He's sitting in his study wearing his sweats. His workout gear. But he's not using the exercise bike in the corner today.

Turns on his laptop. Waits longer than seems fair. Starts a new document and gets to typing.

It's not the public send-off he could've had, but it's gonna have to do.

The story needs sharing.

How he felt lonely that time his wife and daughter were off visiting her family down in Scotland.

How he'd felt at his lowest.

He knew about Davie's side business. It's a small place. People talk. Everyone had to know about it. Everyone who ever felt lonely must've given him a call.

Moira was the girl who he picked up outside the café.

A pretty little thing.

Okay, a rounder face than his might've liked, but that personality was incredible. The fire behind the doll's eyes.

He'd cooked her dinner. Rack of lamb. Red wine. The chocolate puddings had been from a packet, but it hadn't mattered by that point.

He'd only wanted to talk. Find out a little about the girl. About that way of life. Why did she do it? What did these girls want out of life? That kinda thing.

But talking leads to other things, when you drink enough wine to fill up a bathtub.

He had no complaints about her. Beautiful. Wild. Willing. Happy.

He had dropped her off a little late, but she'd said it was okay. She'd liked her evening. Should they do it again?

Definitely.

Every time his wife was out of town, as it turned out.

They talked. Sometimes that's all they did. No bedroom trip necessary.

She spoke of her goals. Ambitions stifled by her brother.

She wanted out. She wanted a better life. Hell, she'd take *any* other life.

But Davie had ways of keeping her here.

But wait! He could help! He had money. He had contacts.

He could get her off the islands. Set some money aside for her.

They spent the next few visits talking. Where should she go?

But this was not a fantasy anymore. This was a planning session.

He loved the girl. It would be the hardest thing to let her go. But that's what you did, wasn't it?

Hell, he shouldn't keep loving her like he loved his wife, anyway. She was only a couple of years older than his own daughter.

That was where the shame kicked in.

Had his wife noticed? She hadn't said anything.

Had she picked up on his being so keen to support her visiting her family?

Had she noticed the different perfume on the bedsheets?

Things had grown colder. Of course she'd noticed.

But his plan failed. A tragic end. The girl had died. Davie had gotten wind of something.

If his wife hadn't known before, she'd have been certain after Moira's body turned up. He was meaner. Quiet. Cantankerous when he finally did speak.

He finishes his frenzied typing.

It's all there. All of it. Warts and all.

Time to finish with the age-old line about resignation.

His wife will leave him.

His daughter might never speak to him again.

He wouldn't blame them.

But it has to be done. Even if Davie says nothing. Does nothing.

He can't live like this anymore.

He can't hold all of this inside and keep pretending.

He hits print.

A strange sense of freedom. Comes out of nowhere.

Almost gleeful.

Is this what it felt like to be free of the burden of guilt?

All those years he'd missed out on that feeling.

He collects the pages from the printer.

He's not missing out on that feeling anymore.

Not for one second.

48. SOMETIMES, A FELLA REAPS WHAT HE SOWS

It ain't difficult in a place like this to find out where someone lives.

Even if they've only been there a few nights, someone's watching. Someone talks.

The talking, the gossiping he overheard at church was the best.

All kinds of things he hadn't even imagined were happening away from prying eyes.

But that didn't make any of it secret. Not up here.

But so many things that should not be happening. Not on remote islands. The people here should be better. Untouched from the monstrosities that afflict society in the UK and in the rest of the world.

So, how to put things right? How can Orkney be cleansed, restored to its simple, glorious life of yesteryear? Well, that seems to be down to him.

Everyone else calls this modernising. You fail to change your outlook? You're old-fashioned. You hang onto your morals, things that meant something a few years back, you're a bigot. Prejudiced. Outdated.

What does the bible say? Woe unto them that call good evil, and evil good? Something like that. For an old book, it hits the nail on the head a lot these days.

He's had an impact too, sure. Maybe not the impact he might've expected.

But people are running scared. They don't know what to

think, or who to fear. That was job done.

That's what the mysterious bosses had wanted. It's what he's delivered.

This is the home straight. This is the big time. This is where he really makes a difference.

He's not gonna hide his approach to the house. Rumour has it, the guy's gonna be drunk by this time of day anyway. Especially now he's got nothing else to do.

Walks straight up to the house. Only one person inside.

Peers in the front window. They're doing something on a laptop. Hopefully a suicide note. Would make things nice and neat.

Except, that's too easy.

This person wanted to be a public example of how to live. Keep their misdeeds in the dark. Well, now's the time for them. Soon to be the most public of examples.

The front door's locked.

The back door too.

But they've left a bathroom window open on the ground floor. He can get in there.

It's a squeeze and a struggle.

Heaven knows how he's not made enough noise to get the guy's attention. The stories of their night-time drinking must hold some water.

He exits the bathroom. Sees the guy lying on the sofa. Giving up for the night.

"Nice place you have here!" Graham's too loud. Too cheery.

The man's arms and legs flail like he's an attacked spider. Scrambles to his feet with the elegance of a one-legged ballerina.

That look. He recognises the intruder.

"What are you doing here? How'd you even get in?"

Graham shrugs. "Does it matter?"

"Hell, yeah it matters. Why are you here? Why now?"

He sits on one of the guy's arm chairs, positioned either side of a generous sofa. All some cream flowery pattern. All one set. Not cheap, by the looks of it. Not very nice, either.

"I came here so you could thank me personally," Graham says.

The drunk man sits on the sofa. The air expelled from flopping down comes out as a laugh. "Why would I thank you?"

He shrugs. "Took care of your problem. You're welcome."

He tries to point at Graham. If he were aiming a weapon, he'd not come close to hitting his target. "Well, you are very *un*welcome. Get the hell out of my house."

He sits back in the armchair. Clear defiance.

"You hear me? Get out!"

"I heard you," he says with a smile, "but it doesn't mean I'm going anywhere."

There are tears now. He's hunching forward. Rests his head in his hands. "I didn't ask for this. I didn't tell you to do this."

He shrugs. "She fit into my plans nicely. It wasn't a difficult change to make."

He's beyond crying now. He's slobbering. Not an attractive sight, but then, he's never been an attractive man. "She was my sister. I didn't want this!" He's full-on sobbing now. It's unbecoming.

Drunkenness could've been added to the deadly sins. Hell, what if that list was being drawn up now? There'd be twenty things, maybe two hundred on it. Screw the more liberal folks who say we've got to be part of being a progressive society.

Graham leans forward in the chair a little. "You know what they say, careful what you wish for."

It's a funny thing when a drunk guy comes at you when you're stone cold sober. They think they're moving quickly. They think they're doing everything right.

Avoiding the first punch is easy. Laughable, even.

"I got arrested because of you," he says with a slur as he goes for him.

Graham's out of the chair. A quick shove and the guy who's had about six too many's face-planting it.

"You got arrested because of *you*, idiot," he says in reply, as if the attempted punch hadn't happened. "At least you've got enough on someone that they let you out."

For a moment, Davie Wallace's eyes clear. It's like he's pushed all that drunkenness to one side for a moment. Forcing one moment of clarity. One moment when he can strike, get his revenge.

He charges in a kind of slow motion. Again, just a nudge is all it takes. Sends him into the coffee table.

The thing looked pricey. It collapses into splinters and shards. Must've been cheap, made to look expensive. Certainly not worth much now.

Blood's coming from the side of Davie's head.

The sight of it prompts an idea.

Drunkenness ain't pretty. It ain't smart. It's far from the worst thing this guy's done.

Whoring out your own sister. Where did that rank?

What else had he done to her? What kind of incestuous relationship did they have before he stumbled on this new way of making a quid or two?

"You wanted Moira taken care of," says Graham Craigie. "I took care of her."

He bends over Davie, lying there. Groaning in pain. The kind of sharp pain that registers. Doesn't matter how plastered you get.

"And I'm gonna take care of you too. You're gonna be a little something extra for the locals. An example. A monster, brought to light and then slain."

Another groan.

He needs something to collect the blood. Could be useful. He goes hunting through the kitchen.

The people of Orkney need this. Davie's victims, slaves, whores need this too.

So does Graham.

More than he ever knew.

49. THAT FRIDAY MORNING FEELING... SICK

A beautiful, clear morning. A rare thing around here, this time of year.

A little cold, sure. A touch of frost in places.

But when the wind dies down, and the sun comes out, who cares about a little chill in the air?

It's been a while since she's started the day with a run. Used to be a daily thing.

The bad weather had set in. Put her off exercise outside. She traded the running shoes for a bowl of porridge. That runner's high for some ill-advised flirting with a guy who could've been her father.

Not that she knew who her father was. She could serve him in the café every day for years and not even know it.

Wouldn't that be a cute little story? He shows up one day. Confesses all. Says he's here now. He can put stuff right in her life and give her the home and the place in society she's always dreamed about.

Today would be a good day for that kinda thing.

It's a good day anyway.

Davie has disappeared. Been gone for a few days.

No more late nights. No more enforced dates. No more evenings in the company with men she and the others would rather avoid. No more putting on that fake smile. Those fake noises and shudders. It's done. All of it.

Even if he comes back, she's not doing that anymore. The other girls are gonna agree. He doesn't stand a chance, one against five. Six if you include Flint.

She's worked alongside a couple of them since. Naomi, as the oldest, had kept the café going. Made shift rotas. Organised food deliveries. No one would know any different.

The girls all have something different about them. Confidence. More personality. The glazed look in their eyes has gone.

What a difference a few days can make. What a difference Flint's helped to make.

Still got no idea why he's doing it. He's not asked for money. He turned her down when she offered a different kinda thank you.

Maybe sometimes, a white knight rides into your life if you're lucky. Fixes things, and goes on their way. Moving on, ready to fix something for someone else in some new place. They shun thanks and refuse payment or reward. Their payment is that justice is done.

She's got her head up for maybe the first time as she walks through the side gate.

She's early for work at the café. Way too early. It just feels like the kinda day where that might be okay, for some reason.

Her chin's up as she unlocks the door. She steps over the threshold.

Her foot slips.

She looks towards her feet for the first time. Something red on the floor. Someone spill some sauce and not clean it up?

She looks back outside. Red drops leading all the way along the path. If she'd walked in with her usual demeanour, she'd have seen it straight away.

It's too dark for sauce. Got a copper, some kinda stale smell.

Far from pleasant. Someone hurt themselves?

She walks back outside.

What happened? What caused this?

The trail heads right, out of the gate. Down the high street. She follows.

She doesn't wanna believe it's blood. This kinda bleeding ain't from a small injury. Not from someone catching themselves on a blade or hitting their head. There's too much of it. A steady flow.

She follows past a bunch of still-closed stores.

Keeps following it.

Who loses this much blood without someone doing something about it?

She keeps walking. Looking at the ground. Following the trail.

Past Moira's old place. Still going.

There's a spot a little way down where a tree's kinda growing out of the pavement and the road. Someone built the road around it. Decided it was old and needed protecting. To this day, shoppers on the high street carry on around it like it ain't even there.

Today, folks are gonna notice it.

She's reached the tree. The end of the blood trail.

She looks up.

A scream's stuck in her throat.

She runs to a nearby waste bin and chucks up whatever she'd eaten recently.

Looks back at the tree.

Davie. That ogre of a boss. The guy whose disappearance made life so much better.

He ain't coming back. Even if he's right there.

Got a rope around his neck. Strung up against some part near the top of the tree.

His arms are outstretched and nailed to tree branches.

A torn piece of cardboard's got some string attached. It's looped around his neck, avoiding the rope. There's some stuff written in thick, black marker.

WHOREMONGER

EPH 5:5

His shirt's missing. Thank God he's wearing something below the waist. It would make this worse, somehow.

Except the person who put him here, didn't stop there.

They got six Polaroids. Five are the girls. Moira included. No clue who's in the other one. Don't know where those photos came from, but he had them. They've been stuck to his torso like the six spots on a die.

She looks a little closer. No, they're not stuck on. They're attached. With staples.

What kind of horror has she stumbled into? What does any of this mean?

Her head spins. This man, her boss, her landlord, her abuser, her deceiver. All of it. Now none of it.

He got her here with a lie and a promise. He broke that promise. She's working in a café that's suddenly got no owner. She lives in a house with no landlord. She's got no job. No money. Nothing.

She can't stop looking.

Soon other people are gonna spot it. Join in. Wonder why this happened.

Who did this?

It wasn't one of the girls, was it?

Couldn't have been. They all kinda hated him, but he had a strange hold on them. They all kinda loved him a little too.

She takes a step back towards the safety of the café.

She's taking a couple more. Not even aware of what her feet are doing.

She breaks into a run.

Someone's screaming. Someone else has seen the body.

The screams are so loud. Worse than any horror movie. Chilling.

Enough to make you wish for everything in the world to come crashing down, just to make that sound stop.

She's slowing down. She's nearly back at the café.

That scream's just as loud. How can it be?

She sees her reflection in a window.

She's the one screaming. Tears are flooding from her eyes.

It's all gone wrong. Horribly wrong.

She stands there, right outside the café. Brother and sister now dead.

What happens next? Who's gonna even care about her and the others?

Is she even supposed to think about herself right now? Is it selfish? Callous?

Her feet are kind of numb.

Her hands too.

Her arms and legs have stuck. They're not willing to move.

It's like they're not hers anymore.

Nothing's hers.

The café's blurry. Why does it look like that?

Everything else is replaced with blackness. The café seems like it's avoiding whatever apocalypse might be occurring.

The café succumbs to the blackness.

Bella's lost everything. Including consciousness.

Who knows what her life's gonna be, when those eyes of hers open up again.

50. A BIG CHEESE CAN LEAVE A SOUR TASTE

"You did what?"

DS Inness is angry. Not inquisitive. She's leaning on the mayor's desk from our side.

He was a man with such confidence and charisma yesterday. Now he looks like the kid who stole a cookie.

"I cancelled my security team," he says. A nervous smile follows hot on the heels of those words.

"Why would you go and do a stupid thing like that?" she asks.

He waves a hand towards the window. That tree ain't exactly visible from here. Partly on account of the massive cathedral in the way.

"It had a little something to do with your man, nailed to the tree out there," he says.

She stands up. Her hair's tied back, so it stays out of the fight. She steps back. "Of all the bone-headed, idiotic, brainless, stupid things you could do."

"Something wrong with my assessment?" He asks. A little more earnestness in his voice than his face wanted to put in there.

She points through the window in the vague direction of the tree too. "First, he's not been on that tree for a while now. Second, there are no guarantees this means what you think it means."

He sits forward. He's not taking that reclining all the way back. "You said I was victim number six. You now *have* a victim number six. All the numbers on the dice. I'm free and clear."

She turns around. "You're something and something else. They're not the adjectives I'd choose."

Stephen steps in. "We don't know what we have there yet. There are key things that don't match the MO... the method the killer has used the previous times."

He shrugs. "So he changed his methods. He knew the police were on to him. Maybe he was spooked. Who knows? Surely that happens."

"The sixth deadly sin. Supposed to be pride," I say. "This scene's about something else."

He spins. Gets out of his chair. Walks towards a bookshelf. "What was that bible verse?"

"Ephesians five, verse five," I reply.

He takes down a huge, thick, fancy leather-bound bible. Brushes a little dust off it. The thing looks like it ain't moved in years. The mayor finds the passage at an impressive speed.

"For this ye know," he says. Clears his throat and keeps on reading it aloud. "that no whoremonger, nor unclean person, nor covetous man, who is an idolater, hath any inheritance in the kingdom of Christ and of God."

He stops. Puts the book on the desk. Jabs a forefinger into the passage like he's poking it's eye out. "There you have it."

Stephen says, "There we have what? I didn't hear anything about pride."

He prods the verse again. "What's an idolator if it's nothing to do with pride? It's right there."

Stephen looks up at the ceiling and sighs. "We don't even know if this is the same person yet. Could be a copycat."

His Hollywood smile takes a hit. Looks a little dented. "A copycat?"

Stephen nods. "Happens with serial killers more than you might think."

The mayor shakes his head. "No, I don't believe it. You've got victim number six. I expect you'll find him with DNA or CCTV or something."

"Kirkwall's CCTV," DS Inness says, "is not worth the name. More like vague guesswork, given the age of the cameras. We've appealed... to *you*... for better cameras. More of them. You've told us there isn't a budget for them."

He nods. "That's right."

"But there's a budget for new Christmas lights? Keep going like this, we won't only refuse to protect you, we'll make sure we get out of the way if the guy comes."

She storms off.

Just the three of us left in the room.

"Who does she think she is?" Mayor Tait says.

Stephen shrugs. "Oh, just the new Area Commander."

The mayor looks at him. Puzzled. Head tilt and everything.

"Yeah, DCI Grant Flett resigned this morning, apparently. I know nothing more than you, but she's in charge until Police Scotland decide what they're doing."

"What? Just up-and-gone? At a time like this? A killer on the loose?"

Stephen laughs. "I thought you weren't worried about the killer now."

He couldn't back-pedal anymore if he was sitting on a bike. "Well, as you say, it's best to be safe about these things."

Stephen shakes his head, looking at the floor. "I'll have a word with DS Inness. See if we can get a couple of uniforms sticking by you for the next few days. The local council's gonna pick up the cost, though."

The mayor's shoulders slacken. Like that's some kind of a blow. He says nothing.

"You know I've got a busy day, don't you? There's the Christmas lights installation to finish. Thankfully I restricted it to just Broad Street. But they started yesterday. Ladders. A cherry picker. They need direction. I won't be later than seven this evening with this."

"You're still going ahead?" I ask. "Given the risk?"

He gives me his best stern look. It ain't tearing anything off me.

"Might be better to put this thing on ice until we've got the guy."

A chuckle from the chair. "When will that be? You've had long enough. How close are you?"

I shrug. "Might be closer when you put yourself on public display, like you're gonna do tonight."

"As I recall," he says, "the last murder we had before you landed was about twenty years ago. An old woman and her cat. People were more upset that they killed that cat too. A domestic thing gone wrong. Now you show up, and the body count's rising like a Rambo movie. A fine one to speak to me about danger."

He turns to look out the window. Can't quite see the chaos

of workmen outside the church from here. "You know, you could call it a sting operation or something. Draw him out, you know? Like all those TV shows."

For a second, I think I'm gonna have to hold Stephen back from finishing the job on behalf of the killer.

"We protect, Mr Mayor. We don't put people, anyone in harm's way just to catch someone."

He huffs. "Maybe you should. Might have caught him earlier."

We give him the politest smile we can manage.

"Let us know your plans for this evening, so we can plan any protective measures accordingly," I say.

He nods.

Pretends to pick up the phone and urgently call someone.

We leave him to his imaginary conversation.

Damn sure he ain't very good at the real-life ones.

***

"You know anything about Grant resigning?" he asks me on the walk back to the station.

Gotta walk all the way round the cathedral. No shortcuts.

The air's still as cold as it was when I got up. The sun's out. The sky's blue. Means nothing, for some reason.

The way the light hits the red sandstone's just an everyday thing to folks here. There are sights here worth the visit, without a doubt. But if I come back, it'll be July or August. Or whenever the locals tell me I'm gonna hit their summer.

I shake my head. Almost forgot he asked a question. "Best

ask DS Inness. She's gonna know."

He nods. We head in through the entrance and we go straight to her new digs.

The door's open. He does a gentle rap with his knuckles.

She looks up from a piece of paper she's staring at. Waves us in.

He sits down. I lean on the wall next to a window.

"What do I call you now?" asks Stephen.

She smirks. "Whatever you did before, but maybe with a ma'am thrown in there somewhere."

He's confused.

"In here, it's Fiona. Officially, I'm still your sergeant."

He nods. Much clearer.

"I was surprised by the news about DCI Flett... er... Grant."

She sits back in her chair. "You and me both."

She picks up some sheets of paper from a drawer and lets them fall on Stephen's side of the desk. "His resignation letter. Sent to the Chief this morning. Printed it out for me to see. Said it shouldn't be a state secret what happened. He might even go to the press if he still feels guilty."

"Guilty?" Stephen says as he starts reading. There are a couple of sharp intakes of breath. Some muttered words, barely audible. Not the kind for publication.

He's on the final paragraph. DS Inness looks over at me. "What do you think?"

"I've got a thought or two," I say, pushing away from the wall so I'm standing where both can see me.

They both stare at me.

"DCI Flett was being blackmailed by Davie Wallace. Obviously got himself mixed up in his escort business. Even with Davie out of the picture, his conscience got the better of him. He couldn't live with the lie anymore."

I swear, their jaws are about to fall off if they drop any lower.

I shrug. "Makes sense, doesn't it? You look back over the way he's behaved about Moira Wallace and her brother. For all I know, Moira's the gal he's been seeing on the side."

They're still staring. A quick glance at each other. Right again.

"He's been shutting things down. Trying to turn us down blind alleys. Of course his head had been turned. But now, we can get back to where we should've been. Pull out all the stops to find this guy before he can do anything else."

Stephen says, "The mayor's got a sting kinda idea in his head."

DS Inness swears in reply.

He carries on, "I told him we'd station a couple of PCs with him. The council picking up their wages for the next few days."

She nods. Approving that's a no-brainer.

Quiet for a moment. Sometimes around places like this, you can forget what that's like.

"Right," she claps her hands. "Can't sit around chatting to you two. Got stuff to organise for tonight. Assuming you don't find the guy before then."

Stephen gets up and smiles. Does some ridiculous micky-take salute. "Thank you ma'am. You're already talking like the top brass. Wanting us to do the impossible with meagre resources."

She smiles and shakes her head as we're walking out. "Not too late to stick you back on a beat in uniform," she says when we're still in earshot.

We've got to head back to the CID office. See what we can do to help things along.

Find enough on Graham Craigie before he finds and deals with Mayor Tait.

51. YOU THINK YOU KNOW A CRIMINAL

All the talk's about DCI Flett.

Those who aren't bumping gums over him, are yapping about the mayor. His blind desire to lead a normal life in the face of a credible threat.

They're usually pretty busy in the CID office, from what I've seen. Today's it's like someone closed with windows, filled the place with wasps and shook the hell out of it.

They're working on murders one to six. They're picking up the phone and calling people. Searching for something to do with some clue online. Some are making wild pointing gestures at pictures on the wall. Wasn't so long ago that that was me.

How many times have I been kicked outta here since then?

I'm back at Stephen's desk. He's got something that looks vaguely familiar on the screen.

"Results of the logical exam of Wallace's phone" He glances at me.

I nod. "Quick work."

He looks back at the screen. "Yeah the physical one, the one that's gonna get the rest we can't see, that's gonna take longer. Got to send it away. The basic stuff we can do here now."

I'm looking at a screen divided into three. Whatever's clicked on the left shows up something to the right. He clicks a search box and starts typing.

A phone number.

"Graham Craigie's number," he says. "Wrote it down before I was ordered to give the phone back."

Three results. Messages received from that number.

> This is what you wanted.

Sent the night Moira died.

> We should meet.

Received around the time I showed up, asking questions.

> What have you done? VIRTUS aren't happy.

Received yesterday morning.

Stephen nods. "Looks like we've got a partial admission for Moira," he says, pointing at the first message.

I nod "Not enough to bring him in again."

He sighs. "No."

"Shows that Craigie and Wallace knew each other," I offer.

He shrugs. "For whatever that's worth."

He looks at me. "Suppose your number should be on here somewhere."

He types it in. Hits search. A couple of outgoing calls. A couple incoming. Back in the early days, when I was gonna keep him updated.

He points at the screen with the lid of his pen. "This one's not from either of you. Unknown number."

> Got someone who fits. New P.I. Known to make a mess.

Then my number.

"That's the day before he called me," I say.

I slump a little in my chair.

Hiring me was suspicious. No reason for it.

Could've seen me on the news. Could've read about my medal of honour. No. Here's a new guy who's gonna screw things up.

I was a smokescreen. Nothing more. Someone to get in the way of the police investigation.

"Flint," Stephen's looking at me. "You know as well as I do, how valuable you've been. The guy clearly didn't know you. What you can do."

I nod.

He clears the search results. Maybe to stop me seeing that message.

Most of the remaining messages are the stuff I knew about already. Lending money. Asking for repayment. Veiled threats when they're skint.

Messages about the sleepy-time gals under his employ. Setting up meetings.

Another sharp intake of breath from Stephen. "Some messages to DCI Flett. I recognise the number."

> Moira. You know the time and place.

Seems to be the first meeting. Months ago.

> No one will know what you've done.

The reassurance of an astute blackmailer.

> You want to keep a lid on your secret? Better do what I want.

> If the police knock on my door again, I'm gonna bring your world crashing down.

Threats galore. A series of calls, to and from. They spoke a few times in recent days.

No wonder DCI Flett was getting out from under this.

I leave him to searching.

I pull out my phone and look up VIRTUS. That's got to mean something.

Some data solutions company in London.

Some getup that sells body armour.

A Wikipedia entry. A specific virtue in ancient Rome. More Latin. Of course it was gonna be more Latin. Valour, manliness, courage. Anything to do with being a man and being strong.

Probably explains the body armour.

Commercial construction.

Can't get any further.

A random call comes in from a withheld number.

I answer and hold it to my ear.

Nothing.

A vague hiss.

A bit of a rustle, like someone moving around.

I hang up.

Busy with a murder investigation. Ain't got the time nor the patience to wait for some two-bit telemarketer to figure out their headset.

The only other thing in my search list is a boring-looking Volkswagen saloon.

Nothing that fits the suspected meaning.

"Ever heard of VIRTUS?" I ask.

He shakes his head. Asks around. More shakes of heads.

He searches police intel. Nothing.

"I figure, if we can figure out VIRTUS, we've got a key to getting to Craigie."

He looks at his watch. "The way time's going, he's gonna show up tonight. Finish what he's started. *He'll* be coming to *us.*"

52. IT AIN'T A LIGHT THING

The cold, bright weather disappeared with the mayor's foolhardy optimism.

The day got grey during the afternoon. Then it got greyer still.

About the time it's getting as grey as you'd think it could get, it started turning something closer to black.

The air's thick with a fine rain. A fog with a vendetta. The kind that you can't escape. Even if you catch a couple of ferries and planes, it's gonna still find you and soak you to the skin.

I don't suppose my ridiculous hat and thick coat are gonna keep the weather out. Even with the addition of a woollen scarf and gloves.

The bells of the cathedral are ringing. Not that anyone can see the spire. Or anything much above ground level. Or anything more than about six feet away.

If you could choose the worst possible weather for a lights switch-on, this would be it.

A podium's positioned right outside the cathedral doors.

The mayor's approaching. He's in a sharp suit. A slightly blunter long coat over it.

A chunky gold chain around his neck. Every mayor I've ever seen's got a chain like that. Like someone robbed Mr T and melted it all down.

Must be some ancient symbol of power. Maybe it started out that the guy with the biggest gold chain was in charge. That got some folks making gold chains bigger and bigger. One day, someone's got one that looks a little like Adam West's Batman utility belt. It's just been deployed a little higher up the body.

PCs in full uniform are either side. They're at least a little drier than the rest of us. The huge, inset, ornate gothic-style entrance provides at least partial shelter.

He's pompous, he's arrogant enough to think a killer won't take him down, but he's punctual. Gotta say that for him.

There's a rough semicircle of temporary protective metal barriers. They keep the crowds back about three metres.

There are gaps. They're not so used to setting these kindsa things up. At least the gradually moistening public respect the barrier. Even if parts of it have gotta be imagined.

In any other place, you might get a crowd of fifty. Short notice. Poor weather. Annoying host.

Not here. At least, not tonight. Gotta be over three hundred. That's a damn good crowd for anything other than a pub opening.

Gonna be hard to find our killer in this lot. If he's even turned up.

Wouldn't blame him for being a fair-weather killer. Takes one look out of the window. Sees how miserable it is. Decides he's gonna wait for it to clear up.

Could still have got it wrong, even if he heads out in all weathers. What if he's more of a private killer? Likes to take lives in the comfort and privacy of a victim's own home. Only puts on the public spectacle later. Less pressure, I guess, in doing it that way.

I'd be happy if either was true. Count me among the happiest here if this guy waffles on, I get soaked to the skin and we all go home with a pulse.

The bells finally stop.

"Welcome everyone. Thank you for coming." Off he goes.

A gentle ripple of polite applause.

"I moved here about the age of ten, with my parents. It was quite a change from Edinburgh."

That explains the different accent.

"I immediately found the people to be warm and welcoming."

He talking about the same place?

"Since that day, I've loved the place. The hills. The cairns. The great outdoors doesn't get any greater than it is here."

This is becoming a little self-indulgent.

I'm scanning the crowd. No obvious threats. Hard to tell when there are so many hoods, hats and umbrellas. No one's wearing a hat like mine. Not surprised.

The mayor's prattling on about his teenage years.

He's gotta shout everything. He's got a voice that carries. No one was gonna risk a dance with a few thousand volts to fit a mic and speakers for this.

Stephen's on the other side of the crowd to me. Some other officers are dotted around. Some in uniform. Some dressed to blend in, which they almost manage.

The mayor is now talking about the tourist sites he's visited. For all I know, he's listing them alphabetically.

The good news is that the drizzle's taking the rest of the night off.

The bad news is that a full-blown downpour's taken its place. It's coming down hard enough to bounce off the stone slabs and still be shin-high.

The mayor could take a hint. Wrap up. Hit a button. Call it a night. But no.

He's talking about the history of the islands.

The crowd's gotta thin if he carries on. They're gonna want to get anywhere else. Maybe some pub, so they can dry their clothes and wet their whistles.

Can't be worth standing through this, in this, to see a few lightbulbs glowing. They're gonna be on every other night anyway. Just come out and see them some other time. Maybe when the weather's a little less like the world doesn't want you outside.

The guy in the gold's now saying something about Christmas on the islands. Something about community spirit. Togetherness. How it's needed now, more than ever. The kinda thing you could steal from an old royal speech or a greetings card.

The rain eases off a little. Not a whole lot, but a little. Still think I've been drier in the shower than I am standing here.

There's a shout from behind me.

Another one.

Some kinda commotion.

I don't get time to turn around. I'm shoved forward. Pinned against the metal barrier.

The crowd's trying to squash me here for some reason.

Someone darts from the crowd. Runs through a gap between barriers.

I manage to clamber over the wet barrier. Slip a little when my shoes hit the stone paving.

I'm back on my feet. I charge the guy. Lunge. Grab his legs and take him down rugby-tackle-style.

He hits the ground hard. He's the cushion against my own hard landing.

I turn him over. Pin him down. Remove the hood.

A face squints back at me through falling rain.

It's not the right face. This ain't the guy.

The closest PC comes to my aid. Gonna put the cuffs on him. Get someone to haul him away.

Out of the side of my left eye, there's another runner.

Clears the barriers. Stephen misses him.

I run and throw myself in the assailant's direction. I grab only one leg. It's not enough to soften my landing.

He turns. Looks at me. It's Graham Craigie.

Kicks out like he's the focal point in a game of Buckaroo. Gets the top of my head.

I cling on, despite the pain.

He pulls his leg back and manages a stamp-like kick which lands in the centre of my face.

Can't keep hold after that one. Letting go's a reflex when it gets too much.

Tears fill my eyes. I make out the shapes of the mayor disappearing into the church.

He had a getaway plan after all.

Craigie's after him.

I know what might've happened to my face. I ain't touching the nose or anything around it for a few minutes.

One or two others charge past me, after the guy. Can't see clearly enough to make out who they are.

Let's hope they're gonna do a better job of stopping the killer than I managed.

***

She sees the first person to clear the barriers.

Sees Flint charge after him. A decent take-down.

No one expected the first. They certainly weren't expecting a second.

He comes from somewhere. Closer to the middle.

The officer that's usually kicking around with Flint reaches for the guy. Misses.

Flint gets the second guy. At least enough of him to allow the mayor to run. He makes the relative safety of the church.

Flint gets a foot to the face for his trouble. Has to let go.

Whatever gets in the girl's head at that moment, no one knows. Least of all her.

Flint is someone who's showed her kindness. Compassion. Respect. She doesn't remember anyone else treating her so well. It isn't fair that he's down on the floor holding his face.

Plenty of spaces in that cathedral. Halls away from the polished floors. Spots where smaller folk are better at getting through in a hurry.

These big police officers won't even make it down some of

those passage ways. Might even get stuck on the stairs.

She's smaller. Thinner. Quicker. She's a runner.

For no sensible reason, maybe for no reason at all, Bella runs at the guy now heading towards the cathedral door.

***

Okay, there was one decoy runner.

Should've thought of that.

Flint took him down.

The second runner was too far away from where he was standing. A good view of Flint's take-down, though.

DC Stephen Sutherland would have stood a chance of reaching him within a couple of steps. Problem was those damned wet stone paving slabs. Might as well have stepped on a wet bar of soap.

Still, he's up on his feet again.

Can't stop Flint from taking one to the face, though.

He grabs a leg when Flint's on the ground, but he slips straight off.

Next time the mayor wants a public outing when there's a killer on the loose, he should consider a tank of eels as a venue. Might be less slippery than this place right now.

The mayor's gone for the safety of the church. Probably got in the door and shouted something about a sanctuary. Don't think Craigie's gonna listen. Don't think that's worked for centuries.

Craigie slams into the other uniformed PC. Elbow up near his face. Smashes the guy against the massive, hard wooden door behind him. Bounces off him and runs in through the everyday, more human-sized door to the left.

The PC keels over. Starts falling as Stephen wants to get past. A crucial delay of a few seconds.

But he's inside.

The mayor's running off to the right. That gold chain's bouncing all over the place. Heading for the tower steps.

Craigie's following.

Someone else, looks like a woman by the shape. She's sneaked in, and she's catching up. She's a slender thing. She ain't gonna overpower anyone. Gotta have a reason to be in this chase.

His feet are still slipping around on this floor. How are the others running on this? Might as well be on an ice rink.

Careful steps. Pick up the pace. Soon he's got some speed in his legs. Not exactly close, but he'll catch up.

There were doubts that Craigie would show. That he would try to take out the mayor so publicly.

He's been ramping up the public side of these killings for the past few days. It shouldn't have been a surprise when he darted out of the crowd.

All he can do now is put a stop to him before something bad goes down somewhere in that cathedral tower.

53. RUN! RUN, LITTLE MAYOR!

Damn these mayoral chains.

Why'd people insist he wore something like this?

The thing always gets in the way. Looks ridiculous. It isn't like he's sponsored by Chanel Number Five or anything.

Should've ditched the chain before he started running. Might not have looked good to the public, though.

But screw the public. He's spent years serving them. What was his payment? Some nutcase is chasing him, trying to kill him. For what? Because he fits into some crazy, warped religious idea? Hardly a good motive.

Maybe the stairs up the tower are a bad idea.

Should've paid attention on one of those five enforced tours. Something useful could've been said during his official duties over the years.

Could've been another way out. But where?

The basement was a bad choice. Another side room led to that weird dungeon-thing. Some corridors up a level or two could make a good hiding place. If he can remember where they are.

The side door was an option, but running towards it, the thing was huge. No easy way to open it in a hurry. The killer would have been on him like white on rice before he got anywhere.

No, the tower was the only viable option.

Make life difficult for the chaser. Hope the police earn their money and catch him first.

If they don't? Well, it leads to nothing but dead ends.

He shakes his head. Why *that* expression? Why now?

Forget it. Keep climbing these stone steps.

The spiral goes on forever. Someone's added twice the number of steps since he was last here. Must've done. Maybe there always seems to be more steps when you're faced with your own mortality.

The steps are getting smaller. The walls are already closing in. Either that's panic, or things are actually getting smaller up here.

He's cleared the first opening. Nothing there but a kind of mezzanine to nowhere. It's where the tours take people. Show them a load of old artefacts that some might find vaguely interesting. The hangman's ladder. The old stained glass windows of dead people.

Loads of stuff about death in here.

If he gets strangled in here, does that make him a martyr? Does he get a new headstone stuck to the wall with skulls, crossbones and hourglasses carved into it?

Forget it. Don't find out the answer to that question. Keep climbing the steps.

The steps get less even. The walls are definitely getting narrower. It's getting harder and harder to keep going at speed. The damn necklace isn't helping.

Gets to the next level. Some smaller passageways. All lead nowhere, as far as he knows.

No, his best bet is to keep heading up into the tower. Some open spaces up there. Places to hopefully give the killer the runaround. Get past him. Come back down.

He gets to a larger, squarer room. Wooden floor. A kind of

balcony to his left with a load of clock mechanisms on it. More of it in a cabinet underneath. The floor's got a trap door. Dead centre.

He winces. Why'd every thought in his head right now include words about death?

The trap door's how they got the huge bells down for cleaning, repair and replacement. At least they've got a kind of wooden railing around it now. Less chance of some unsuspecting member of the public walking over them. Plunging a couple of hundred feet to their death.

The old clock mechanism's against the far wall. Replaced early twentieth century. The hands of the old clock face too. A strange thing to stop and dwell on. Is his time running out?

He runs past it. There's a doorway or something over there.

Goes nowhere. Of course it goes nowhere. It's a tower. He's cleared the roof of the rest of the building. It's a covered area the other side. No idea why it's there. Just gives someone like him false hope of finding another way down.

Got to head back to the stairs in the other corner. Make his way further up before anyone catches up.

He runs across.

He's too late.

The man the police warned him about is right there. Anger etched onto that face.

The man reaches for him. Misses somehow.

He takes the chance to run past, up the stairs.

The next level up's the platform for the bells. The seat and the mess of ropes that ring things in the way they're always rung on a Sunday morning.

Isn't there a curtain up there? Might be able to hide. Use that to his advantage.

And where the hell are the police?

Why haven't they caught up yet?

***

She can certainly move faster than the two men in front of her.

Yeah, it would be easier on flat ground. Open space. But no, she's in this narrowing spiral staircase.

She's at least gaining on the guy. The one that hurt Flint. The one that wants to take out the mayor.

She manages to reach out and grab an ankle. Yank the guy back.

He groans as he hits the floor, and the stairs.

He scrambles up onto the floor, just a couple of steps above.

She hasn't got a clue what to do next. She can delay the guy, but he might be capable of doing worse to her.

The first instinct is to turn around. Head back down those spiral steps.

She turns, but she doesn't get to start going down.

Pain fills her entire scalp and the back of her head.

He's got hold of her hair, and he's pulling her upwards. She's got to get her feet underneath her. Walk with it. No choice.

She's within arm's reach.

He grabs her round the neck. Squeezes.

She's clawing at thin air. Wants to scratch him. Stop him. But it isn't working.

She gets to scrape some fingernails of her right hand down his arm.

He screams out. Thrashes around.

Throws her sideways.

She clatters into something wood. It breaks around her. Hurts like hell.

The floor under her moves. This ain't a good place to be standing.

He grabs her hair again. Drags her off the unstable floor.

She's at a wooden handrail at the side. Built to stop some idiot falling the entire height of the roof onto the church floor below. Built better than the last wooden rail, anyway.

He's pressing her against it. Hands around her throat again.

She's trying to stop herself going over the edge. Trying to fight back. Trying to keep breathing.

Seems to be failing on all counts.

This daring attempt at intervening hasn't gone well. Using her speed to someone else's advantage hasn't worked out to hers.

Should have thought it through.

Sure, she's got nothing to lose. Not really.

The job's gonna go sideways now that the boss has been canned.

The home's gonna go with it when someone else takes over as landlord.

No family. No friends. No money.

What's she got to live for anyway?

Not that she's got a lot of choice in the matter, right now.

She's getting weaker. She can feel it.

Can hardly move her arms now.

It's too late to start a new life. Too late to find some hope in the future.

Someone else (probably this guy) threw away the rest of her life by taking out Davie Wallace.

She threw the rest of it away in some stupid chase to the top of St Magnus Cathedral.

Bella Johnson. Anonymous waitress. Adequate escort. Poor bounty hunter.

The mechanisms of the clock make some noise behind her.

The bells start ringing. Loud. Too loud. Then quieter.

Her time's about up.

***

Stephen reaches the floor with the clock mechanism. The bells have finished chiming.

Someone's holding a girl against a railing like they're trying to snap her in half.

The guy doing it's Graham Craigie, wanted killer.

The girl being strangled and pushed is Bella from the café.

She's the one who snuck in ahead of him. Why?

What was she hoping to achieve, other than maybe a dramatic death?

Honestly, it's a struggle getting to this height. When you've got wide shoulders, you've gotta turn sideways near the top of that staircase. No clue what he's gonna do if he's got to get any higher.

Those old stone staircases were made like this on purpose. Wider, heavier at the bottom. Better access. Less people needed to come up so far. Those who needed access must've been smaller than your average person. The steps were smaller, narrower. Saved on weight. Someone had to carry them up here at some point and fix them in place.

He's grateful for room to breathe, even if his first task is saving the girl.

He runs over. Leads with his left elbow into the side of the guy's face.

He soon lets go of the girl. She collapses on the side of the railing without the huge drop.

She's coughing. Crawling around. Looking for some air from somewhere, like it's held in secret little boxes below knee height.

Craigie's got a fire in his eyes for this fight.

He's gotta recognise Stephen as the DC from the arrest and the interview. Upset that his plan was nearly thwarted too soon. Livid that he's here right now, still getting in the way.

They're trading blows like football stickers. Neither seems to be coming out ahead.

Craigie lands a good punch to the side of Sutherland's face. He staggers back.

Must've been a good punch. He feels unsteady on his feet.

He looks down. He's on the huge trap door. The one they'd

built a barrier around to stop folks from falling through. That barrier's missing around this spot for some reason. The thing had better hold his weight.

He's still swaying a little from the punch. Reaches out for a piece of broken wood nearby. Swings it like it's a battle axe.

Craigie backs off. Walks off to the corner, where the old clock mechanism sits. Disconnected. No longer useful.

He picks up a large, straight bit of metal by its side. It's shaped like a giant arrow for a massive bow. The old minute hand for the old mechanism. Sitting there. Waiting for someone to pick it up and stab someone with the pointy end.

He uses it to bat away Sutherland's piece of wood. Sweeps the other pieces out of the way.

Comes closer. Keeps swinging the thing. Sutherland can't get fully out of the way of it. Takes the hit on his right arm.

Then something jabs into his right knee. Then his left.

The pain screams within him. Gotta do something to relieve it.

He drops to his knees. The uncertain floor's still holding.

Craigie's now swinging the thing downwards. Hitting him over the head. The shoulders. The back.

Where's Flint?

He should be here by now. Should be stopping this guy.

If not him, someone else must've come in to help.

Hell, the girl over there, choking, could do something.

He hears footsteps on the stone stairs.

Here he comes.

About time.

The hitting's stopped.

Has he got to him already?

No such luck.

Craigie's jamming the metal in the gaps of the trap door. He's standing clear.

Something springs open.

The floor's become more precarious, but a bolt or something the other side's still holding. Just.

Flint's just coming into view on the stairs now. He'll stop the guy.

Craigie's got an evil look on his face. A murderous, playful look. The kind of look a cat must give a bird that it's about to drop off as a present to its owner. Once it's stopped moving.

Craigie steps right to the edge of the safe bit of floor.

He thumps his foot down on the join between the two doors.

Leans and steps back as the doors fly open.

Stephen's right in the middle.

There's nothing for him to grab onto.

The floor's literally been ripped out from under him.

Maybe a running motion can keep him suspended in the air, like all those cartoons he watched as a kid.

No such luck.

Those three final words from the conversation with DS Inness come back to haunt him.

For our sins.

Maybe this is what he gets for his own. Unless he's the latest to suffer for Flint's.

He's already heading down. Nothing to break his fall but the solid, polished stone floor, way beneath him.

No one falls from this height and lives.

He ain't gonna be the exception.

He sees Flint's face for part of a second before he drops.

A look of shock. Horror. A look that says he was right all along. Everyone he gets close to ends up dead. Says a hell of a lot.

He's got a lot of time to dwell on that face. That apologetic expression. Sorry I didn't get here sooner. Sorry I got you so involved in all this. Sorry you met me. Sorry we're not gonna share another drink at a nearby pub and talk about our respective divorces. Sorry for everything.

The fall takes forever. How can that be?

It's only gotta be a drop that would take maybe three to five seconds.

Why are these seconds stretching out like taffy on a hook at a confectioner's store?

It's like some final punishment. Some final moment of torture. You've got seconds to live. Let's drag them out. Make you dread. Make you terrified. Keep you falling until you're resigned to your fate. Until you've made peace with the world.

The floor's getting closer.

The patterns in the cathedral floor look quite spectacular from above. Hadn't noticed that before.

He's too close again to appreciate it now.

Too close for anything, other than hitting that floor. Way too hard.

That's it. End of career. End of the adventure.

So long world.

He hits the floor.

Nothing else can go through that mind of his when it's splattered all over the place.

54. SETTING HIMSELF UP FOR A HELL OF A FALL

There goes kill number seven.

All he can think as he watches the guy fall.

If it all works out, he could hit double figures and still come out of it still sucking in air.

That'd be something.

You should get a chip when you hit ten, like one month sober in the AA.

He's got to deal with this detective. He's getting closer. Only then he can think about finishing the job with that whore. Finally, onwards, upwards, and deal with the mayor.

A simple checklist. If only murder was always so easy.

With the trap doors open, one wrong move and he's joining the copper in a matching wooden box.

Most of the wooden barrier around it's still intact. It's not up to much, though, clearly.

He'd swept some chunks of wood to the corner where he's standing. He picks them up one at a time. Lobs them in the direction of Enoch Flint. That thorn in his side. That nosey nobody. Here to ruin the party.

It was all supposed to be so neat. So clean. Then someone got the mayor to make some stupid changes. He was left with no choice. Instead of a public display of a body at town hall, it has to be a very public death at the cathedral. So be it.

Flint's the other side of the gap. It's a little like one of those comedy chase scenes. Irate family members chasing each other around a dining table. They just keep going round and round.

Except here, no one's laughing.

If Flint goes right, he goes left. He can get out of here without throwing or receiving a punch, if he's clever.

Flint runs at him to the right of the gaping hole.

He turns left and beats his feet.

Past the gasping girl. Except she reaches out. Grabs his leg.

Stupid woman. Could've made him trip. Have one long fall.

He stops. Lays the boot in. Once. Twice. She's not gonna try stopping him again.

Runs past her and up the stairs. The others will come after him, but the mayor's the real prize. He's the one that needs to die for any of this to work. Forget the others. The girl's gonna stay there. Flint's sweet on her. Might decide to stay and help her.

Up the narrowing stone steps. Can barely move in the stairwell now.

Not too many of them left, though.

Soon, he's on the next level up Another huge trapdoor. Huge bells overhead. A wooden staircase over the far side.

What's that cowering underneath the stairs?

Bingo!

***

She watched him fall. Not a damn thing she could do.

She's watching this killer try to knock Flint down the same hole.

Still nothing from her limbs. Stupid body. Stupid fear. Stupid recovery time from nearly being killed.

If only there was something she could do to stop this monster.

One thing's for sure, if he takes out Flint, she's next.

She grabbed his leg. One feeble attempt to stop him escaping.

Not something he liked very much.

Now he's gone, and she's had a couple of hard kicks to the ribs for her troubles.

Flint runs over. Crouches down beside her. "You okay?"

She croaks out, "I'll be fine." Waves a hand in the direction of the stairs.

He's got better things to do than to help her through her pain.

He's running for the stairs.

She's gingerly getting back to her feet. Mild injuries. Especially when compared to what could've happened.

She's already moving around better than she might've thought possible a moment ago.

He's out of sight.

There's another life to save.

If he can get up there quick enough.

**

That scream's gonna stay with him for a while.

The sound of a man knowing there's nothing he can do but die.

The thud as he hits the floor below.

Nothing hit anything harder.

No dull sound ever sharpened the mind more.

One dead. He could be next.

He died coming after him. Defending him.

Nothing he could've done. That's what he's got to tell himself if he ever wants to sleep again.

First, he's got to get out of this tower. Avoid the big sleep.

There are no curtains to hide behind up here. Must've remembered wrong. Just bells, a seat, and a wooden staircase. It leads up past the inside of the glass clock face and on to the viewing platform and the spire.

He's hidden in the only spot that looks a little like a hiding place. Under the first section of the wooden stairs.

Not a great hiding place, as it turns out.

The killer's seen him as soon as he's in the room. It's obvious in the man's eyes.

Nothing left but to make a break for it.

He scampers out. Stands up as he starts to run up the stairs. They're roomier than the stone ones had gotten by the top. They turn twice, leaving him facing the clock face.

Still ticking. It'll carry on ticking, regardless of whether he's around to know about it.

The guy's already coming after him.

He can hear his steps on the wood.

Louder.

He's a lot faster.

Only thing left to do is run as fast for a door out the tower as possible.

He reaches the top of the stairs. A small room. Maybe a little like Mr Eiffel's office at the top of his tower.

Opens one of four doors out to the viewing platform. One on each side. Only one's dead ahead of where the stairs go. He cringes again. Stop using that word!

He bursts out. Get out, run a lap of the tower, beat the guy back inside. See if you can lock the door again. That's the idea.

The cool, wet night air is like a hosepipe to the face.

Rain hits him hard.

Until that moment, he had no idea how hot under the collar he'd become.

He barely gets a lungful of cool air, though.

The killer's not caught up. Not entirely.

But he's grabbed the damn chain. He's pulling it backwards.

He uses it to walk himself towards his target.

Tries to wrap the chain round a second time. It ain't quite long enough.

He turns the excess chain over into a figure of eight. Pulls each side. It's tightening more and more around his neck.

His head feels like it's getting bigger.

Eyes start to bulge out.

His cheeks are burning. Even the rain ain't helping.

The other guy's arms are longer. Stronger. He flings his arms the best he can, but he can't reach him. Can't reach the hands holding the chain.

He could force an arm up through the gap if he was using his hands. This stupid chunk of gold's left no room for that. Not for his hand. Certainly not for his airway.

All he can do is move his feet. He's shuffling backwards. Not sure why backwards is the better idea. Forwards might've closed the gap. Might've been more sensible. Too late now.

But he's moving, at least. The attacker's moving with him.

His back hits a low wall. He's met the corner of the tower. Opposite the one where a friendly bird often sits to greet visitors.

If only there were a flock of birds up here. If only they'd start pecking the guy's eyes out.

His feet are slipping on the wooden decking beneath his feet.

He's sinking to the floor.

At least he's not being shoved over the edge.

His arms are going limp.

His heart's beating like crazy, but it's not gonna do any good. At least it's getting a little more to do before it stops for good.

His feet are going numb. His legs aren't far behind.

He's now feeling pretty much nothing.

A curtain's coming down on his vision.

A few more seconds and it's the final curtain call for the mayor.

He's blacking out. He can feel it.

He's heading down a tunnel where there's no light at the

end.

His strength is failing.

His eyes close.

But he can still hear just a little.

The ears. The last things to go. Who knew?

There's some kind of collision.

The gold chain breaks after one final go at choking him. Seems to break behind him. Somewhere other than the front, anyway.

A shout.

Another frightening scream. Getting quieter.

Quieter still.

Pretty faint by now, but still there. Can still just hear it above the rain hitting the copper spire.

Then a thud.

Seems someone else has joined the officer on a fast trip to ground floor level.

For all he knows, it's him.

Now he can't even hear anything.

He's out.

55. WHAT'S AHEAD OF YA CAN'T BE WORSE THAN WHAT'S BEHIND YA

Can't seem to catch my breath.

Plenty of air around me up here.

Bella's up here too.

Both of us struggling to take in the oxygen our lungs want.

One on the floor, not even trying.

Bella's looking at the mayor with wide eyes.

His are closed. Might be a good sign. I'm no paramedic.

She nods her head towards him. "Is he...?"

I crouch down. The chain's gone. Bruises and red marks where it used to be. The thing went with Graham Craigie when he left in a hurry for some face-time with the ground.

I feel around on the mayor's neck. There's a pulse. Faint, but it's there.

I shake my head. "Still alive. Got here just in time."

She looks at me. Rain's got us both dripping wet.

I expect her to throw her arms around me. Try to turn this into some romantic thing again.

If she's doing all that, it's only happening in her head.

There are footsteps way down underneath us. Shouts coming from the stone stairwell.

I look down at the unconscious mayor. "We've got a few seconds to get our story straight."

She looks at the mayor. Looks at me. "What shall we tell them?"

I look at her. I shrug. "Whatever we like. It ain't like anyone else knows what happened but us."

She smirks at me. Nods. I could swear there's a wink. "I know what to say."

***

The air tastes a little sweeter at ground level.

Not something I ever noticed before.

Someone's got a couple of ambulances on scene.

They've put a thin silver blanket on me. Another on Bella. We're sitting side-by-side at the back of an ambulance. I think we're well past shock, but they've got a job to do.

They put Graham Craigie in a body bag.

Detective Constable Stephen Sutherland goes in another.

It doesn't take them long to take a few pictures. Declare a time of death, and a reason.

Graham Craigie managed to miss the roof of the cathedral and fall straight down the corner of the tower. Might not have done him any good if he'd have hit the roof. Just might've been bad for the roof.

"That's your story?" DS Inness asks Bella.

She nods.

I shake my head. "It ain't a story, DS Inness. It's what happened."

She frowns at us. "He slipped. Fell right over the edge."

We nod.

"He was strangling the mayor with the gold chain, and it snapped, and his own strength was misdirected? No help from either of you over the side?"

"How could there be?" I ask. "We'd only just got to the top of the steps. Just stepped outside when it happened."

"And I suppose you were too far away to try to grab him so he could face justice for the murders he's committed?"

I nod. "I'm a fan of justice, being a police officer. Of course I'd want him to answer for his crimes."

Bella looks at me. Tries not to smirk.

"Besides," Bella says, looking back as DS Inness. "It was really slippery up there. Even if one of us had reached out an arm, we'd have been more likely to go over the side with him."

DS Inness looks up at the tower from the ground. "But he cleared the cathedral roof completely."

She looks back at us. "You telling me his own momentum from slipping sent him clear enough to fall the whole way? Without a push?"

I nod and point. "Really, you look at the angle. It wouldn't take much if you fell right from the corner, which he did."

She looks at me. A serious nod.

"I assume you found the broken chain somewhere?" I ask.

She nods again. "Believe it or not, he was still clutching it when he hit the ground. Didn't end up far from him."

She looks at us again. The closest she can manage to a death stare. She's gonna have time to work on that on her way up the ranks.

There's the slightest hint of the slightest of smirks.

"Okay, DC Flint. On the basis that you're both saying the

same thing, and that there's no evidence to the contrary, I've got no choice but to believe your account."

The mayor wanders over.

After some smelling salts and a few moments of wooziness, he was very much as he had been before. Maybe less of a Hollywood smile. Might be more of a Pinewood Studios expression. Still classy. Not quite as flashy.

His hair's ruffled. His eyes are a bit bloodshot.

He'll live. Before too long, he'd look like his old self again.

"Thank you," he says to the two of us. "From what I hear, you were coming up to try to save me, but it wasn't even needed. Of course, I remember the chain breaking, and I heard the guy fall."

DS Inness can't resist. "No one intervened?"

He smiles at her. "How could they? They were too far away. Haven't they told you what happened?"

DS Inness shrugs and walks off.

Mayor Tait winks at us and shuffles off with his new silver blanket around his shoulders.

"They find my gold chain anywhere?" he shouts at no one in particular as he walks.

He'll have no idea how pathetic he looks in this very moment.

It's of no matter.

The man who wanted him dead has met the same fate himself.

But he took another victim with him.

I get up. Turn a little.

Stephen's body is bagged up and being loaded into an ambulance.

Goodbye, friend. So sorry you met the same fate as so many others have.

I haven't killed any of the folk close to me. Could never be that kinda person.

But I'm responsible for so many deaths, nonetheless.

Whatever people tell me, those faces are still gonna haunt me.

Got another one to show up in my nightmares now. Things are gonna start getting a little crowded.

"What do I do now?" Bella asks. She's got that vulnerable, could-be-twelve look on that mug of hers.

I shrug. "You do whatever you want to do."

She laughs. "I wouldn't even know where to start."

I shake my head. "Not true. You've worked in that café for a long time? A few years?"

She nods. Stops and looks at me. "Can't see myself doing that again, though."

I raise my eyebrows. "What *can* you see yourself doing?"

A slow shake of the head. No words.

"The beauty is," I say, "you've got plenty of time to figure it out."

She looks at me like that's no answer at all.

"How many people do you know, who are doing the same thing they were doing thirty years ago?"

She purses her lips. Frowns a little. Looks at me. "None, I guess."

I nod. "There you go then. No one path gets you where you wanna go. Find something that drives you. Do that."

She gives me a resolute nod. "I've got it," she says. "I'm gonna train to be a police officer."

If I'd been drinking anything, I'd have done what they call in the movie business a spit take. "You wanna do this kinda thing?"

She shrugs. "Didn't know I did until I started chasing that guy. A rush I've never had in my life."

I wanna tell her it's more like a slow crawl than a rush most days. I ain't got the time.

My phone rings in my pocket. Managed to stay there through the whole ordeal. In a few seconds, I'm gonna wish it hadn't survived it all.

I see a few missed messages. Some voicemails. A couple of text messages I can get to later.

I take the call and I hold the thing up to my ear.

A hiss. A little louder than the rain. A shuffle.

I'm gonna hang up again.

But I hear something that's not supposed to be on the other end of the line.

Right now, a hundred silver blankets ain't gonna stop the shiver that runs through me.

56. I'M STARTING TO WISH I DIDN'T HAVE A PHONE

A minute later, I'm off the phone again.

I run to DS Inness.

She's talking to someone. Couldn't give a damn.

"I've gotta get home," I say. "It's gotta be as soon as possible."

She looks at me. Concern in her face.

I've maybe gone a bit paler in the last few seconds since she last saw me.

"What's the matter?"

I'm a little breathless. She was only a few feet away. This ain't exhaustion. This is something else.

"Toby."

She looks at me. Then it registers.

"Your kid's still missing?"

I nod. "Just got a phone call. Withheld number. Care to guess what I heard?"

She nods. "You heard him. Someone's got him?"

I nod again. "A couple of seconds of Toby squirming. Trying to call out. Then some other guy. Maybe one of those altered voices. He says I've gotta stay outta things if I wanna see him again. Said something about going after Flick next."

She's puzzled again. "Flick?"

"My partner. His mother."

Her eyes are wide. "What have you gotten yourself into, Flint?"

I shrug. "I have no idea. Starting to think this might be linked to things here. Some bigger picture none of us are seeing yet."

"Wait here," she says.

She hurries off in the direction of the mayor.

57. MY WORK HERE IS DONE

"Anything he needs," I hear Mayor Tait say. Got his authoritative voice back already.

He's got a phone to his ear.

"You know who this guy is? What he's done? If we can't make an exception for him, then for who?"

No idea who he's talking to.

He paces around close to me.

"Thank you. I owe you one... I know, probably a lot more than one."

He walks over.

"Sorry to hear about your family, Flint."

I nod.

"Got off the phone to the guy who runs the airport. Flights have started again."

I still find it kinda funny that an airport can be run by one guy. Would make me smile at any other time. What a place this is.

"Their last flight of the day to Aberdeen is about due to go. Got an empty seat because of a no-show. I got them to hold it. You ready to head straight to the airport? They'll hold it for a while, but you're gonna have to be quick."

I nod. "I'll go grab my things. Thank you."

He puts on that sympathy smile. The one we've all seen. What other look is there for a time like this?

I shake the guy's hand.

"You're always welcome back here. Just give us a warning so

I can make sure we've got forensics on-hand for whatever turns up when you do."

I can't argue with that. Death follows me. Seems to leave me the hell alone. No clue why. It's a tormentor. A stalker. One that only takes down those by my side.

I get Bella. Get back to the car. One stop at hers, then off to the airport.

They ain't trips that take any time at all.

Before I know it, Bella's waving me goodbye outside her place. Gonna be interesting to see where she ends up. And the other four. Maybe they'll take on the café together. Without the side business.

It ain't long before I'm dropping the car keys in a drop box and heading through departures.

It's a tiny airport. When they wanna get you through in a hurry, they can manage it.

They waive the security checks. When the mayor and the police area commander call and tell them I ain't a threat, these folks believe it. More than any other airport staff might.

I'm straight out onto the runway. Climbing steps on to the plane, all within maybe ten minutes of getting there.

The same hostess who offered me shortbread and a drink is standing there. Same smile on her face. Bet she's been doing this so long, she wouldn't know a genuine smile if it ran up behind and gave her a wedgie.

She takes my bags. Stashes them and points me to a nearby seat.

Not a single spare seat now. A lot of people willing to fly this time of night. Might be time to consider some bigger planes.

The door's closed. The loud propellers are speeding up.

My seatbelt's fastened.

The safety announcement's in full-swing.

We're off the ground before you can say UNESCO World Heritage Site.

With any luck, I'll be home in time to see what's going on.

Fix things. Protect Flick. Get Toby back.

58. HOME, HOME IS A PAIN

The influence of the Orkney bigwigs only got me as far as the flight outta Kirkwall.

Didn't get me anything on the Aberdeen end.

No matter how I hurried, whoever I asked, I wasn't getting beyond the outer limits of the granite city any time soon.

Getting out of there and home quick was as easy as greasing up a live turkey.

Still, I got the earliest flight back to London. Some of those leave crazy early.

I'm stepping off the last of the tiny, tubular death traps with wings at a quarter to five in the morning.

A taxi's happy to take my fare straight outside. Gatwick to Cookston's gonna rack up one hell of a bill. Good job they take card payments now. Might need to take the rest off my pension if we hit traffic.

The familiar buildings of Cookston come into view. The old police station, now SITU offices, looms large over the buildings around it.

I see streets I've driven along with since-departed colleagues.

I see the park where I was told about the death that seemed to start it all. My old trainer, colleague and mentor Tobias Hutchins. Since then, how many have bitten the dust while I'm sniffing around on the edge of it all, looking for scraps?

Like something dropping through me like a white-hot stone, it comes back to me. In truth, it never left.

Toby. My kid. Named after my old friend. Missing. Not just missing, but gone. Taken.

Wish I could tell Flick what I know. About the phone call. That it's my fault, not hers that Toby's not there.

If only she'd answer her phone. I've tried calling so many times. Can't even leave a voicemail anymore.

I'm so far past the day I was gonna get home, I ain't surprised she's not taking my calls. Probably changed the locks on me too. I'd be tempted to do the same if the roles were reversed.

Who would do this though? Who would stoop so low as to nab a kid near their house?

If that call's to be believed, it's got something to do with my interfering with things. But the stuff in Orkney? Just a mad man who was trying to make a point.

Wasn't it?

Can't ask the guy now.

Then there's the message. VIRTUS. What did that have to do with this?

Could it be possible that someone got into Graham Craigie's head? Set him to thinking the way they think?

Could be there's some plan. Orkney might've been a starter.

What the hell's gonna be the main course?

Gets me thinking I might've done something else to put the noses of these people out of joint.

Old cases.

Can't ask Jasper what he thinks. Just another one pushing up daisies because of me.

But that last case with him. The guy we took down. Elias

Wilkins. He's still living it up, prison-style. Still a walking, talking CO_2 machine.

The motivation seemed a little off. Money? Maybe that's at the root of all of it. What if there is something more? What if he knows something?

Gotta get the resources of SITU onto this. It's only a whiff of a rumour. A hint of some overlord-funded wrongdoing.

If I'm right, there are people out there. Planning big things. Throwing local lunatics and wannabes under the bus on their way to achieving their goals.

I've gotta know the truth of what's going on.

Might be the only way I get my family back together again.

59. SOMETHING OF NOTE

My musings get me to my front door.

The place looks just like I left it.

But so many things have changed.

Gotta get inside. Tell Flick what I know.

Maybe she got a call too.

I get my key in the lock. I'm in.

She hasn't changed the locks on me. Small mercies.

Still early. Still dark. No lights on.

"Flick?" I call out.

No answer.

No movement.

I dump my bag on the floor and run upstairs.

"Flick? You asleep?"

I hurry into the bedroom.

Empty. Bed's made.

Maybe she's slept in Toby's room. Feels more attached to him when he ain't there.

She's not in there either.

Room to room, she ain't in the house.

Where is she?

I check the rooms downstairs.

She's got to have left a note. Wasn't looking for little things when I got here. Was hunting for something person-sized.

Kitchen. Nothing.

Lounge. Not a thing.

Dining room. Empty.

I check my office. Turn on the light.

A single sheet of lined paper from a notebook. Torn out badly. Sitting right there in the centre of the new desk.

I sit in the chair. Pick up the note. It's hand-written.

> Flint,
>
> Your meddling has gone on long enough. Your son going missing wasn't enough of a hint? We've got another one of yours too. Maybe now you'll butt out of things that aren't anything to do with you. Don't try to find us. We'll be in touch when the time's right.
>
> Get some sleep. You must be tired after such a long journey.
>
> V

I hold the note in my hand. I look back at the desk.

Something else there. Right under where the note was.

Two individual drops of blood. Left there to dry.

I can get someone from work to test them. I know what they're gonna find.

60. GOTTA GET BACK TO THE SHOEBOX

A phone call to someone I've barely spoken to in months.

Holly Chamberlain.

She knew about Toby. Hadn't heard a peep about any of it in days.

She ain't just the Inspector. She's the one who stuck her neck out for me. More than once. She's the one who talked me down when I handed in that letter. The one you don't come back from. Persuaded me to wait around. Take a couple of months. See how I felt.

It worked.

I'm back.

Not how I wanted to walk back through those doors.

She's there by the entrance. Willing to give up her Saturday. Can't ask for more than that.

"A hell of a couple of weeks, hey Flint?"

I shrug. "About the norm these days, I guess."

She puts on a sad smile. Shakes her head.

We walk towards her office.

"I got someone in local forensics to test the blood on your desk. As you say, I think we know what we're gonna find."

We reach her room. She sits at her desk. Points at the other one for me. "There's a whole heap of tests they can do on one drop of blood these days. I'd lost track. One of them can tell you if it's from a living source."

I wince.

She looks down. "Sorry. I should be a little more sensitive."

I shake my head. "We've gotta deal with this the way we deal with anything else if I'm gonna hold it together."

She pouts. Nods once.

We both look out the window at a few different things that add up to nothing.

Quiet for a moment. No words said, but we know what we would've said. That's enough.

"This mean you're through playing a private gig?"

I nod. "Too much trouble comes attached to it. Turns out."

She opens her drawer. Pulls out my ID badge and warrant card. "You'll be needing these."

Drops them on my side of the desk. "I've been keeping them to hand. Figured the moment would come."

"Glad you've got faith in me," I say.

She smiles. "Always had faith in you, Flint. Tried telling you enough. You just needed to stop beating yourself up for things that go on around you. You walk into less when you keep your head up."

I shrug. "Not sure that stacks up, but I know what you mean."

We both move to get up.

"No time to waste then," she says. "Let's find your family."

Simon Whitfield

FLINT WILL RETURN SOON AS HE GOES IN SEARCH OF HIS FAMILY.

Simon Whitfield

ABOUT THE AUTHOR

Simon Whitfield has previously written under the pseudonym Will Thurston. This is his sixth novel.

Simon works in an office in a less-than-perfect building with a sea view, when he's not working and writing in his home office (which is actually a renovated caravan). He lives in Suffolk with his wife and two adopted children (and a dog), and longs for the day he can write full-time. He may eventually have his own website and social media stuff, in his own name.

Blog and social media details are below, along with an email address for feedback from readers.

Website: https://simonwhitfield.uk/

Twitter: @willbthurston

Instagram: whitfield_author

Facebook: www.facebook.com/simonwhitfieldauthor

BOOKS BY WILL THURSTON

THE REPLACEMENT PHENOMENON

Jake Hingham gets his wish to rewind time to save his brutally murdered little family. When time continues to unwind he seeks to find out why, and to trace the events that led to the death of his wife and two boys.

THE TALENT SCOUT

Brian Townley must save his brainchild, the Talent Scout, from falling into the wrong hands. A device that can detect natural abilities in anyone's DNA could be used for good or evil. Will he survive the fight against organised crime to protect his research and his prototype?

THE DOLL COLLECTOR

When PI Dan Castle gets a message that his teenage daughter has been captured, he embarks on a rescue mission in which he hopes to find and bring the Doll Collector to justice. His chase through the disturbing underworld of child abuse could save more lives than one, but can he save his own daughter before it's too late?

DEATH BY CHAPTERS

Sam agrees to be the protagonist in Larry Llewellyn's next gruesome novel. She knows the character will die, but has the man's killing spree merely been confined to the printed page? Horrible truths suggest otherwise, and now she must find a way to stay alive.

ENOCH FLINT INVESTIGATIONS

1. **The Departure Lounge (2023)** – Flint investigates a murder which becomes apparent when body parts show up in holidaymakers' luggage all over the world, but is there something bigger about to go down?

2. **The Dark Isles (2024)** – Flint is hired to find a missing person, but uncovers a series of murders that are designed to push the island community to its limits. Can he find and stop the killer before they strike again?

3. **Breaks Like Flint / Dying To Find You (Due later in 2024)** – Flint must succumb to the whims of a secret organisation to find his family. Can he track them down, against huge odds, before it's too late to save them?

4. **Dead Ahead (Due 2025)** – Flint is called in to investigate a murder that happens in slow-moving traffic. How does someone get shot when there's no one else in the car, and the windows are undamaged? What will it lead to?

Printed in Great Britain
by Amazon